THE REBELLION OF THE HANGED

B. Traven

The Rebellion of the Hanged

ALLISON & BUSBY
LONDON · NEW YORK

This edition published in Great Britain 1984
by Allison & Busby Ltd,
6a Noel Street,
London W1V 3RB
and distributed in the USA by
Schocken Books Inc.,
200 Madison Avenue,
New York, NY 10016

Originally published in Spanish as *La Rebelión de los Colgados*

British Library Cataloguing in Publication Data
Traven, B.
   The rebellion of the hanged
   Rn: Otto Feige   I. Title
   II. La rebelion de los colgados. *English*
   833'.912 [F]   PT3919. T7

   ISBN 0 85031 444 5
   ISBN 0 85031 445 3 Pbk

Printed and bound in Great Britain by
Richard Clay (The Chaucer Press) Ltd., Bungay, Suffolk

The Rebellion of the Hanged

Prologue

Cándido Castro, a Tsotsil Indian, his wife, Marcelina de las Casas, and their two little sons, Angelito and Pedrito, lived on a plot of ground in a district of small agricultural holdings called Cuishin, on the outskirts of Chalchihuistán. Cándido's property amounted to about five acres of arid, powdered, stony soil that required back-breaking work from him if he was to wring enough food from it for his family. The big landlords—called finqueros—of the districts of Jovel and Chiilum had tried several times to persuade Cándido to abandon his miserable piece of land, take his whole family, and go to work on one of the fincas as a peon.

The finqueros were forever on the hunt for Indian families, essential to them for labor on their fincas. They were completely unscrupulous about snatching the Indians from their own villages and districts. The finqueros contested the possession of such families as though trying to establish the ownership of unbranded cattle. Quarrels over the possession of Indian families went on and on, were handed down from fathers to sons, and were prolonged even when the cause had long since been forgotten and no one could guess what had started the deadly hatreds among the finqueros.

The political bosses and other minions of the dictatorship, naturally, were always on the side of the powerful finqueros. When a finquero asked them to deprive some Indian family of its shred of land, declare the Indians devoid of rights, or take advantage of any criminal method whatever, the representatives of the government carried out his wishes immediately, leaving the victims at the finquero's mercy. He then undertook to pay off the family's debts and take care of the exorbitant fines inflicted—most often for no reason, but useful for drowning the Indians in debt to such a depth that the finquero could acquire absolute rights over them. That a finquero was related to a political boss or friendly with one or could help to assure some other employee of the tyranny a long and easy existence was enough to guarantee that Indian labor would never be lacking on his finca.

Cándido had been able to preserve his independence and live in freedom thanks to his innate peasant caution, his natural good sense, and the line of conduct he had imposed on himself: to be concerned only with his land, his work, and the well-being of his family.

The small community was made up of five families belonging, like Cándido, to the Tsotsil tribe. Their patches of land were as poor as his. Their miserable hovels were made of adobe and thatched with palm leaves. They led the kind of hard existence that only humble peasant Indians can endure. All the finqueros' efforts to turn them into peons had failed, nevertheless, as they had with Cándido. The Indians were not unaware that life on a finca would be less harsh for them; but they preferred to stay on their dry and sterile land—because of which the district was called Cuishin, which means "burning"—preferred to live their precarious lives full of the constant anguish of seeing their harvests ruined rather than lose their liberty for an Eden in servitude. They preferred dying of hunger as free men to getting fat under an overseer's orders.

If the Tsotsils had been asked the reason for their preference, they might have replied like the old Louisiana Negress who had been a slave in her youth, before the Civil War. In the old days the slave's masters had taken care of her existence. She had eaten as much as she wanted. Now she lived in a miserable shack and in order to make a living had to take in neighbors' washing. She never knew whether she would be able to eat the next day or would be driven to robbery in order to feed herself and would then be thrown into jail. One day they asked her: "Now then, mammy, didn't you live better when you were a slave?" And she answered: "Sure, I lived better before—but now I'm happy—a man's stomach's not the only thing that makes him happy."

And in Cuishin the stomach alone did not give orders. If it had, there would be no explaining why those Indians accepted their painful lives instead of turning over the care of their stomachs to a finquero in return for simply obeying his orders.

1

 In the depths of his soul the Indian believes more
in the power of his destiny than in that of any god
whatever. He knows that, do what he may, he cannot escape
that destiny. When he senses its approach, the Indian comports
himself like all human beings: the purely biological instinct of
self-preservation drives him to resist by all available means, by
whatever methods he imagines can help him, including invoca-
tions to the saints—who communicate, as everyone knows,
with God. But he understands perfectly that he is like a lost
sentinel and that if he opposes his destiny, it is merely to delay
its action a little.

When Marcelina, Cándido's wife, fell suddenly ill and none
of the usual remedies proved effective in easing her pains, Cándido felt intuitively that he had reached a decisive moment in
his life. Marcelina had a horrible pain in the right side of her
belly. She said she felt as if she was swelling up so much that it
seemed she was going to burst. The old family midwife declared that her intestines had got themselves into a knot. To
untie them she prescribed purges strong enough to empty the
belly of an elephant, but they only doubled the sick woman's
pains and wails. Marcelina felt as though her intestines were on
fire and about to be torn apart.

The midwife then gave it as her opinion that this was the
sign of approaching death, and advised that they send one of
the children to Mateo to set him to making a coffin so that poor

Marcelina should have a Christian burial. But Cándido was far from satisfied by this solution. He loved his wife and was not disposed to see her taken from him so easily. He decided to take Marcelina on muleback to Jovel to see a real doctor.

He collected every centavo he could find in the house. He counted and recounted the money and convinced himself that his fortune consisted of eighteen pesos. Cándido was not unaware that doctors are like priests and never do anything for nothing. Besides, he knew that Marcelina's illness was not one of those for which the doctors accepted the usual fee of one peso.

Every step of the mule tore cries of pain from the unhappy woman. When the trail became rougher, Cándido decided to carry his wife on his shoulders and lead the mule by the bridle. But this did not improve matters for Marcelina; on the contrary, it made them worse, for now the weight of her body pressed her belly against her husband's body, and her sufferings were so atrocious that she begged Cándido to put her back on the mule. Finally she begged her husband to put her down on the road, where she could stretch out to die in peace, for she felt that her end was near.

They remained thus for more than half an hour: she stretched out on her back and he seated by her side at the edge of the road, not knowing which saint to invoke. Every now and then he went to fetch her a few swallows of tepid water from the brook on the other side of the road. At last a group of Indians came along—men, women, and children returning from the market. They were Tsotsils belonging to the same village as Cándido. They all stopped to refresh themselves at the brook.

"Where are you going, Cándido?" one of them asked. "The market stalls were closed quite a while ago."

"Marcelina is very sick. I think she's going to die. I wanted to take her to Jovel to see a doctor who can take the knots out of her intestines. But I can't carry her on my shoulder because she screams, and on the mule's back she suffers so. She's already half dead. Now I'm just waiting—because if it happens I'll be able to put her on the mule and take her back to the house.

What a pity—she's so young and so amiable! She keeps our house so well, does so much work! Furthermore, the children will be left without a mother."

"No need to give up hope, Cándido," replied one of the Indians. "Naturally, if Marcelina has to die, she'll die. But that's not certain yet. Wait a minute, we'll give you a hand." He called his companions together. They talked among themselves for a few moments and then walked back to Cándido. "Look, we're going to carry her to Jovel. We'll do it so carefully she won't know we're carrying her."

Cándido thanked them silently with a movement of his head.

The men went a little way into the underbrush, cut branches, and wove and fastened them together, improvising a stretcher on which they placed the sick woman. The women and children meanwhile took charge of the various objects carried by the caravan, which began the return trip to Jovel.

Night was already falling when Marcelina finally reached the house of the doctor, who, after feeling the painful spot, declared: "It's necessary to operate immediately. I must open the belly to remove part of the intestine that is infected and will bring about her death in less than twelve hours if I don't operate. How much can you pay me, fellow?"

"Eighteen pesos, my doctor and patron," Cándido told him.

"But don't you realize that just the cotton, the alcohol, and the iodoform gauze cost me more than eighteen pesos? Not counting the chloroform, which will cost ten pesos at least."

"But, for the love of God, my doctor and chief, I can't let my wife suffer like a dog!"

"Listen, fellow. If God our Lord will pay my back rent, my account for light, my debts to the provision store, the butcher shop, the bakery, and the tailor shop, then, yes, I could operate on your wife for the love of God. But you must know, fellow, that I have more confidence in the silver and in the solid promises you can give me than in the love of God our Lord. He takes care of lots of things, but not of a poor doctor overwhelmed by debts. I got myself into these debts in order to study, and if I have not been able to pay them it's because here there are many doctors and few sick people with any money."

"But, my doctor, if you don't operate on my wife, she's going to die."

"And I, fellow, if I operate without charge, I'm going to die of hunger. All I can say to you is that an operation like this costs three hundred pesos. But just to show you that I'm not a wicked man capable of allowing anybody—even the wife of an ignorant Indian—to die, I'll do something for you. I won't charge you more than two hundred pesos. It's a scandalous price, and I run the risk that they'll throw me out of the association for lowering the price so much. Nevertheless, I'll do it for only two hundred pesos. But you must bring me the money within three hours at the outside, for otherwise the operation will be useless. I'm not going to tell you pretty stories or perform an operation for love of the art. If I take your money, I'll give you my work in return and restore your wife's health. If she doesn't come out of the operation well, I won't charge you. That's the most I can do. You don't give away your corn, your cotton, or your pigs. Isn't that true? Then why should you want me to give you my work and my medicines?"

While this conversation was taking place, Marcelina remained stretched out on a straw mat on the floor of the portico. The Indians who had brought her on the stretcher loitered near by, talking in low tones and smoking their cigarettes.

What could they have done? Even by putting together all the money they possessed they could not have raised the two hundred pesos—no, nor even by selling all their sheep. As for Cándido, he knew neither how nor where to come by the sum demanded.

Having fixed the price of the operation and assured himself that nobody else was waiting for him in his consulting room, the doctor picked up his hat, put it on, and went out to the street. He felt the need to assure himself once more that the town's old houses were still in their usual places and, above all, to learn whether in the last three hours some event worthy of

comment in the cantina had occurred. Perhaps Doña Adelina
had at last found out that her husband spent every second evening in the house of the amiable Doña Pilar, who had been a
widow scarcely four months. The fact that Doña Pilar glad-
dened herself with Don Pablo, though he was married, was not
the most scandalous aspect of the thing. What was deplorable
was that she had not waited to do so until at least one year of
the mourning she should have observed for her husband's death
had gone by. The whole town was up to date on Don Pablo's
evening visits—except, naturally, Doña Adelina. As sensational
events never happened in the town, and as the only thing
worth discussing was an occasional robbery, the townspeople
were eagerly awaiting the moment when Doña Adelina would
become aware that she was neither the preferred nor the only
woman with the right and pleasure of consoling herself with
Don Pablo for the sadnesses of this poor world. If two men met
in the cantina, if two women ran across each other in the market or chatted in front of a door, they came, after a brief consideration of the temperature, to the inevitable question: "Has
Doña Adelina found out at last?"

Nobody found anything immoral in the extramarital visits of
Don Pablo, because everybody was healthy enough in spirit and
normal enough to admit that Doña Pilar was doing nothing
more than take advantage of a natural right; and as nobody
before Don Pablo had undertaken to console the solitary lady,
he was playing the providential role. In the bottom of her heart
every married woman of Jovel rejoiced that the place had been
taken by someone other than her own husband. The neighbors
awaited the scandal, not for love of scandal, but because they
wished ardently to be present at the scene that Doña Adelina
would feel obliged to stage in order to safeguard her dignity.
Nevertheless, there was one black spot. It was very possible
that she knew already and was deliberately avoiding scandal. In
that case all hope of witnessing a tragicomedy was gone.

Before going to take a stroll through the plaza, the doctor
called at the house of Don Luis the pharmacist, his best friend
and associate, to wish him good evening. When pharmacist and
doctor thoroughly understand one another, business is profit-

able for both. If on the other hand they are at loggerheads, invalids get fat and live to old age and German manufacturers of pharmaceutical products discharge their workers.

When Cándido saw the doctor leave, he wondered again what he ought to do. He decided to go out to see where the doctor was going. He did not for one moment think of consulting another doctor, as he knew very well that in the matter of fees they were all the same. He had sought out this one because he was the one whom the Indians of the town and the surrounding villages were accustomed to consult. The Indians do not change their medical man except when he has killed one of them. Then they try another until the next death comes, and so on, successively. At the end of a few months they have gone through the whole local membership of the medical profession, and there is nothing else to do but to go back to the first doctor.

The Indians were the preferred patients of Jovel's doctors because they paid spot cash and were never given credit. At the exact moment when the Indian crossed the threshold of the consulting room, and even before the doctor spoke the slightest word to him, the Indian had to deposit his peso or whatever portion of it corresponded to the special price the doctor usually made him.

Cándido had left Marcelina lying in the portico in the care of his friends. He himself stood immobile in the middle of the street, not knowing which way to go. Obsessed by his wife's sufferings, he set out instinctively for the nearest drugstore with the idea that the pharmacist could give him some remedy. He nursed the vague hope of being able to buy some beneficent medicine with his eighteen pesos. On seeing Cándido enter, Don Luis asked him: "What do you want, fellow, ammonia or camphor?"

"What good would that be to me? I want something for my wife, who has a terrible bellyache on the right side."

He explained the situation. When he finished, the pharmacist told him that he had no remedy for a case like that. He was an honest man. From Cándido's account he understood the illness

Marcelina suffered from, and in his opinion only an operation could save her.

"Ask a doctor," he told Cándido.

At that precise moment the doctor entered the drugstore with the object of hearing from Don Luis what sensational event had occurred during the four hours since they had last seen each other.

"I know this fellow," the doctor said. "His wife is laid out in the portico of my house. She has appendicitis. I've put ice on her belly, but that can't cure her. If I don't operate, she'll die. But how can I operate if this fellow has only eighteen pesos?"

The pharmacist let loose a roar of laughter.

"That's clear. How could you operate on her at that price? But tell me, fellow, don't you know anybody who will lend you two hundred pesos to save your wife?"

"Who's going to lend me two hundred pesos?" replied Cándido in a voice that betrayed neither his despair nor his emotion, a voice so neutral that it seemed to mean: "So it is, and there's nothing I can do."

"You could get yourself engaged as a coffee-picker in Soconusco. The hiring boss won't refuse to lend you two hundred pesos," suggested the pharmacist.

Cándido shook his head, saying: "No, I don't want to go to Soconusco. There are Germans there. They own the coffee plantations. They're crueler than animals in the forest and treat one like a dog. That's impossible. If I went to work on the coffee plantations I'd kill some German with my machete if I saw him mistreating one of us."

"In that case, fellow, I don't see any possibility of helping you, and your wife will die."

"She'll die, there's no doubt, my chief," declared Cándido in as indifferent a tone as though he were discussing a stranger.

Then, leaning against the door jamb, he passed his hand through his hair and spat out into the street, which was lighted by a few lanterns that blinked sadly here and there.

With his two arms perilously leaning on the showcase and the cigarette traveling from one side of his mouth to the other, the pharmacist also looked toward the street from time to time. It ran into the plaza, and his shop was located on a corner. The big square was shaded by century-old trees with thick foliage. On the west side arose the Municipal Palace; on the north the cathedral; the other two sides were lined by the illuminated windows of the town's principal stores.

The doctor sat back on the safe. He felt the need of relaxation after the fatigues of a day's work. Languidly he too placed his elbows on the showcase and put his right foot on a package that had been brought to the shop that morning and had not even been unwrapped.

"How goes the matter of Doña Amalia?" asked the pharmacist.

In reality Don Luis scoffed crazily at the question of that old woman's health: she had never entrusted him with the smallest prescription. He put the question merely for the sake of saying something. It is a curious fact that the majority of men who know one another find themselves uncomfortable if they have nothing to talk about. That is why they indulge in so many stupidities when they get together that their words are even more empty than the gossipings of women.

"Doña Amalia?" asked the doctor. "To which one do you refer?"

"To the one who has an old cancer of the womb."

"Well, if we were to go by the scientific laws of medicine and have faith in the prognoses of the best disciples of Aesculapius, Doña Amalia ought to have been under the ground for at least ten years. But there you have her, with as much energy as you and me put together. One has to admit that the people are right when they insist that medical science is no more advanced than it was three thousand years ago. Speaking frankly, that's what I think."

The doctor was getting ready to propound other philosophical truths when he was interrupted by the arrival of a man who emerged brusquely from the darkness of the street.

"Ah, Don Gabriel!" exclaimed the doctor. "Where do you come from? Did you come to take a little walk around town?"

Don Gabriel stood still, hesitated a little, and then decided to enter, saying: "Good evening, gentlemen." Then with a movement of the hand he pushed back the brim of his hat and said: "What a mess! I came in just to cash the lumber camps' checks, and I find that Don Manuel hasn't enough cash."

"Can't he give you a check on his own bank?" asked the pharmacist.

"Naturally, and he's willing to. But what I need is hard cash, and that he won't have for six days. In the meantime I'll have to wait; that'll mean wasting too much time."

To raise Don Gabriel's morale, Don Luis said: "I'm going to make one of those famous cocktails which only we pharmacists know how to fix, and which have the virtue of making everything come out all right."

He went into the prescription room, his sanctum, as he called it, where he compounded his pills and mixed the potions ordered by the doctors.

"What's that fellow waiting for?" asked Don Gabriel.

"His wife has appendicitis and has to have an operation. I have offered to relieve her of a bit of guts for two hundred miserable pesos. If I don't, her number's up. But where can this boy get such a sum?" said the doctor.

Don Gabriel immediately seemed to take a deep personal interest in the Indian's case.

"Don't you know anybody in the city who would lend you the two hundred pesos?" he asked Cándido.

"No, my chief, nobody," replied Cándido, underlining his answer with another energetic expectoration. Then he pulled hard on his cigarette and seemed to regard the matter as finally settled.

Don Gabriel was a good Christian and a still better Catholic. He religiously observed the precepts of the Bible and lent his services to his neighbor every time the opportunity occurred. "Listen here, fellow. I'll lend you the two hundred pesos, and even fifty more, and besides that I'll give you two bottles of aguardiente so that you can treat the friends who helped you bring your wife here. You're not going to let them go home without showing them your gratitude, are you?"

Cándido could neither read nor write. He did not give the impression of being either more or less intelligent than the majority of his kind. On the other hand, he possessed one faculty more precious for everyday life than all the sciences. He had the natural gift of discerning what men's words might conceal and a wide experience of his fellows and, above all, of white men. He knew, without fear of ever making a mistake, that if a white man offered him one peso and he tempted bad fortune by accepting it, he would have to repay at least ten pesos; so he did not have to beat about the bush much before going straight to the point: "If it means working in Soconusco with the Germans, I won't go. I wouldn't do that even for five hundred pesos."

Just then the druggist came out of his sanctum shaking a mysterious beverage in a great tumbler and, blinking his eyes like an enamored crow, said: "Gentlemen, here's a cocktail you won't forget for a week, I give you my word. And I wouldn't give you the recipe for twenty-five pesos. So that you can get some idea how complicated it is, it's enough for you to know that it contains rosewater and an infinitesimal quantity of benzoin."

But when Don Gabriel was dealing with a matter of business, not even the most mysterious drink in the world could distract him from the juicy profit he foresaw. A new cocktail is delightful, but a substantial profit comforts the heart.

"To Soconusco with the Germans?" he said in a tone of surprise. "But, fellow, there's no question of the coffee plantations. Those people don't know how to pay, and they behave like brutes. They're always carrying a whip in their hands and landing it on the backs of the poor Indians who die in order to earn a few miserable pennies."

"You're right, my chief. But where am I going to get the two hundred pesos if not on the coffee plantations?"

"I'll be able to get you a job in the lumber camps."

Don Gabriel calmly rolled a cigarette.

"You are going to find me a guarantor. You'll surely find one among the friends who carried your wife. Tell me your name and where you live so that I can draw up our contract immediately. As soon as you've signed it, I'll give you the two hundred and fifty pesos without further formalities."

"You'd do well to accept right away," the druggist put in. "The doctor has already told you that it's necessary to relieve your wife of a piece of rotten intestine within two hours. Otherwise by morning you'll have nothing to do but bury her, and you'll be a widower."

"And your children won't have any mother," added the doctor, who, as was natural, did not lose sight of his own interests.

Even while Cándido's brain was undergoing the hard test of weighing the pros and cons of Don Gabriel's proposition, he did not forget that he was not the only person involved in the situation. The remark made by the doctor had turned his thoughts back to his wife and his children. A means of salvation was being offered him. This means, apparently sent by God and His saints—could he reject it to spare himself an arduous life without thereby committing a great sin? If he refused to sign, he would be allowing the providential help to escape and would be condemning to death the mother of his children. He would be her assassin. But if he accepted, long years of labor awaited him in the lumber camps, far from his wife, his children, and his land. And if, as a consequence of his refusal, his wife died, who would be able to save him? His conscience would give him no peace. Night and day the specter of the dead woman would torment him and overwhelm him with reproaches. In vain he looked for a way out. What would happen to his wife and children when he was away? No, he would not abandon them. He would leave to God the responsibility of his wife's death.

But Cándido had not counted on the astuteness of Don Gabriel, who had also seen the way by which Cándido could escape and who hastened to block it.

"Who told you that you'd have to abandon your family, fellow?" asked Don Gabriel, raising his eyebrows in surprise. "I never said anything of the sort."

Cándido stood looking at Don Gabriel, his mouth open, his expression questioning. He did not believe in miracles. Nevertheless, would it not be a miracle to find the means of obtaining the money for the operation and at the same time be able to remain at home with his family? How could it be possible? Evidently Cándido could not understand it quickly; it was too difficult. Furthermore, before he had time to ask any questions, Don Gabriel had got ahead of him, saying: "It's quite simple, fellow. You'll take your wife and children with you to the lumber camps."

Cándido was surprised by this solution, which had not remotely occurred to him. He realized immediately that it would be impossible for him to turn it down, because at one stroke it closed the last exit left him. For a moment he was struck by the idea of claiming that he could not abandon his land because he would lose it forever. But he felt that this argument would carry no weight—Don Gabriel would take care to let him know nobody would want to acquire his land, not even if it were for sale for fifty pesos: it was nothing but stones, and anyone could find a piece just as good whenever he wished merely by paying fifty centavos survey tax.

Furthermore, Don Gabriel did not give him more than one second for reflection, immediately asking his name, that of the place where he lived, and that of the friend he wished to act as his guarantor. He made careful notations in his little book and took off the leather belt that he wore under his shirt, in which, like the merchants, cattlemen, and landowners who travel about, he carried his money.

Don Gabriel slipped fifty silver coins out of the belt, counted them, and put them in a pile on the counter.

"Here you have an advance of fifty pesos. As regards the rest, I'll arrange with the doctor, to whom I'll deliver them tomorrow. Do you agree, doctor?"

"Certainly," said the doctor, and added, addressing the pharmacist: "Don Luis, will you make up this prescription immediately?" handing him a piece of paper on which he had just scribbled some hieroglyphics.

"Of course; in ten minutes you'll have it at your house. And now, gentlemen, we can at least honor this cocktail on which I have spent so much work and talent."

"Excellent," said Don Gabriel, clicking his tongue after he had emptied his glass in one swallow.

"There's some left," said Don Luis, filling the glasses a second time.

While the gentlemen were singing the praises of the cocktail and its creator, Cándido was busy placing the fifty pesos in the folds of his red woolen sash. When he had finished, he slipped toward the exit and, without taking leave of anybody, disappeared into the night.

Cándido met his friends in the portico of the doctor's house. They were huddled together and seemed to be watching over Marcelina, but they maintained so deep a silence that Cándido thought they were asleep, as it was not customary for any group of people from his village to remain silent, looking stupidly at one another. On the contrary, when Indians from the south get together, they talk interminably. They talk late into the night, and when sleep overtakes them, some will wake up every half hour to make remarks about those who are sleeping. On the day following, they will hardly have opened their eyes before they loosen their tongues again. Only when they are on the road, during their work, or in the presence of strangers do these Indians withdraw into an obstinate, ferocious silence that gives the impression that they are mutes.

Cándido, approaching the group, could scarcely make them out in the light cast over the portico by a little oil lamp in one of the windows. He stumbled among the squatting men and became aware that they formed a circle around his wife's stretched-out form. He realized immediately that something had happened. He sat down beside the nearest Indian, touched him lightly on the shoulder, and asked in a feeble voice: "When did she leave me?"

"About half an hour ago. She woke up and began to complain greatly of the pain. Then she asked: 'Cándido, my husband, where is he?' Then she stretched herself out and died."

The doctor arrived, opened the heavy entrance gate, and shouted in the direction of the Indians: "Bring her into the consulting room. I'm going to operate on her." And not stopping, he went with long strides into the interior of the house, opening the door and calling out: "Hi! Rodolfa! You cursed sleepy hen! Put six candles in the necks of empty bottles and bring them to me. I've got to do an operation. And a bucketful of hot water, too. Hurry! Do you hear?"

The doctor left the door of the consulting room wide open while he lighted a candle fixed in a pewter candlestick from which the enamel had been chipped away on all sides. Against the wall was a small glass cupboard in which could be seen rows of bottles filled with dark liquids and bearing labels marked with skulls. Those small bottles produced an extraordinary effect on his patients, and for that reason he had placed them in the front of the cupboard. Elsewhere in the cabinet could be seen, carefully laid out, his instruments, which seemed to be mostly scissors and pincers for pulling teeth rather than surgical instruments. When they were examined closely, it could be seen that the nickel plating had all disappeared and that many of them were rusty. On a little table half painted white and covered with a piece of oilcloth of doubtful cleanliness, larger instruments were spread out, looking like a blacksmith's tools. But vague traces of nickel plating among the rust indicated their obscure origin.

The doctor lit a cigarette and went over to the cupboard. From it he took a bottle of considerable size, on the label of which the inscription "Hennessy" could be clearly read. He raised it to the level of the candle flame, looked through it to verify its contents, poured a half-tumblerful into a mug, swallowed it in two gulps, smacked his tongue, and coughed to clear his throat.

"The devil," he murmured. "I'll have to buy another tomorrow. This is like hot oil. Unless that sow of a servant is helping herself while she does the cleaning. I'll stick a label on it marked 'Poison.' Then she won't dare."

He coughed vigorously and went to the table on which were the scissors, pincers, and blacksmith's implements and began to rub them with gauze. He was about halfway through this work when he remembered that the sick woman was still stretched out in the portico. He went rapidly toward the door, shouting: "What the devil's the matter with you? Are you going to bring her in or not?"

Nobody replied. Then he crossed the threshold, went out to the portico, and approached the circle of Indians. The men looked at him without uttering a word. He bent over and let the light from his candle fall on Marcelina's face. He smacked her cheeks, raised one of her eyelids, and said: "Well, well, it was to be expected."

His face betrayed a deep disappointment. He felt himself somehow frustrated by this woman. Still hoping to carve up her body, he placed a hand on Marcelina's breast. Then he quickly withdrew his hand and began vigorously pinching her cheeks. But he could not make one drop of blood flow. Brusquely he asked Cándido: "Why didn't you come sooner?"

"But, doctor, I arrived on time!" Cándido protested softly.

"To hell with it! Shut your mouth. And you—all of you—take this away from here."

"With your permission, doctor, we are going to take her home."

Cándido caressed his wife's face and covered her naked breasts with his sarape. The other Indians wrapped the body in the straw mat it had been lying on, tied it up like a bale, and placed it on the improvised stretcher. Cándido went toward the gate and showed the way to the others.

They were about to leave when the doctor called to Cándido: "Listen, fellow, are you thinking of leaving without paying your debts?"

Cándido retraced his steps. "I forgot, doctor. Excuse me. How much do I owe you?"

"Five pesos for the first consultation and five for the post-mortem examination—that is, for having verified the death."

"Excuse me, doctor, but you didn't cure her. You did nothing to ease her pain."

"Didn't I examine her carefully and tell you that it was necessary to operate on her?"

"Yes, my chief."

"Good! You don't call that work?"

"Certainly, doctor, it was work, but work that served no purpose. As you see, she died in spite of everything."

"Friend, I've enough other things to do without arguing with you. Either you pay me the ten pesos you owe me, or I'll put you in jail. Is that clear? And your wife's body won't leave here until you've paid your debts. I'm a reasonable man, and I have the kindest feelings toward the Indians and toward you in particular. Any other doctor would have charged you ten pesos more for having kept your wife in the portico. Don't overlook that I must have the place where she died cleaned with disinfectant. That's an order of the health department, of which I am director. And you can be sure that nobody will make me a present of disinfectant."

The doctor held out his open hand toward Cándido to make him understand that he must not argue further and that the open hand must be filled. Cándido began to unroll his woolen sash. He took out ten pesos, which he deposited one by one in the doctor's hand. As he was counting the money and thinking of what he had to do to earn a single peso by selling in the market the produce from his miserable patch of land, his friends, bearing the body, passed through the gateway. They would wait for Cándido in the street.

Funeral establishments are open day and night, because the climate demands that a corpse be interred within twelve hours, and sometimes sooner. So Cándido easily found one open. The cheapest coffin was a rectangular wooden case badly painted black. The artisan who had made it received a laughable wage, and he satisfied himself with a few brush-strokes, leaving the natural color of the wood showing through in many places and the bottom not even daubed.

"This coffin costs four pesos," said the employee.

"Good. I'll take it."

"But I'm afraid it's very small for your wife," the salesman continued, seeing that Cándido had enough money to buy one costing more.

One of the Indians measured the body and the wooden case with his arms and declared: "The coffin is big enough, Cándido."

The businessman felt that he was going to lose the opportunity of making a more advantageous sale. Slapping Cándido's back affectionately, he said: "Listen, fellow, you can't bury the mother of your children in a coffin as ugly as that. What would the holy Virgin think when she saw her in it? She is quite capable of not letting her enter heaven, and I don't believe that you're ready to leave your wife hanging around the gates of paradise in the company of sinners, bandits, and assassins. This box you want to buy is intended for corpses of unknown people found on the roads. Look at this other coffin, how pretty it is. You're not obliged to buy it, but at least look at it. Don't you believe that your wife would rest better in it? And I assure you that when the most holy Virgin sees this lovely box, she'll go up to your wife and take her by the hand to lead her into paradise herself. That's sure, because she'll see immediately that the deceased is not a lost sinner but a good Christian who was baptized. I suppose that your wife was baptized?"

"Yes, my chief, when she was a child."

"Then you can't bury her in that common coffin. The other box is well made, beautifully painted black outside and white inside; it's lined with lace paper, fine Chinese paper."

"How much does it cost?" asked Cándido.

"Twenty pesos, fellow."

The Indian looked at him in consternation. Whereupon the salesman immediately abandoned his commercial tone and said to him in a voice full of compassion: "It's hard, my friend, to lose one's wife. I know that better than anybody, because I've been widowed twice, and as I'm being considerate of you, I'll let you have the coffin for only seventeen pesos. At that price I make nothing. I swear by the most holy Virgin that it cost me sixteen pesos and fifty centavos."

They began to bargain, and when at last the Indian could lay the body of Marcelina in the bottom of the coffin, it was because he had paid out thirteen pesos. He still had to buy blessed candles and the aguardiente needed if his friends were not to leave with dry throats.

2

　　From the day on which his wife had fallen sick until a week after her death, Cándido lived in a kind of
daze. His thought had stopped, his sensibility had become
blunted.

To buy the pretty coffin, the wax candles, and the five liters
of aguardiente so as to be able to refresh his friends and those
who came to offer condolences, Cándido had depleted his sash
without thinking one single moment of the way he had obtained the money, not to mention the consequences that the
possession and dwindling of such a sum would have for him.
Even if he had not had a single centavo in his pocket, he would
have found the means to bury his wife decently. At the worst,
his friends and other Indians would have helped him to roll
Marcelina up in two sleeping-mats and to fell a tree and hack
from it some boards to make a box. Cándido had begun to
spend without keeping account from the precise moment at
which the doctor had insisted on the payment of the ten pesos,
with the threat of retaining Marcelina's corpse if he did not
pay up. Vain threat, because the doctor would not have been
able to keep the body more than ten hours, at the end of which
he would have been obliged to let the town take care of the
burial. But Cándido had not hesitated to reduce his store of
pesos. The idea of leaving Marcelina's body in the doctor's
house, of returning to his home and appearing before his two
little boys without having brought their mother, dead or alive,

horrified him. Afterwards, as if seized by giddiness, he had continued his reckless spending.

Although scrupulously honest, at this time he would have spent even funds entrusted to him by someone else, his grief being enough to prevent him from telling good from bad, just from unjust. During the three weeks after the death of his wife it never occurred to him for a moment that his expenditures would decide his destiny. The money was of no use in the village, for the land produced enough to prevent death from hunger. But it was necessary to buy three suckling pigs. These little animals are as necessary for the subsistence of the Indian peasants as cows are for Dakota or Minnesota farmers. Unfortunately, Cándido, in trying to dig a stone from the earth, had broken his machete so close to the handle that what remained of the blade was useless. He made his calculations: a new machete would cost him three pesos. As for the little pigs, he could find them at four reales each, provided he took the trouble to look for the smallest ones in the market at Jovel. Altogether he needed four and a half pesos.

On the market day he made up his mind and got together the sum required. Like all the Indians of his tribe, he had the habit of wrapping his money in a rag and burying it in the earth floor of his hut. When they need to take out a few centavos, they disinter the cache, extract the coins, and bury the cloth again, but in a different spot, usually under the hearth. Cándido dug in the floor, took out his bundle—and could not restrain a cry of surprise at finding before his eyes twenty-six pesos.

In the preceding few days he had been emerging little by little from his torpor. Work in the field, urgent because of the approaching rains, and looking after his two children had brought him back to reality. As the clarity of his thoughts had vanished when he took his wife to Jovel, all that had happened afterward, including his negotiations with the doctor and the druggist, seemed to him like a nightmare, and he remembered only the eighteen pesos he had saved earlier. His stupefaction did not last more than a minute. Suddenly he remembered the reason for his wealth, the amounts he had disbursed, and that he not only had lost his wife, but had pawned his freedom forever. He had turned himself into property, into the slave of Don Gabriel, who would send him to the lumber camps, uprooting him from the soil in which Marcelina rested.

He was struck with the idea of running away with his two little boys, but two considerations held him back: one of his fellow Indians was his guarantor, and if Cándido broke his promise, his friend would have to take his place. He could not do such a thing. Furthermore, if he fled, he would also be separating himself from the land that was flesh of his flesh. There was nothing to do, then, but wait for the day when the soldiers would come looking for him to force him to go to the mahogany camps. The faint hope struck him that perhaps Don Gabriel might have forgotten him. That was possible, seeing that Don Gabriel had not sent him the two hundred pesos, to which the doctor had no right whatever. And in that case Don Gabriel himself had not fulfilled his part of the agreement.

On the following day Cándido, without even waiting for the sun to rise, set out on the trail with his two children. He carried a great bundle of corn on his back. The older boy was doubled under the weight of a bale of fodder, and the little one carried a sack of wool. Cándido intended to sell his products in town and, with what he could get for them, buy salt, sugar, and a piece of sheeting. As a precaution he was taking five pesos with him.

He completed his deals quickly, obtaining as usual a ridiculously small sum. Then he bought the little pigs and put them in a sack, which he slung over his shoulder. The little animals squealed and struck him with their feet, which pleased Cándido, who knew that such vigorous behavior was a sign of good health and that they would be easy to raise. Then he turned his steps toward the hardware shop called El Globo to buy a new machete. He left his sack outside the door and told the children to watch it. He went into the store with as much timidity and embarrassment as if, instead of being a customer with money who was gong to bring profit to the merchant, he was a shameful beggar, to be received with kicks.

He had scarcely entered the shop when he heard someone calling him. "Ah, see here, fellow, I was just looking for you."

Cándido raised his eyes and saw Don Gabriel, the labor contractor, the trickster.

Like all the white townspeople, Don Gabriel spent the day now in one shop, now in another, chatting with the tradesmen and looking for familiar faces. Between one stop and the next he went to the saloon to quench his thirst and commune with his friends. It was clear that his political opinions were of considerable importance. When he had refreshed himself the way he liked, he returned to his occupations and thus passed the day. Then he had a good excuse for returning to the saloon, and on this visit he was not satisfied with a modest little drink, but needed at least a dozen. Then he went out for a stroll through the plaza until time for the evening meal. As supper could not be enjoyed without a reasonable quantity of liquid, he had to make another call at the bar. The work of real gentlemen, indispensable for the progress of civilization, is intermittent. They know how to alternate serious matters with pleasant pastimes, while they have work done by those who are not gentlemen—and, indeed, they could not live at all without this arrangement.

It had been during one of those very brief periods of activity, generally lasting only a few minutes, that he had been able to trick Cándido, tying him up in the knots of a contract whose terms he was recalling during another of those periods. The business of strolling around the shops and letting the hours pass uselessly did not turn out as unproductive as might have been supposed, seeing that if Don Gabriel had not been (apparently) idling away his time in the hardware shop, he would not have met Cándido and would not have been able to take up this important matter with him.

"Listen, fellow, don't forget that the group leaves for the lumber camps Monday and that you'll be going along."

"But, my patron, I didn't use the money—my wife died before the doctor arrived."

"The two hundred pesos are at your disposal. You can ask the druggist for them whenever you like."

To be sure, the money was not in the drugstore or anywhere else, but Don Gabriel thought that if Cándido claimed the money, of which he now had no need, there would always be time to deposit it or to cover up the whole matter by fine words.

But Cándido resisted, saying weakly: "No, my chief. Because I haven't taken the money there is no contract for the lumber camps."

"You took fifty pesos—yes or no?"

"Yes, but I can return them."

For a moment Don Gabriel was disconcerted. He was afraid he might lose his man. Yet he became calm almost immediately at the thought that it was impossible for the Indian to have those fifty pesos, seeing that he had paid the doctor and bought the coffin. Also, Don Gabriel was sure that Cándido could never have saved that much.

"Do you think I'm going to pay attention to your stupidities? Even if you were to give me back the fifty pesos, you would not be free from your obligations. You've signed the contract before witnesses and you also received an advance payment before witnesses. Even if you'd taken only three pesos, it would be the same thing. You can't duck your obligation. Do you want me to take you to the police station for them to tell you which of us is right?"

Cándido did not reply, and a fear struck Don Gabriel.

"Oh, no—so that's it! You intend to try to clear out. . . ."

Immediately Cándido understood what was happening. He rushed to the door and doubtless would have succeeded in getting away had it not been for his children, whom he could not abandon in the town. He shouted to them to follow him, but by then Don Gabriel had seized each one of them by an arm, and in a stentorian voice was shouting: "Police! Police! This way!"

The Municipal Palace was just on the other side of the plaza. The fourth door led to the police station, where a few policemen were always waiting for orders. In response to Don Gabriel's shouts, three of them ran up with clubs in hand.

"What's happening, Don Gabriel? Have these boys stolen something from you?"

"Take this pair of lousy brats into the station and lock them up. I'm going to speak to the chief right now."

"Right you are, Don Gabriel, at your orders," the policemen replied servilely, grabbing the children, who were screaming with fear: "Papa! Papa!"

In spite of the load hindering him, Cándido had been able to cover a good distance. He was almost across the plaza, thinking that his children would follow him, for he knew they were quick-witted and accustomed to chasing rabbits and iguanas. But on hearing them scream, he turned and saw them being taken to the Municipal Palace. There was nothing to do but go back. When he neared the station door the policemen let go of the children, who immediately rushed toward him and held onto his knees, begging for protection. A man seated at a table was looking profoundly bored, staring out toward the plaza, doubtless because he had nothing better to do.

"Stay here, fellow! Wait until Don Gabriel comes. He seems to have something against you."

Along the walls of the portico there were two large wooden benches on which offenders sat resignedly to wait until they were called. In the big building were housed not only the municipal services but also the town council, the police, the civil judge, the criminal judge, the federal and local authorities, and the tax offices—and there was still room in the patio for the jail cells.

Policemen awaiting orders were sitting on one of the benches at the entrance. Cándido remained standing for a short while in the hall. Nobody seemed to pay the least attention to him. Then he went into the patio and sat down in a corner. He could not think of escaping with the police covering the entrance. A quarter of an hour had passed when Don Gabriel, in no hurry, strolled in and asked the drowsy clerk: "Is Don Alejo in?"

Don Alejo was the chief of police.

"No, not just now, Don Gabriel. He went out to have an aperitif with the deputy. But he won't be long."

"Good. Then I'll come back. Until then!"

"At your service," said the clerk, bowing.

Don Gabriel went out of the room and slowly lighted a cigarette. He glanced around the patio and deigned to notice the presence of Cándido huddled in his corner.

"Get this into your head, fellow: neither you nor anybody else is going to slip through my hands. When I've caught a fish, I hold onto it tight."

He held out his cigarette case to the policemen. Each of them took a cigarette and thanked him courteously.

Before going out Don Gabriel added: "Keep a sharp eye on that Indian, boys."

"Don't worry, Don Gabriel, he won't get away."

Cándido pulled toward him the sack in which he had the pigs, and patted the little creatures, which squealed and tried to get out. "Quiet, quiet!" he said. To the children he added: "They're full of life. They'll grow to be big pigs."

"Yes, papa," replied the children, "they're beautiful little pigs."

Cándido took five centavos from his sash.

"Here," said he, holding out the money to the older boy, "take this and go to the corner of the market. Buy a measure of corn for them to eat. They're hungry."

Angelito obeyed. He returned a few minutes later with his shirttail full of corn. Although Indians' money has exactly the same value as that of the townspeople, they are never given a piece of paper or a bag in which to wrap their purchases. What end would such generosity serve? They can just as well keep their things in their hats, in their shirttails, or in the folds of their sarapes. The Indians could not expect any attention from shopkeepers even when without sales to the Indian peasants commerce would be ruined and the tradesmen would have to shut their doors: the Indians who came into Jovel each week or fortnight to do their buying and selling numbered twenty or twenty-five thousand—that is, twice as many as the population of the town, for which they provided a livelihood.

The suckling pigs ate the corn voraciously, to the great satisfaction of Cándido and his boys. Meanwhile the commandant had returned. He paid no attention to the Indians huddled in the corner of the patio. The patio was full of them constantly. They came to settle some matter with the authorities or simply to rest or to wait for friends whom they had agreed to join there for the trip to their homes.

A few minutes later Don Gabriel reappeared.

"How are you, Don Alejo?"

"As usual, Don Gabriel."

"Don Alejo, out there in the patio is an Indian whom I'd like you to lock up for me until Monday. I'll pay you for his keep."

"On what grounds, Don Gabriel? You know that you must make a formal charge. Without that I can't lock up anybody, because it all has to be entered in the record. . . ."

"Breach of contract, Don Alejo, or rather, attempted breach of contract."

"Good. How did it happen?" The commandant gave an order: "One man—here!"

One of the policemen sprang toward the door, saluted in military fashion, and said: "At your orders, chief."

"Bring in that fellow of Don Gabriel's."

The policeman returned to the door and in the same imperious tone used by the commandant shouted: "Hi! You! Come this way, and hurry if you don't want me to come get you!"

Cándido stood up, put the pigs in the sack, closed it, put it over his shoulder, and followed the policeman.

"What have you got in that sack, fellow?" asked the commandant.

"Some little pigs that I want to fatten up, my chief."

"Right. You can keep them with you in the patio."

The commandant turned toward the two heavily laden boys, who were trying to hide behind their father's knees.

"And those kids?"

"They're mine, my chief, and your humble servants," Cándido replied politely.

Don Alejo looked at Don Gabriel.

Don Gabriel did not show the least embarrassment. "It would be best to lock them all up together, Don Alejo. The kids can't return alone to the village."

"You're right, Don Gabriel. But on Monday? What are you going to do with the children when the father leaves for the lumber camps?"

Don Gabriel started laughing.

"Quite so! Their mother is dead. I think the only solution is to send them along with their father to the lumber camps."

The commandant made a gesture of approval. He looked at the children distractedly, as if a thousand other preoccupations were running through his mind, and said: "In fact, Don Gabriel, I believe that's the best, the most humane solution. It's not right to separate children from their parents. Now that we've decided that, I think that we can go over to Don Ranulfo's bar and have a little drink."

Once in the street, Don Gabriel said to the commandant: "Now, you know, Don Alejo, that I make something out of this, but I also allow others to earn a little."

"I know it well, Don Gabriel, and it's precisely about that I wish to say two words to you."

"Say them, Don Alejo. You know that I'm always at your service."

They went into the saloon.

"Those children," continued the commandant, "are healthy and strong. Why not make them cowherds or shepherds? They would work beside their father and help him, as is their duty and as God has prescribed."

"I'm of the same opinion, Don Alejo, above all because to tear them away from their father's side would be an unpardonable cruelty, a sin for which we'd find no pardon."

"Your health, Don Gabriel."

"Yours, Don Alejo."

The tequila cleared their throats. Don Gabriel sucked a lemon to dilute the strong taste of the alcohol. Then he said: "Fill them up again, Don Ranulfo. You have here two gentlemen dying of thirst in the desert."

While Don Ranulfo turned away to get the bottle, Don Gabriel whispered into the ear of Don Alejo: "Twenty-five pesos, eh? I think that should settle the matter."

"Accepted, Don Gabriel. And always glad to be able to render a service."

The police chief put the money in his pocket, emptied his glass at one gulp, put a pinch of salt in the hollow of his hand, and took it with one lick of his tongue.

"Damn it!" he exclaimed. "I must hurry along. Excuse me, Don Gabriel. So long, Don Ranulfo." And with a friendly wave to the bartender he went out.

3

     On the following Monday the Indians set out on the march. There were thirty-five of them, including Cándido's two little boys. There were four women in the caravan. They had not wanted to abandon their husbands and now were bravely following them to the lumber camps, ready to face the worst fatigues in order to behave as good companions. Before reaching the jungle, the caravan was joined by small isolated groups of workers belonging to the villages or districts along the route. Some were villagers. Some were from estates where Don Gabriel had ensnared them earlier, and they had been awaiting the coming of the caravan in order to join it. The troop increased with every passing mile.

On leaving the last village before entering the empty regions, there were one hundred and twenty men, fourteen women, and nine children younger than twelve years of age. Children who were (or seemed to be) older than that counted as adults but were paid half-wages.

At the little village the ranks had been swelled by three strange-looking men who had asked Don Gabriel to take them to the lumber camps. Don Gabriel had looked at them a long time before deciding to take them on.

"So be it," he said at last. "If you have made up your minds to work hard, I think I can give you jobs."

To tell the truth, he would have liked to embrace them. Three husky youths like this were an unlooked-for gift, all the more because he did not have to advance them money or spend anything on them except for the small rations of black beans they would consume on the way. On the contrary, each of them would bring him a commission of fifty pesos, money that could be considered as having dropped from heaven. He noted down the names they gave him without for a moment questioning their authenticity. One does not look a gift horse in the mouth.

The three men were out of the ordinary. To judge by their appearance, they must have been like rolling stones in the region for some time. None of them possessed a scrap of luggage, whereas all the Indians in the caravan were loaded with packs, showing that they were coming from some sort of homes.

"You seem very tired and out of everything," said Don Gabriel.

In truth he said this for the sake of having something to say in front of the foremen, and to fortify himself beforehand against the blame they might place on him for having signed up vagabonds or perhaps fugitives from justice. He knew ahead of time the explanation the men would give him, and it was with a certain pleasure that he listened to it.

"We were waiting for you to pass by, patron. We knew that you would have to pass by here, but we did not know the day. So as to live in the meantime, we had to sell all our belongings."

"Yes, to be sure, that's natural enough," said Don Gabriel. "As you understand, it's very difficult for me to be exact about my itinerary. Sometimes we have to stop at various places, and that slows up the march. I'll take you with me. But understand well that I do it out of charity and because I'm a good Christian and couldn't under any condition leave men to die of hunger in the jungle when they've made up their minds to live honorably by their work. Well, then, I'll do everything possible to find you work in the camps. But I don't know if I'll succeed, because there are lots of men in the camps, an endless number of people who can't be employed. On that understanding you can come along."

Don Gabriel added to the list the following names: Martín Trinidad Castelazo, Juan Méndez, and Lucio Ortiz. Don Gabriel was as clever in business as he was a good judge of men. He took good care not to register the contracts of the recent recruits in Hucutsin, as he was supposed to. He made no contracts with them and judged it entirely unnecessary to present them to the mayor, it being difficult to register nonexistent contracts. He advised the men to go straight to the encampment situated outside the village and not to show themselves unnecessarily.

He was well acquainted with the world and knew that those three would not try to slip away. What they did after arriving at the camps was of little importance to him, since by then he would have received his commission.

At the entrance to Hucutsin, seated beside the road, an Indian girl was waiting. She was barefooted and was carrying a large package under her arm. When she saw the first men in the caravan come out from the underbrush, she climbed up a little hillock to be able to see the whole column of marchers better. With a sharp glance she examined those who were going past. The men advanced, bent under the weight of their packs, tired out, partly covering their faces with their hands, which they held up to lessen the pressure from the heavy leather tumplines that pressed against their foreheads. These long, hard leather thongs from which hung the bundles on their backs made their heads swim after so many hours of marching through mountainous country. They were like steel bands that became tighter and tighter every minute.

The girl looked closely at every Indian who went past. When almost half of the column had filed past her, her face expressed a deep disappointment. Suddenly a ray of hope shone in her eyes. She straightened up, stretched her arms toward the sky, and shouted: "Cándido, my brother!"

Cándido, almost doubled in two, limping, with his head bent toward the ground, was caught by surprise. For a moment he gave the impression of being fastened to the spot. Then he started off again hesitatingly. His sons were following all their father's movements in the secret hope of being regarded as equals by the men in the caravan.

When the girl realized that the man she had called was going ahead without looking at her, she ran after the caravan to reach her brother. Close to him, she shouted again: "Cándido, my brother, don't you know me?"

At that Cándido straightened up, stopped, and looked at the girl with stupefaction. The children allowed the parcels they had been entrusted with to fall to the ground and ran to the girl, yelling joyfully: "Aunt Modesta! Aunt Modesta!"

Each of them seized one of her hands and covered it with kisses. The Indians continued to move ahead. Only Cándido's immediate neighbors took vague notice of the scene, but they were all far too weary to be interested in what did not affect them personally.

Cándido stepped out of the file. He dropped on his knees to relieve himself more easily of his cargo. As the pack touched the ground, the weak squeals of the pigs could be heard. He had been unable to get rid of them, and he had taken them with him because he had not been allowed to return to his patch of land, as he would have liked, to talk to his neighbors and friends and to place in their care the few possessions he was abandoning.

Cándido straightened up, raised his head, and at last recognized his sister, still not entirely sure that it was she, flesh and bone. The excitement and joy of the children at last convinced him, for they loved their aunt with the ardor often displayed by children toward important members of their family younger than their parents and accustomed to pampering them more.

Modesta was the youngest of his sisters. He was the oldest in the family and had a marked preference for this girl, to whom he had shown it especially when, on the death of their father, he himself had become head of the family.

Their mother had died of smallpox, leaving him the entire care of Modesta, their older sisters having married and followed their husbands to their respective villages.

Modesta had insisted that Cándido should get married. He had long hesitated on her account. When at last he decided to take a wife, obtain a piece of land, and raise a family, his first care was to place Modesta as a servant in the home of a businessman in Jalotepec. This man paid her a mere two pesos a month but gave her permission to go and see her brother every second week. It often happened that she did not have this freedom more than once a month, because her mistress, like all mistresses, always discovered something urgent to be done at the last moment, or found that she had to go visiting on that very day or was expecting friends. But their meetings, rare as they were, were enough to strengthen even more the bonds that united Modesta with her brother and her sister-in-law. When Cándido had his first son, she devoted her whole existence to her brother and his family. Life did not begin for her until she was in Cándido's home, in the miserable hut he had built, beside which her master's house could have passed for a palace. Everything indicated that Modesta, so that she might devote herself to Cándido and his family, would never marry.

The stragglers followed at a distance. Epitacio, the overseer, came up on horseback at the rear of the marching column and forced the laggards to catch up with the others.

"Get on there, fellow! Move on, keep going!" he shouted at Cándido. "We're there. The camp's nearby, and there you can curl up as much as you wish and rest. Come on, now, get ahead!"

He cracked his whip and repeated the same words to another straggler.

Cándido adjusted the leather straps across his forehead and got up. The children again took up their bundles. Modesta ran to the place where she had left her bundle, put it under her arm, and rejoined her family.

"Are you going to Hucutsin, little sister?" asked Cándido, advancing painfully.

"Yes, brother, I'm going there."

"Have you found a good job there? They say that Hucutsin is very big, bigger than Chamo, as big as Vitztan. I believe they'll pay you better there than in Doña Paulina's house."

Modesta didn't answer. They walked as fast as they could to

catch up with the column, which was now crossing the town. The inhabitants stood in front of their houses to watch the exhausted Indians pass by, feeling the pleasure they had felt earlier when a regiment marched through. For this column of Indians meant profitable business to them. Their town was the last inhabited place before the forest; that is to say, it was the last opportunity the Indians had of buying necessities, in exchange for which they would leave here the money that had been advanced to them. From here on they would not see a centavo until their contracts were worked out. In the camps there was nothing to buy, and money had no value. So at this point they all spent every last centavo they possessed. This explained the joy of the inhabitants of the town.

The column had to cross the town to reach the camping grounds, installed in a poor meadow, the grass of which disappeared among stones. Later the laborers would be summoned to the Municipal Palace, where the mayor had to stamp the contracts. Not until this formality was completed were they free to walk around and make their purchases.

Cándido rejoined the file, with Modesta and the children near him. When they had passed the last houses and the cemetery and had finally reached the encampment, Cándido asked: "Where, then, is the house where you're going to work? I thought it would be one of the big ones in the plaza."

Modesta replied in a soft, somewhat mournful voice: "Good heavens, this pack is heavy! It's lucky that we've arrived."

Cándido set about making a fire.

"Let me help you, brother. I've rested a long time and I'm less tired than you."

She unpacked a brazier and an earthenware bowl and got ready to make coffee and heat the tortillas.

"You children, go look for some wood and bring water."

Cándido, seated on the ground, set himself to rolling a cigarette. He looked at his sister for a moment and then stood up and said: "I'm going to town to buy corn for the little pigs. They're hungry."

He found a stake lying near by, drove it into the earth, and tethered the pigs to it. The little animals, having been squeezed in the sack on Cándido's shoulder during the whole march, squealed with pleasure on feeling the ground under their feet. They rooted in the soil, scratched about with their feet, and bickered fiercely over roots they found.

Cándido returned in a few minutes with a handful of corn that he threw to the pigs. He was amused to watch them push one another aside. He puffed vigorously at his cigarette and said: "They're gluttons, those little pigs of mine. Soon they'll be fine and fat."

Then he raised his head and seemed to come out of a dream. He watched his sister fanning the fire, saying to himself that even now he still did not understand how she happened to be there or how she had come.

"Now it's ready. Boys! Come here!" she called to her nephews, who had gone over to another hearthfire to watch an Indian skin and cook a rabbit he had caught on the way.

The four of them sat down around the brazier and ate their meager supper. When they had drunk the last drop of coffee, Cándido lighted the cigarette he had rolled before eating and puffed at it.

Modesta cleaned the utensils, put them in order, and took some tobacco from a pouch, making a cigarette by rolling it in a small corn leaf. Overwhelmed by fatigue, the children lay down near the fire. Modesta covered them with an embroidered sarape that she took from her bundle.

"It's getting late, little sister. You'd do better to go to your new masters' house to sleep."

"Tomorrow will be time enough. I can even go there after you have left. I don't think that will be before a couple of days."

"That's right. Don Gabriel told me so."

"I'll go look up my masters when I like. They don't know whether I'm arriving today or next week."

Cándido made a movement with his head which indicated: "Just as you wish."

They remained silent a long time. Night was near. It fell

heavily, brutally, like a hammer striking. They sat still near the fire, smoking, their eyes fixed on the burning wood, lost in their thoughts. Around them on all sides fires shone. Of the men huddled near them, some were talking, laughing, arguing; others, the majority, were quiet, as close together as possible, like dogs in search of warmth.

The thickets that bounded the camp became blurred in a slight mist. Clouds riding in the sky allowed a few stars to be glimpsed at intervals. The rainy season was not far away. From the little town human voices reached them, confused and apparently happy voices. From one corner of the camp the nostalgic melody of a harmonica arose, and farther away, perhaps in the cathedral plaza, a marimba sounded. Among the thickets a frightened or pursued bird drowned with its cries the amorous buzzing of the cicadas and the song of the crickets.

The hearth beside which Cándido and his sister were sitting was nothing but a heap of dark-red coals gradually dying out. Cándido went to cut some branches, broke them in pieces, and threw an armful on the embers. The fire became still darker. Cándido bent down and blew on it. A flame suddenly reached a dry branch, blazed, and—surprised to find itself alone—sank back into the dark green, shifting smoke.

"I went to see you on Sunday, you and the children," Modesta said suddenly.

She was but a few inches away from Cándido, separated from him only by the fire. The smoke prevented him from seeing her expression. He puffed his cigarette without replying.

"Your neighbor Lauro," continued Modesta, "told me that you and the children were in the jail in Jovel. He didn't know anything more, and I set out. I met Manuel, who had returned from Jovel the day before."

"Yes, Manuel knew what had happened to me. He was outside El Globo when Don Gabriel pounced on me and ordered me to be ready on Monday," replied Cándido, as though evoking a far-off memory.

"Manuel told me everything and I understood that you would not be coming back. I went at once to find Uncle Diego and told him the whole story. Later he came over. He has promised me to look after your land and your house. He and our aunt will live there until you return. And so you will be able to go back to your house, your goats, and your sheep. In the meantime Cousin Emiliano and his wife will live in Uncle Diego's house. He will easily be able to look after his own land as well as theirs."

"Very good. That's the way I'd like things to be. That night in the patio of the jail, I couldn't sleep for thinking about what would happen if I had to leave everything without arranging for someone to take care of it."

"We did all we could, the natural thing to do," replied Modesta in the tone she might have used to speak of the changes a family undergoes when the father or mother dies.

The tone impressed Cándido and gave him courage to say: "I am glad that Marcelina is dead. At least she doesn't know what has happened. She can't see what is happening now. How sad she would be if she saw all this, to know that I had to sell myself to save her life. It would be impossible for me to make her happy again, and she would die of grief."

"She would have gone with you to the lumber camps."

"I'd never have allowed it. She could easily have found another man."

"You know very well that she would never have loved any other man. I would have gone to live with Marcelina, and together we'd have cultivated your land, taken care of the goats and sheep, so that when you returned you'd have found the house all in order and the children grown and healthy. We would have waited for you and thought of you day and night. We would have set up a little altar in a corner of the house, with a light for the most holy Virgin, and we would have prayed to her every day to have you return safe and sound."

Cándido poked at the fire. It was too small to give enough heat, and there was hardly any light from it, but it gave the spot a feeling of intimacy and awakened in those two beings a comforting feeling that for some hours helped them forget their griefs and their sad destiny.

At neighboring fires other people sat, worn out or excited, vague, less defined than shadows, their voices mixed in conversation, rising suddenly to call someone and fading immediately into the night; insects buzzed incessantly in the bushes, and branches groaned, agitated by the wind—all these sounds intermingled, fusing into a fantastic reality in which Cándido and Modesta felt themselves isolated from the world, linked to it solely by the fire.

The children slept, wrapped up in the sarape. One of them was breathing deeply, and the other, dreaming, was saying some unintelligible words. Soon they fell silent. Modesta arranged their sarape, not so much to prevent the cold air from getting at their half-naked little bodies as to make them feel that, even while they were asleep, a loving hand was taking care of them.

"Tomorrow you can go to start to work, little sister," said Cándido after a long silence.

Modesta slowly rolled herself another cigarette as though she were particularly interested in doing it well. She lighted it and took a few puffs. Then she slowly lowered the hand in which she held it, letting her gaze wander toward the underbrush where its black shadow was marked off in an irregular line against the dark, clear sky, in which some stars were shining. She sighed deeply and said: "I won't go into service, brother. I'll not be a maid to people like that any more. I'll go with you to the camps. From now on, the only work that interests me is serving you and the children."

Cándido leaned above the fire and said in a very low voice: "You ought not to do a thing like that, little sister. The camps are no good for women, and still less for girls. It's not for me to give you orders, but I advise you to go back. If you don't want to work any more with the city people, you can stay with our uncle in my house, which is your house, and where you have a perfect right to live."

"Uncle Diego and our aunt said the same thing to me. So did the neighbors. But the more they insisted, the more I felt that I would never be able to live quietly and in peace and that I ought to go with you and the children because you need me."

"You don't know how hard life in the forest is, Modesta, and how much harder still in the camps. You are only a young girl, and you'll have to live surrounded by men among whom not one amounts to much."

"I was told all that before I set out. But remember that life didn't begin to be hard for you until you had to take charge of me when I was a tiny orphan. How, then, can it be hard for me to help you, to be at your side now that your children are small and have no mother? Some day we'll go back home, and then I'll look for a good man like you and marry him."

These were the last words they exchanged. They pulled the wool blankets more tightly around them and smoked, their glances lost in the dying fire. Thus they awaited the new day.

The dawn came slowly, enveloped in a damp, heavy fog that fell on the thicket and the field when the sun rose. The sun appeared on the horizon suddenly, without warning, as if with one leap it flung itself into the universe.

4

      "The devil take you, you pack of nobodies! That's
the way you rob me of the money I've worked so
hard to make. For three months all you've done is scratch your
asses, and I haven't been able to send off even one load of mahogany. God and the most holy Virgin are witnesses that I've
paid you down to the last centavo, that I don't owe you anything. And now I come to the end of three months and find
nothing in the dumps, not one chip of mahogany worth men-
tioning. Expecting to find logs piled up as high as hills, or at
least as high as the cathedral in Villahermosa, I find nothing!
But, by God and all the saints, what have you been doing all
this time? Now scratch your bellies, you sons of bitches! Now
answer me, and don't try lying or I'll punch you each one in
the nose. Come on, let's see! What's your answer?"

In these choice terms Don Severo directed himself to his two
overseers, El Pícaro and El Gusano—the "Rogue" and the
"Worm." He shouted so loud that he could have been heard
over a mile away, and nobody hearing his shouts could have
helped choking up with fear.

The more Don Severo thundered, the redder and more con-
gested his face became. No doubt he was afraid of bursting, for
suddenly he muted his fury, though in such a way as to an-
nounce clearly that this was merely a short respite and that
when his two overseers had given him their explanations, he
would return to a display of his vocabulary's shining gems.

Don Severo was the oldest of the three Montellano brothers, owners of this great mahogany camp and of two smaller ones situated on the other side of the river. The most important was called La Armonía, the others La Estancia and La Piedra Alta.

La Armonía covered an area so large that it had been found necessary to divide it into four regions or camps: north, east, south, and west. The boundaries of the exploited territory were very vague; it had been difficult to determine them clearly because the property was all buried in the jungle. Streams ran near its edges, and these had sometimes been taken as its natural boundaries. From one frontier of the exploited territory to the other, it measured at least fifty miles as a bird flies, a distance that seemed easily doubled in walking or on horseback because of such natural obstacles as rocks, gorges, rivers, and swamps.

The north camp was under the personal direction of Don Severo. Each of the other camps was in charge of trusted overseers, foremen, and some assistants.

Don Félix, the second brother, looked after the accounts in the central office of the administration, known as "the village."

The administration office was not situated in the center of the camps, but at one extreme edge, near the bank of the river that carried the wood to the sea. This allowed the management to supervise and control the cargoes of wood set going down the river, make a reasonable estimate of their extent, enter their number in the books, and calculate their value. This location also allowed the personnel to circulate more easily between the central office and the various camps, using canoes called *cayucos* and paddling along tributary streams, all other means of communication being precarious. To tell the truth, it was often impossible to paddle up the small streams, but the owners of the camps had chosen this site as best for their central office, their chief reasons having been strategic. The exploitation of this area had been begun by an American group, which in time, having found a richer region, had ceded it to the Montellano brothers.

The youngest brother, Don Acacio, managed the camps on the other bank of the river. That completed the organization of the business as settled by common agreement among the three brothers.

Don Severo had so much to do in his own camp that he could not go to inspect the other camps every two or three weeks. The routes between them were so bad and so long that a tour of inspection of the three camps, not counting his own, would have taken him fifteen or twenty days, especially if he should wish to visit the dumps. He had, then, to be satisfied with an inspection every three months, and that was anything but a pleasure tour. It was, in fact, a penance that ought to have merited divine indulgence and direct admission to paradise.

Don Félix could not undertake this inspection because it was impossible for him to leave the central office, the heart and brain of the camps.

To the office came the customers. It was there that tools and equipment were received, that everything required for the existence of the workers was stored. The invoices were received there, as were official communications from the tax office, letters from banks and from customers, and reports from agents in New York and London, with information about the state of the market in mahogany and of the timber trade in general.

Thanks to his energy and to his long experience, Don Severo was clearly the man to direct the exploitation and hauling of the mahogany. It was for this reason that the hardest job had been given to him, leaving to Don Félix the more agreeable administrative work.

In his distant post Don Acacio was as indefatigable as his brothers, but he was even more greedy than they—and more irritable. From the time the three Montellanos had bought the camps, he had hardly set foot in the central office or even risked sending a messenger across the swampy roads. For long periods of time at a stretch his brothers did not know whether he was alive or whether his corpse was rotting somewhere.

It was not certain that Don Severo and Don Félix would have grieved much to know that their brother Acacio had been murdered, that fever had carried him off, that a jaguar had devoured him, that a scorpion had mortally stung him, or that he had drowned in the swamps.

Very probably if he had left the dumps well enough supplied with mahogany logs—this was the only thing in the world that interested the Montellanos—the other two would not have been able to shed one small tear over the premature end of their younger brother. In any case, they would have consoled themselves quickly by thinking that the profits from then on would be divided into two parts instead of three.

Don Severo was making his inspection in the south camp and was directing his amiable words to El Pícaro and El Gusano. He had set out very early on horseback, accompanied by El Pícaro, intending to note the quantities of mahogany felled and collected in the various dumps and ready to be sent floating down the rivers. At each dump he estimated with a quick glance the number of piled-up logs and then let loose his fury.

"So this is all the work done in three months! How is it possible to have produced so little in three long months? It's a crime, a sin against all the saints!"

And every time this happened, El Pícaro gave the same reply: "But, Don Severo, there are still other dumps where you will find plenty of logs."

This did not stop Don Severo from declaring at the next dump that it had fewer logs than the one before, so that as his inspection progressed, his anger grew. This anger was slowly changing to a mad fury, a demented rage. When, on returning to the camp office after an exhausting ride, they found El Gusano stretched out full length on the floor and helplessly drunk, Don Severo struck him with his whip, lashes that El Gusano did not even appear to feel, being in a world in which grief and pain seem as sweet as syrup.

Then Don Severo began to bang the crude wooden table, and each phrase of his discourse, emphasized with disgraceful oaths, was underlined by thwacks of his whip on the table, the other pieces of furniture, and the door: "I ought to tear your guts out! There's no excuse for bastards like you! Hell would be too good for the two of you."

In his rage he rushed on: "But, by the devil and all the carrion-eating curs, what have you been doing these three months? Scratching your asses and picking your noses? Answer me!"

El Pícaro stayed on the other side of the table, where he had barricaded himself against Don Severo's anger. As things went from bad to worse, he cautiously moved nearer the door, ready to escape.

"Are you going to speak up, you rat?"

"All the trunks of the trees were cluttered up with roots."

"With roots! With roots! Is that a reason?"

"We had to build scaffolds at least two yards high to get at the trunks," argued El Pícaro.

"Anybody would think it's the first time that has happened! As if I myself didn't have to do it for years and years with nearly every tree. I myself have built scaffolds because the branches and the roots were nearly ten feet up. That didn't prevent me from making the men produce up to three and four tons every day. But you, you pair of good-for-nothing overseers, whom I leave in charge of the simplest work in the world in return for wages as high as a contractor's—you find a way to produce four times less. You're a pair of bandits, thieves who take my money to drink yourselves silly. Hardly one ton a day per man!"

El Pícaro sidled a little toward the door and said: "Pardon, but the amount is more than two and a half tons a day per man." He spoke in a frightened tone as if to defend himself.

"Shut your mouth when I speak to you. Understand? Two tons! Did I or didn't I order you to produce at least four? And to top it all, the rains are coming. Within four weeks we'll be beginning to haul them to the water, and what am I going to dispatch? A ton and a half! That's not the way we'll be able to pay the sixty thousand pesos due on the first of January."

He looked round the room furiously, unseeingly. His blood-shot eyes falling again on El Gusano, he rushed at him and kicked him in the legs: "Pig, pig of a hog!"

El Pícaro decided that the moment had come to take up the defense of his pal: "This is the first time he's been drunk for six weeks, for the simple reason that we haven't had even a drop of aguardiente. Until yesterday, when the Turk came, we couldn't get any bottles. It was natural, then, for him to drink a little."

"A little! Magnificent! Where's your bottle?"

El Pícaro went to a corner of the office and from under the bed drew out a half-empty bottle. He thought that Don Severo would snatch it from his hands and smash it on the floor, but that was not what happened.

Don Severo had shouted so much that his throat was dry. He seized the bottle, looked at it against the light, shook it, and took several good swallows. He cleared his throat, shook the bottle again, and drank from it a second time. It seemed to calm him a little.

"Refreshing!" he said more calmly.

But his calmness was of short duration. It disappeared almost immediately when he remembered the reason for his presence in this place.

Three days before, Don Severo had received from Don Acacio the first and only letter he had written since he had been in the camp. He had sent the letter by a foreman who had traveled on horseback. Don Acacio informed his brothers that the exploitation of the small camps he managed must be suspended for the time being. Deeply shut in between two hills and two mountains, the camps had been turned into two swamps by the recent heavy rainfalls. The oxen could not walk without getting bogged down, as a consequence of which it was impossible to transport logs to the dumps. Even more serious, the cutting had had to be interrupted because the cutters were being drowned in mud.

This short letter brought Don Severo the disastrous news that the cutting in Don Acacio's camps must be regarded as lost that year. The loss was all the worse because it represented more or less half of the total production. The deficit would probably prevent them from meeting the obligations they had contracted in order to buy the business, and in that case it was possible that the company that had sold it to them would fore-close on their property and resell it to others, as it had a right to do by the contract, the terms of which were very hard be-cause of the small down payment made by the Montellano brothers.

Immediately, Don Severo and Don Félix had met in the cen-tral office to discuss the situation, and both had reached the conclusion that there was only one method of saving the year's production.

They admitted that Don Acacio, the youngest, was the most energetic of the three when it came to obtaining the maximum yield from the men. If he wrote that his district was temporar-ily unexploitable, that must be the case, and nobody in the world would make more effort than he to obtain something. In these circumstances, then, seeing that the two small camps could not produce anything, it was necessary at least to double the production of the big camp or, if it was possible, quadruple it. It was entirely a question of yield, because the mahogany was abundant enough in La Armonía to make up any deficit. Nobody could be better qualified than Don Acacio, assisted by the foremen he had trained, to obtain this result. Don Severo and Don Félix knew Don Acacio would run grave risks, but they had to have recourse to the last possibility if they wished to win the game.

Don Acacio's messenger returned with their reply inviting him to move to La Armonía with his men to start new dumps.

Don Acacio, at least as intelligent as his older brothers, was a step ahead of them: he was already on the way toward La Armonía when he met the messenger, fortunately for the latter, who was on the verge of being bogged down, together with his horse.

When Don Acacio and his men arrived at the principal camp to get provisions and tools, Don Severo had left for the south camp, administered by El Pícaro.

The aguardiente seemed to have a soothing effect on Don Severo, but only for a short time. He was thinking that all hope was lost as far as the other two camps were concerned. On the other hand, he had counted on an output double what he had found in El Pícaro's dumps.

"If I had not wanted more tons of mahogany, do you think that I'd have sent two foremen here? For what? The boys would have done the work by themselves and probably would have produced more than under you two lazy pigs. But tell me, how have you managed to get only half the work that I expected from you? You must surely have slept more than you worked."

"But, chief, what more could I do? I've whipped them like dogs, to the point of tearing the hide from their backs. But they soon got used to it, and the more you whip them, the less they work."

"I've already told you that if you abuse the whip, it's no use for any God-damned thing. They get obstinate, they lie down and don't do any work. Why didn't you hang them more often? That's what we do in our camp. There's nothing like it. It really scares them."

"But we're only two, El Gusano and me. And to hang half a dozen isn't so easy. They resist and fight back. To pull it off there would have to be three men for each boy."

"What use then is that gun hanging on your rump? Do you wear it to look pretty or for hunting pheasants?"

"Actually, it's no good for anything."

"You have only to flash it in the face of anybody who gets insolent and you'll see how they'll cool down."

"That used to be true, chief. But now they just laugh at me when I stick the gun in their ribs. 'Shoot, you bastard,' they say. 'Why don't you shoot? Your day is sure to come somehow. Just wait a bit and we'll get even with you and El Gusano.' What's more, they sing all sorts of songs against us, especially at night."

"Then you've only to plug one or two. That way they'll see that you're not joking."

"All right, chief, if you say so, that's what I'll do. After all, it's not my funeral. Do you know what they say when I put the mouth of a gun against their hides? 'Go on, shoot, Pícaro, you big fool—and then you'll find yourself with one less cutter and you can stick the contract up your ass.' That's just what's terrible about it: they would really like me to shoot so that they wouldn't have to work any more."

Don Severo remained silent. He put his head out of the door, looked in the direction of the workers' hovels, then came back into the room, picked up the bottle of aguardiente, took another good round of swigs, and lighted a cigarette.

"Tomorrow," he said after a moment, "Don Acacio will be here with his men and his overseers. Then we'll take energetic measures. You'll see how to deal with these guys and how to make every one of them turn in four tons a day. Maybe we'll get it up to five."

"Sure, chief," replied El Pícaro.

"Damned right! What are you thinking of? All this you've been telling me is just child's play compared with what my brothers and I have seen in other camps."

He raised the bottle again, as if it contained nothing but water. Then he put it down and again looked at El Gusano.

"Bring me a bucket," he ordered.

El Pícaro fetched him a full pail of water. Don Severo seized it and threw the water on the drunken man.

"Bring another," he said to El Pícaro, handing him the pail. "One's not enough. At least six are needed to put him on his feet. And when he stands up, you'll flay the skin off his ass with this horsewhip. Then maybe he'll be of some use. But do it later. I have no interest in being here during the punishment. Take him a little way off so that I don't hear him yelling."

"Very well, chief," said El Pícaro, who, to save himself the trouble of fetching more buckets of water, lifted El Gusano onto his back, carried him to the arroyo, and doused him in it until he began to recover his senses.

"But listen, pal," muttered El Gusano, "you're not going to beat me up? Aren't we friends?"

"Of course we are, you pig. But why must you get drunk just when the old man arrives? There's nothing I can do about it. I have to give it to you whether you like it or not. It's better for me to do it in a friendly way than to call one of the boys,

Gregorio or Santiago, for example. For then, my friend, it wouldn't be any fun, I assure you."

"You're right. Get it over in a hurry, while I'm drunk and won't feel it so much. Can't you fetch me a swig before—to make it easier for me to bear?"

"Not a bad idea. I'll have a little myself."

El Pícaro ran to the office, slipped through the door, took the bottle, and made El Gusano drink a lot before he began to lash him.

On the following day a little before sunset Don Acacio and his column arrived at the south camp. Don Severo received him with these sweet words: "Everything's going as badly as possible here, Cacho. They've done no more than two tons per cutter."

"In that case there's nothing for us to do but eat shit," replied Don Acacio. But he was not a man to waste time idly. Even when he had made a hard journey, he did not seem disposed to rest. Still less was he likely to sit and listen to useless speeches. He called his overseers.

"Get going, you pack of mules! Hurry—get the huts up. We haven't any time to lose. If you don't want to spend all your nights under the stars, start now, because tomorrow we won't be able to bother with that."

The foremen, followed by their men, made their way into the underbrush to fell some trees and cut palm leaves for building the huts. But night surprised them before one hut was finished.

The men took shelter in the huts occupied by the camp workers, but there was not room for them all. It was hard spending the night stretched out on the ground. It rained torrentially and the ones who slept on the ground awoke in a bath of mud. They were called to their work, as usual, before the first rays of daylight.

"Good morning!" said Don Acacio. "It seems to me that building huts won't be necessary. In fact, we're not going to stay here—we're going to settle in the forest. We're leaving right away. You can boil your coffee and cook your beans later when we have time. Now you can eat on the way. Let's go."

"That's the way to talk," said Don Severo to El Pícaro, who stood beside him at the office door. "If you had been able to function like him, you and your drunken assistant, we'd have had our four tons a man right now."

"Certainly, chief. But if I'd done that, I'd have lost my life before night, or I'd have had to leave two or three of the boys laid out somewhere with bullets in their ribs," El Pícaro said, laughing derisively.

"That's just what makes the difference. There are overseers who know how to make their people work and others who don't know their job. You're one of those who don't understand and never will learn. And, by the way, where's El Gusano?"

"Hi! Gusano!" shouted El Pícaro into the darkness. "The chief wants to see you."

El Gusano came running, and without stopping to get his breath said: "At your orders, chief!"

"You and El Pícaro are going to break camp with all your loafers. You'll leave with Don Acacio. Get your things together. On your way!"

The two overseers called their men and followed Don Acacio's column.

A week later Don Gabriel, arriving at La Armonía with the caravan of men he had recruited, stopped on the wide embankment in front of the bungalow that housed the administration.

Don Gabriel had demands for labor for four different camps. He was considering the project of staying at La Armonía, of establishing his center of operations there and dividing up his men. On the very day of his arrival Don Severo was there, and Don Gabriel took advantage of the opportunity to have a talk with him. As a result of their conversation all of Don Gabriel's Indians were taken on by La Armonía. The other camps would have to wait until other men were recruited or Don Gabriel should take pity on them.

Don Severo and Don Félix had a look at the newcomers and seemed to be satisfied.

The caravan of Indians was dead with fatigue. They fell on the ground, forming little groups. When Don Severo and Don Félix went up to a group, those who formed it immediately stood up. Don Severo felt their arms, the muscles of their legs, and the napes of their necks, as he would have done before buying a yoke of oxen.

"What's your job, Chamula?" he asked Cándido, whose place of origin he recognized by his hat.

"Farmer, sir, and your humble servant," replied Cándido modestly.

"In that case you'll be a good cutter."

"At your orders, sir."

"Who is that woman with you? Is she your wife?"

"She's my sister, chief. My wife died."

"And the two little boys? Are they yours?"

"At your service, chief. They're here to serve you."

Don Severo felt their arms. "I believe they'd be good herd-boys."

"I beg pardon if I contradict you, chief, but they're still very little and won't be able to work in the jungle. One of them is only six years old and the other only seven years and three months."

"If they want to eat, they have to work. You'll eat all your ration yourself, and if you want a double ration you'll never finish paying your debts."

"We can work. We're strong, chief," said the older boy, realizing that he and his brother might be the cause of their father's finding himself in one more difficulty.

The younger boy took a step forward, planting himself in front of Don Severo and doubling up his arm to show how the biceps stood out. "Feel that, my chief, and see how strong I am. I'll be able to work more than my brother, who's bigger than me. And the job of looking after cattle pleases me. With your permission, papa."

Cándido said nothing.

"That's fine," said Don Severo, laughing. "Those are the

kind of kids I like. It has never done anybody any harm to begin work early and earn his bread. I'll send you two boys to the pasture and your father will go on with the cutters."

The two boys were taken aback. "But aren't we going with our father?"

"Your father isn't a cowboy. He's a cutter. So he can't be in the same camp as you. If it's possible, we'll arrange things so that you can be together at night."

Cándido drew the little ones toward him as if intending to protect them with his own body. He caressed their thick mops of hair and said in a muffled voice: "There's nothing we can do, my sons. He's the master and we must obey him."

Don Severo went on to another group.

Don Félix, who had remained behind, made a sign to Modesta, who had withdrawn a little while Don Severo was talking with Cándido and the boys. She obeyed the sign, coming up to him with her head bent forward, her eyes downcast, and her arms crossed.

Don Félix tapped her cheeks lightly and put his hand under her chin to make her raise her head. But Modesta resisted, half closing her eyes and clenching her teeth a little.

"There's no need for you to be afraid, little hen. I don't eat girls, especially when they have pretty legs. I satisfy myself with separating those when I want to. What's your name?"

"Modesta, your humble servant."

"Good, I'll call you Mocha. What did you come here to do?"

"I came with my brother so as not to leave him alone with the children, chief." She spoke without raising her head.

"And where do you expect to eat, little hen?"

"In the camp, with my brother."

"That's impossible. He'll receive only one ration, and if he wants another he'll have to pay for it. Then there will be absolutely nothing left of his wage and only God knows how much he'll be owing us then. We'll pay him fifty centavos a day, and that on condition that he fells three tons of mahogany."

"Two tons, chief, that's the way it's written in my contract.

The mayor told us that in Hucutsin," Cándido interposed, stepping up.

"I spit on what your contract says, and you shut your mouth if you don't want me to call one of the foremen, who'll give you a welcome to the camps. When he's tanned your hide enough, you'll know that here nobody opens his face except when he's asked to. You'll cut down your three tons daily, understand? If you don't, we won't pay you—and give thanks that you don't have to cut four. That will come later."

"Pardon, chief, with your permission, the man who signed me up, Don Gabriel, told me that it would be two tons, and the mayor of Hucutsin, who stamped my contract, told me that, too."

"For you it'll be four tons, you lousy coyote. And watch out for your skin and bones if you don't cut them."

Don Félix took a notebook from his shirt pocket, wrote down Cándido's name, and added the following note: "Four tons, obligatory."

"But, my chief—" Cándido never finished the phrase because Don Félix gave him so violent a blow in the face that blood began to spout from the Indian's nostrils.

"Now I've told you, you sickening worm, that the only right you have here is to shut your trap."

Cándido sat down on the ground and tried to stop the bleeding by applying a handful of grass to his nostrils. Modesta remained standing in front of Don Félix, her head lowered. The incident was more painful to her than to Cándido, but, like the rest of her race, she was accustomed from infancy to bear silently the worst treatment from white men. Not a gesture, not the slightest contraction of her face, betrayed what she felt. The children embraced their father tenderly, trying to console him. The younger began to sob, crying: "Papa, papa, it's not my fault."

Cándido caressed him and answered him with a smile. The older boy had picked a gourd and run to the arroyo to fetch a little water for his father to use on his face.

Don Félix continued his conversation with Modesta. The

fact of striking an Indian in the face was to him something so unimportant that he did not give it a moment's attention. That of killing an Indian by blows or by a shot was an incident forgotten an hour later. He remembered the hunting of a deer or a well-aimed shot at a jaguar more easily than the death of a peon.

"Do you know that you're not entirely ugly, Mocha? But you must eat and for that your brother won't be able to help you."

"I'll put up a little house here in the camp, I'll fatten some pigs, and I'll do the cooking for the workmen." This idea had come to her suddenly. She knew that it would not be easy to put it into operation, but she felt happy to have hit upon it because she had fears about the sort of work Don Félix had in mind for her. She had signed no contract and she could do as she wished, but she had to eat, and here everything was the property of the Montellano brothers.

"Don't think that's so easy, little hen. You can't build a hut unless I give you permission, and as for fattening pigs, you require my authorization for that too. As for cooking for the laborers, if that pleases you— But look, if you want to work, why not do it for me? It's less hard to work for one person than for twenty. Next week I may be going to another camp to skin those loafers. I'll take you with me, little hen, so that you can do everything for me."

He caught her by the point of the chin and lifted her head to force her to look him in the face, but Modesta closed her eyes.

"If you behave well and are amiable with me, it will go well with you. But if you're obstinate, then I'll tan your hide and you'll go back home carrying your lousy rags. You'll have to cross the jungle and who knows when you'll get out of it? At the best you'll meet a jaguar that will eat your legs and all the rest."

"I don't wish to be your servant, chief," replied Modesta in a low voice.

"That'll be decided by me, not you, little fool."

Don Félix turned his back and went to join Don Severo and continue the inspection.

5

The new gang reached the south camp in the middle of the night. The men were dead on their feet with fatigue from the march through the underbrush and a two-hour struggle to get out of the heavy, sticky mud of the swamps. They let themselves fall to the ground with whatever they were carrying, and it was not until almost half an hour later that they began to have the strength to ask for something to eat. The cook told them he had nothing to give them and that unless they had brought their own provisions they would have to wait until morning. He added that he also was tired, that he had not the least desire to work at such an hour, that they should wait for the arrival of the woman he had been promised as an assistant. The foreman, known as La Tumba, who had been in charge of the column, told him that the woman would be at his disposition next morning because for the time being she was with her brother.

Some cutters who had been working for some time in the camp and were loitering in the neighborhood of the cookhouse came to look at the newcomers in the hope of finding some faces they might know. They sat near the fire, lighted their cigarettes, and watched the others prepare their frugal food.

"They won't get fat on that," said one of them.

"Everyone eats what he can," was the reply.

"Did Don Félix come with you?"

"No, he stayed in the big camp to check equipment and get the provisions ready."

"Any of you ever been in a camp before?" another asked.

"Not me," replied one of the men in a voice exhausted by fatigue. "And I don't believe that any of us knows the camps."

Santiago, one of the ox-drivers, broke in, saying: "Well, you'll get to know them. You'll get to know hell and all its devils."

Nobody took up his words. The old hands smoked; the new ones waited for their beans and coffee to get warm. The fire crackled, throwing out sparks, and at last decided to burn brightly.

The Indians lying around the fire suddenly raised their heads as if they had heard the roar of a jaguar in the underbrush.

"What's that noise coming from the jungle?" asked Antonio, an Indian from Sactan, listening intently.

"Do you mean those groans and moans in the underbrush?" asked Santiago, raising his eyebrows.

"Yes, that's what I mean. You'd think that somebody was tormenting gagged animals."

"By God, comrade," said Santiago ironically, "I assure you that you're sharp of hearing. You must be able to hear a flea dancing on a silk handkerchief. With hearing like that, you'll get somewhere! Besides, you're not mistaken."

"No, you're not mistaken, you've heard perfectly," interposed Matías. "They're tormenting animals, and they're holding their mouths to stifle cries that might disturb Don Acacio while he's slipping between the heavy thighs of his Cristina, the girl with the twisted nose. By the devil, she's ugly! But her ass must have some enchantment, for he takes her everywhere with him and buys her boxes of scented soap whenever the Turk comes."

"And why are they tormenting those poor beasts?" asked Antonio.

The ox-drivers laughed uproariously.

"Those poor beasts!" replied Santiago. "Yes, the poor beasts are being cruelly mistreated because in spite of the gags they can hear their screams."

And there was another outburst of laughter.

"But they're not little lambs with white fleece," explained Pedro.

"Beasts, poor beasts! No, those are not animals that are being tormented, you pack of asses! It's twenty cutters, twenty ax-men who are howling. They've hung them up for three or four hours because they haven't produced, either today or yesterday or the day before, the tons of mahogany they'd been told to. You are innocent and ignorant, but within three days you'll know what four tons are. Two tons are the normal production of an experienced cutter who's as strong as an ox. And now that son of a bitch Don Acacio wants us to cut four tons a day. Whoever can't cut that amount is hung from a tree by his four members, and even by five, for half the night. . . . Then the mosquitoes come humming around, because the thing happens at the edge of the swamps; not to mention the red ants, which arrive in battalions. But I don't have to give you any more details. In less than a week you'll know as much as I do—and by personal experience. After that you'll have been initiated into all the mysteries of a camp belonging to the Montellano brothers. You'll be soldiers of the regiment of the hanged."

Somebody said: "I thought that all they did was flog you the way they do in the prison camps and coffee fincas."

It was Martín Trinidad who seemed to be so well informed. Martín Trinidad was one of the three ragged men who had joined the column on the road and whom Don Gabriel had engaged without a stamped contract. During the three long weeks of the trek through the jungle those three vagabonds had hardly exchanged a word with the Indians. They had always remained together in a group, talking among themselves and not appearing to bother about the others. This was the first time that Martín Trinidad had spoken to them.

Santiago looked at him with half-closed eyes and an air of suspicion, with the caution a real proletarian employs in the presence of an informer.

"Where do you come from?"

"I'm from Yucatán."

"That's a long way! How did you get here? Are you running away?"

"Let's say that's right, brother."

"Right, let's say that. . . . When they've hanged you at least three times, I'll begin to believe you. Because, look, if anyone here isn't flogged or hanged we get suspicious—he may be a squealing son of a— And even to receive some lashes doesn't prove anything, but to be strung up, to be well and duly hanged as El Rasgón, La Mecha, and El Faldón know how to do it—that's altogether another matter. After that there's no comedy. I hope you understand what I'm going to tell you. Celso and Andrés will have a little chat with your two pals in order to know more about who you are. Here nobody's afraid of anything, and nobody can match our skill in sweetly slicing the next fellow's neck for almost no reason at all. It can happen within twenty paces of the hut without the interested party's feeling it at all. Nor is any attention paid to how the loathsome soul of an informer goes down to hell. As you'll see, we don't give a thought to anything, not even their bullets—you don't shoot a man you expect four tons a day from. A dead man can't fell trees—isn't that so? The worst they can do is hang us, and we're so used to that now that it doesn't help them any more. They used to beat us savagely when we couldn't cut more than two tons. But we got hardened to beating, and it no longer served any purpose. On the contrary, the more they beat us, the less we produced. At that point the Montellanos thought up the scheme of hanging us. It's horrible, it's terrifying, but only while you're strung up. Next day you can work again, and then you cut your four tons! This new invention has really worked for them, because the recollection, the mere recollection of the suffering, the terror of being strung up again, drives you to try to cut four tons, even though after one ton your hands are skinless. Only now we've almost got to the stage where even their new invention will become useless. There's nothing they can do about Celso there, for instance. When they've hanged him for four hours and El Guapo arrives to take him down, Celso shouts: 'Hi! you son of a bitch, here you come just when I feel fine. I'm sleeping peacefully, and this is the moment you choose, you pig, to come and disturb my dreams!' Celso was the first. Now there are about six of us. This is the secret: human beings can become like oxen or donkeys and remain impassive when they're beaten or goaded, but only if they've succeeded in suppressing all their natural instinct to rebel."

Martín Trinidad did not reply.

The men in other groups finished eating their warmed-up black beans and coffee and soon afterwards came over to the group formed by the ox-drivers Matías, Santiago, Cirilo, and Fidel, who had been working in the camps for some time.

Andrés, the most intelligent of the drivers, was not there. He had been sent with a number of other men to take tired, hungry animals to the big pasture and to bring back oxen in good condition. The pasture was eighteen miles from the main camp, on the shore of a lake, but as the greater part of the way there was inundated, they would not be back in less than three days.

"Do they hang some cutters every night?" asked Antonio.

"No, man, that way they'd contract fevers more easily and kick off too often. Many have died already, and there's never a week when we don't bury two or three."

Pedro interrupted him: "You're talking about things you know nothing about."

Pedro was the oldest hand in the camp and, like all old hands, felt a driving need to show off his knowledge and experience of things, especially now when he saw how attentively they had been listening to Santiago. It was a real joy for the old man to hold forth before people to whom everything he related seemed like a story.

"Yes," he continued, "you don't know what you're talking about. Sure they don't hang cutters every night, and even less do they hang us ox-drivers. The proof of that is that here we are this moment smoking our cigarettes and talking in peace to you new fellows who don't know anything."

"Things are as they are," Cirilo broke in, "and it's only after a lot of going and coming that we get any idea of what's really happening here."

"Don't listen to that preacher," Santiago cut him short, laughing. "This morning a tree trunk fell on his head, and he still doesn't know what he's saying. That's why he's talking through his hat. And tomorrow he'll be still worse. But what I am going to tell you is the real truth. Five or six days ago the youngest of the Montellanos arrived here. His district is flooded and won't be dry before January. That means that his camp won't give them even a chip of mahogany, and what they can't get there they'll have to get here. Don Acacio is the worst of the three. Last spring he took eighty men to his camp, strong and healthy Indians accompanied by a dozen women and some twenty children. Do you know how many of them are left now when he has to abandon his camp? Twenty-three! All the rest died, the majority from bad treatment, after beatings and hangings. Fevers carried off others. Ten disappeared in the swamps. Four fled and one died in the jungle. Others were eaten by animals or bitten by snakes while they were hanging. For how can any man defend himself from a jaguar when he's strung up? You can't move even a finger. Of the twelve women, three went crazy. He shot dead the husband of one, the prettiest one, to get her into his bed. Two ran away with their husbands and shared their fate. They beat another barbarously because she'd urged her husband to escape. She was left lying unconscious on the ground and, as there was nobody to rescue her, she was eaten by wild boars. As for the children, of the twenty, only two survive, and they have the fevers."

"All in all, he's done a good job," commented Fidel.

"You, fellow, you'll speak when you're asked. Well, then, Don Acacio, having merrily buried nearly all his workers, left his camp in a state of flood, and now we have him here with the few who could escape. Five cleared out on the way, and two foremen have been sent to look for them. The poor devils will be caught, for though they know how to run, two horses can always run faster. They may hang themselves or cut their own throats when they're at the end of their strength or about to be captured. If they're brought back, not a square inch of their skin will be spared. Don Acacio arrived here five or six days ago and made his bow with the beautiful ideal of making up the loss. He has given orders that each cutter must fell four tons every day, and whoever doesn't produce four not only loses the day's pay but must be taught how that amount of timber can be cut with the application of a little goodwill. The horse-whip didn't produce good results in his camp, and he knows that here it will be even more useless. That's why he has put into practice his invention of mass hanging. You arrived just in time to enjoy the songs of the first hanging group. We ox-drivers have already received the new orders. Every day Don Acacio goes on his horse to the felling-places and determines how many logs each driver must cart to the dumps if he wishes the day to count for pay. So that, if we are here tonight sitting quietly around the fire telling you pretty stories, it's not un-likely that tomorrow at the very same hour you'll also hear us, nothing but our voices coming from down there in the darkness, and it will be the cutters' turn to listen to our music."

"What can anyone do against all this?" one of the new ar-rivals asked in a voice that trembled. He came from an inde-pendent village and had sold himself to the camps in order to be able to marry later.

"Yes, what can anyone do against all this?" Fidel repeated like an echo. Then he looked at the faces of the men seated near him and, tightening his lips, added: "What can be done? that depends on the sort of men you are!"

"What do you mean?" one of the newcomers asked.

"Nothing," replied Santiago for him, "nothing, except that the other night I heard one of those boys singing amid the howls and groans of the others who were hanging with him. It seemed as if he got relief by singing."

"You must remember his words," said Cirilo, who knew the song, but wished Santiago to be the one to repeat it to the new men.

"Sure I remember. It's enough to hear such songs once in a lifetime never to forget them. It goes more or less this way:

If my life is worth nothing
And I live worse than an animal,
I'd lose nothing by killing
Him who has hanged me,
And I'd gain a lot sending
A condemned man to hell.
Ay, ay, ay, ay, little iguana,
Let's go to the tomb to sing. . . ."

"I don't understand a word," said Antonio.

Matías roared with laughter and then, through compressed lips, said: "You'll understand soon enough. The music will make it clear to you."

Someone else asked: "But don't the men resist when they're going to hang them?"

"When you're going to kill pigs they also squeal," said Prócoro. "But that doesn't prevent you from eating the cracklings three hours later. It's exactly the same with us. What can you do when three or four brutes fall on you at the same time? Suppose you resist. Then they give you three blows on the head, and when you come round, you find yourself neatly hung from the branch of a tree, with an army of red ants strolling around in your nostrils and ears, which they have smeared with lard to attract them better. You feel lucky that they didn't anoint your ass or smear you in front—both mighty pleasant things! As for the mosquitoes, they come without the necessity of lard. The next morning you wake up with your head so swollen and your stomach so sour that next time you take care not to offer the slightest resistance when they want to string you up."

"That foreman called La Mecha, that cross-eyed animal, has discovered a new trick you haven't yet become acquainted with," said Santiago to the old hands. "Tell Prócoro to show you."

Prócoro had no shirt. He turned his naked back to the light of the fire, and to show them better Santiago passed his finger over the lines, like zebra stripes, which furrowed the man's shoulders. "After stringing up Prócoro that stinking coyote La

Mecha scraped his skin with a thorn so that the ants, mosquitoes, and other insects could suck more easily. Now then, boys, where do you think you are? On a finca? In your village, where only the lice and the fleas can eat you? Here you're not just at the entrance to hell; here you're at its very bottom."

"You've said it well, Santos," Fidel interposed, "in the final pit of hell. That couldn't be more exact. The cruelest of the devils wouldn't want to be here. He'd be ashamed."

Thirty steps away, near another fire, Cándido and Modesta were keeping warm in the company of Indians of their own tribe. Cándido's children had fallen asleep. The distance that separated the two groups prevented Cándido and his companions from catching the animated discussions of the ox-drivers and the tale of horrors that froze the blood of those who heard. On the contrary, there was almost complete silence in Cándido's group. The men were exhausted, broken by the long march and perhaps also by the vague fear of what awaited them in the future. They were enveloped by terror. It surged about them from all sides, from the dark night, from the grass on which they were squatting, from the jungle that surrounded the camp, from the dying murmur of the arroyo near by. Like those of the other group, they heard the lamentations and groans rising from the jungle, and when the wind caught the cries and brought them more clearly, they looked at one another with horror because they well understood that those were cries of pain from men being tortured, of their companions in tomorrow's misery. They knew that those who were sitting around the fires, to all appearance in peace, would soon be wailing like the others, who would listen to the cries in turn, helpless like themselves to help their brothers.

They knew that in the other group what those wails meant was being explained anew. They knew it because incomplete phrases, raised voices, reached them. That was why none of them rose to go over and ask the old hands the meaning of the cries peopling the jungle. They did not wish to lose their last hope. They were afraid to know the truth. They wanted to persuade themselves, in their inner beings, that it was not their companions who were being tortured, that those groans were not what they were, that what they heard was merely the soughing of the wind or the buzzing of insects in the under-brush. Not one of them thought of going up to the edge of the jungle to try to see what was happening, especially as they saw that nobody from the other group was doing so. They all knew that here, as on the fincas, in the barracks, in the jails, in the prison camps of Vera Cruz, Yucatán, Tabasco, and Jalisco, it was better not to show oneself too curious or to go deeply into the cause of anguished cries, of wails and groans that arose from wells, caves, dungeons, or ruined convents. The laborers and peons knew by experience that inquisitive persons moved by the cries of the victims and trying to help them would not have to wait long before uttering similar groans.

Furthermore, it was very possible that those groans were without basic reality: in the forest, by night and by day, man is constantly at the mercy of hallucinations, mirages, obsessions. From any point of view, it was preferable not to say anything, not to make any allusion to those noises. After all, it could be pretended that this was happening in a foreign country very far from the place in which they were.

In the office the foremen could be heard laughing and swearing. To the Indians came the sounds of their obscene songs and the sharp cries of drunken women.

In the camp there were only two women to satisfy the appetites of Don Acacio's five foremen. They had followed the men when the flood had compelled Don Acacio to evacuate his camp. They were old women with slack flesh. Nothing about them was attractive, and they knew it. They also knew that they had reached their last stage. They had contracted all, without exception, of the diseases inherent in their profession. Nobody had forced them to follow the foremen. They would have preferred to be carried along by force so that they could have added ten centavos to the price of their favors. But nobody, not even those filthy foremen, had wanted to force them, and they felt happy that Don Acacio had permitted them to follow the men and had assigned them animals for the journey. Put to it, they would have followed the column even on foot, because if it had been decided to leave them in the swamps, they would have had no recourse but to beg the foremen, for the love of God, to give them the *coup de grâce*, to finish them off with a bullet in the head. Thus, they were happy still to see around them men from whom they could extract something, however little, and who would share with them their beans, tortillas, and coffee. And there was still the possibility that when the Turk came to the camp, somebody would buy them a length of muslin without too much grumbling.

They felt really satisfied when they heard someone say in front of them: "It's an advantage to have something here that resembles a woman."

The women began to sing in rasping voices, and two of the foremen joined in with them.

The foreman called El Guapo stepped out of the hut, staggered, and shouted back: "Eh! Faldón, and you, Mecha, come on out. You too, you good-for-nothings."

The good-for-nothings were two Indian boys who worked in the office.

"Take the lanterns," he ordered.

The Indians lighted the lanterns at the flame of the candle on the table.

"We've got to take those swine down. They've been hanging long enough now. If we don't hurry, tomorrow they'll be all raw and won't be able to work," added El Guapo, swaying on his feet.

"Won't you let us go with you to see how you hang the Indians and how you untie them to get them down?" asked one of the women, moving toward the door.

"Go on—let us," said the other, pulling up her blouse, which she had let slip down to her navel, "I want to see."

With one slap El Guapo flung her against the wall.

"Bitches, old whores! You wait for me right here. Don't let me see you hanging around the place where the boys are hanged, or I'll smash in your mouths. Do you need a show in order to be satisfied? Sows! If you value your skin don't go sticking your sows' snouts into that!"

He took a step toward the woman who had expressed the foolish wish. No doubt she knew what was going to happen to her, for she covered her face with her open hands. But he pulled them down with a brutal gesture and gave her half a dozen blows so violent that the unhappy woman's nose swelled up and began to leak blood over her face.

"Get moving," he shouted to the other foremen. "We've got to take them down. They've been hanging in their trees too long."

The three foremen passed among the groups of Indians squatting near the fires without seeming even to notice their presence.

"Where are they going?" asked Antonio in a low voice.

Fidel, to whom he had spoken, replied: "They're going to untie the men who have been punished."

"And what if we went to watch?" one of the newcomers proposed, and stood up.

Matías forced him to sit down again. "Be quiet if you value your skin. If the foremen saw you show your face there, you'd suffer the same fate. When blows are being dealt out gratis, it's better to run before receiving one."

"Patience," said Santiago, his voice lowered. "The day will come when we too will be hanging and unhanging. And when we approach them it will be not to accept blows, but to give them. Those dogs forget that it's not possible to go on striking a man forever. One fine day that man learns to use a whip and strike blows to give a little comfort to his soul."

Having said these words, he fixed his look on Martín Trinidad, who returned his gaze as though trying to pry into his thoughts.

"Why are you staring at me like that? If you're a spy, say so. In any case we'll know it very soon, and then you can be sure you won't squeal any more."

Martín Trinidad replied with a sly smile: "If you don't want me to hear what you say, all you have to do is stop talking before me. I didn't ask you to come here. It was you who came and joined our group."

Santiago inclined his head, contracted his mouth, and took an ember to relight his cigarette. "Tomorrow," he said finally, "Celso will have a good look at you three. And Celso sees clearly. He has a pair of good eyes."

"And we have six excellent eyes," replied Martín Trinidad.

His two companions broke into laughter, and Juan Méndez added: "Yes, we have three pairs of excellent eyes. Without them we wouldn't be here, I assure you, brother," he said, turning toward Lucio Ortiz.

"We three see for six," the latter replied.

"Look, there they come," said Santiago, indicating the foremen with a movement of his head, "as satisfied as hogs."

"Now we can go find the men," said Fidel.

He stood up, and ten workers followed his example.

Fidel and two of his comrades went to the large hut that served as their dormitory, picked up two lanterns, and made toward the underbrush. Eight men, eight shapeless masses, were twitching on the ground. They were incredibly doubled up, as if they had been cooped up in narrow boxes for six months. Each wore only a torn pair of white breeches. They groaned quietly, like sleepers half awakened. They squirmed on the ground and slowly stirred their limbs one after another to ease the stiffness, for their arms and legs were stiff and swollen.

The ropes that had held them to the trees had been simply untied by the foremen, letting the men fall brutally to the ground. The foremen never worried about their victims, because they knew that the men would come to help them. Besides, the foremen were not required to watch over the health of hanged men. They could burst or not during the torture. The Montellanos and their bodyguards were not concerned with the possible death of the hanged men beyond the fact that a death meant the loss of a man's labor. If a cutter was lazy or weak and could not produce three tons of mahogany daily, the loss was not great, the man could die quietly. For the worker, work is a duty. If he is lazy, he has no right to live. After all, if he dies, there is one less nuisance.

The eyes of the hanged men were bloodshot and inflamed. Their bodies were covered with the bites of red ants and mosquitoes. Hundreds of ticks of all sizes had penetrated so deeply beneath their skins that infinite patience was necessary to extract them without leaving the heads behind, for if these were left under the skin the bites produced by the insects' stings would become dangerous. Wherever a tick had worked its way in, there remained, even after its removal, a terrible itching that lasted as much as a week and compelled the victim to scratch himself incessantly. The bodies of the tortured men were still covered with ants, which now began to make their escape replete with their booty of blood or flesh. On and between their toes chiggers had left their eggs deposited deep in the flesh. Spiders had invaded their hair, and some of them had begun to weave webs to catch the flies attracted by the blood and sweat of the hanged men. On their legs could be seen the sticky tracks left by snails.

The old hands picked their comrades up in their arms and carried them, still stupefied by pain, to the bank of the arroyo. They immersed them in the running water to alleviate the burning stings of mosquitoes and to rid them of ants and spiders. After this ducking they laid them out on the bank and began to stretch their limbs, massaging them at the same time.

"This isn't so bad," explained Santiago to Antonio, who was helping him revive one of the cutters, Lorenzo. "It's not so serious when they hang one near the huts. What is dangerous is when they do the hanging far from the camp as a special punishment. Because then the wild boars and wild dogs eat them, and they aren't able to defend themselves in any way."

"There's still another marvelous punishment, an invention of Don Severo," said Matías, rubbing another of the hanged men. "Toward eleven o'clock in the morning they grab a man and take him to a place where there isn't a tree or any shade of any kind. They take off his clothes, tie his hands and feet, and bury him in the hot sand to just below his mouth, leaving only his nose, his eyes, and the top of his head above ground, and all this under the caress of the sun. To you, you innocent lambs who don't yet know anything about these things, I can say that when a man has been buried once in this way, just once, he shakes like a goat's beard when he hears Don Félix say these pretty words: 'Now you'll cut your three tons, or I'll have them bury you for three hours.' Those three hours seem longer than a lifetime."

The barbarous practice of hanging was effective and rarely cost a human life because the Indians were strong and had such powers of resistance that often they were capable of work on the same day that they had been tortured. In the course of their long experience the Montellano brothers had learned that hanging produced on the "lazy ones" as terrifying an effect as the lash formerly had. Hanging and burying did not leave wounds bad enough to prevent working. What remained, giving magnificent results, was the fear of reliving frightful hours, hours that seemed an eternity and terrorized the unfortunates. The fact that their torment occurred in the darkness prevented them from seeing the dangers threatening them, and they were therefore surprised and totally unable to defend themselves. Only the Indians of the region know the horrors the jungle can produce.

But what increased to madness the terror of hanging, of the impossibility of defending oneself in the night in the depths of the forest, was the unspeakable, inexplicable horror, the instinctive and unconquerable fear that the Indian feels of phantoms and specters—his superstitious belief in ghosts, which he sees arising on all sides in the darkness.

A white man shut up at night in a wax museum or in the crypt of a mausoleum suffers less than an Indian suspended from a tree in the forest, far from all light. The Montellanos were sufficiently experienced and intelligent not to hang their workers far from the camp, except some exceptionally tough types. To have hanged the majority far from the camp would have been to find not one of them alive the next day.

When the hanged men were at last revived, thanks to the ministrations of their comrades, they could sip a little coffee

and eat a few warmed-over frijoles. They got up and, staggering like drunken men, moved toward their huts, where they
collapsed at full length. It was nearly eleven o'clock at night.

At four o'clock the next morning La Mecha went into the
huts to kick the sleeping men awake. They were still so full of
pain and fright from the hanging of the preceding evening
that, without washing their hands, they threw themselves on
the pot of tepid beans, which they scooped up with their hands
and ate ravenously. Then each of them drank a few gulps of
coffee and, ax on shoulder, went off into the forest resolved to
cut his four tons that day.

Throughout the entire day they had only one idea in their
heads, an idea that never left them in three weeks: "By all the
saints in heaven, little God, make me able to cut my four tons
so they won't hang me!"

But God, who came to earth two thousand years ago to save
men, undoubtedly forgot these Indians. It is certain that at that
time their country was still unknown. And when at last it was
discovered, the first thing the conquistadores did was to plant a
cross on the beach and say a Mass. In spite of that ceremony
the Indians still suffer.

"Certainly," said Martín Trinidad unexpectedly some nights
later, "the Lord came to the world two thousand years ago to
save men. Next time we'll save ourselves."

"Maybe so," replied Pedro, one of the ox-drivers who had
some ideas about religion and priests, "maybe so. But we'll still
have to wait another two thousand years for our turn to
come."

Celso intervened dryly: "Why wait for the Saviour? Save
yourself, brother, and then your savior will have arrived."

6

"This little tree of yours isn't bad," Celso said to Cándido. "Did Don Cacho pick it specially for you?"

"Yes, look. My number's written in ink on the bark."

"It's just as I thought. It's really a pleasure to look at this tree. From it they'll easily get three tons."

Cándido had laid his ax on the ground and was spitting generously on his hands. Before picking up the ax and beginning to hack he said: "I don't know anything about tons and logs. This is the second tree I've ever cut. El Faldón told me that the first two weeks count as apprenticeship and that they won't hang me even if I produce less than four tons. For fifteen days he'll be satisfied with three. But the trouble is that here I've been at it for more than two hours and I haven't yet succeeded in making a dent in it."

Celso began to laugh. "The devil you say! There's nothing strange about that. If you go on scratching as you've been doing this morning, four days will pass and the tree will still be standing."

"That's what I'm afraid of. I'd like to leave it and look in the forest for another marked with my number that's less difficult."

"You won't gain anything that way. This tree has been assigned to you. If you don't cut it today, you'll have to cut it tomorrow."

Cándido looked at Celso in despair. "Then what shall I do? My ax is good and sharp, but it doesn't sink in. It's as though I'm chopping iron. Every stroke I give bounces back and doesn't even nick the bark. Twice already it's bounced back and hit my leg. You can see the mark."

"It's because you're tackling it wrong. This sort of tree has to be attacked another way."

Celso explained that the tree belonged to an exceptionally hard species. Furthermore, such trees were frequent, and Don Acacio and his foremen found them easily to assign them to workmen whose lives they wanted to make extremely difficult —men like Celso.

A great many trees in the virgin forests of the tropics have around them roots that rise out of the earth at the same time as the main trunk during the first period of growth. These roots form a kind of ribs that reach an inch in thickness at their biggest. The closer they are to the trunk, the thicker they are, and they penetrate deeply into it. Some trees have seven or eight ribs of this sort sticking out from the trunk like rays. The ribs formed by the roots are of a wood much harder in texture than that of the trunk. To fell such a tree it is necessary first to cut away all these ribs, as that is the only way the ax can reach the tree itself. These side growths are often three feet high.

It was against a tree of this sort that Cándido was exhausting himself in useless effort. He realized that at least two days' work would be required to bring it down.

Celso was one of the strongest and most expert cutters in the camps. Cándido's confusion amused him. He saw only the three tons of wood, and in his eyes those long roots were nothing but an insignificant obstacle, when compared with the amount of wood the tree would yield.

"No, you'll never do anything that way. You've got to set about it differently. First you have to build a kind of scaffold high enough so that you can reach the trunk with the ax. You've got to raise yourself above the tree's ribs so that you can strike directly at the tree without touching the roots."

"But just to do that I'll need at least half a day."

"The first time, possibly. When you've got used to it, it will be a simple thing to do. First you must cut a few small branches and join them together with vines. Don't try to make a platform that'll last a lifetime. Even if it only holds you up until the moment you've made your first good stroke, that'll be enough. I'll tell you what you've got to do after that to keep yourself up."

Celso cut a few small branches. These Cándido lashed together to form a makeshift foothold. In less than an hour they were able to surround the trunk with a primitive scaffold.

"Now you see, little brother," said Celso, contemplating his work with a satisfied look. "You certainly can't stand on that as solidly as on the ground. You have to brace your feet well against the crossbranches. If you don't steady yourself firmly, you'll fall, and you'll have to climb up all over again. Now then, try it so that we can see."

Cándido climbed up and began to swing his ax. He had made three strokes with the ax and was getting ready to give the fourth when he fell full length on the ground.

"Very good," said Celso, laughing. "Now at least you know how it's done. Wait a minute, I'm going to show you a good trick. Put that rope around the trunk. Now tie one of the ends to your belt. Now make a knot, neither too tight nor too loose. This way, if you slip you won't fall all the way—you'll just hang there. And if the length of rope you've left between the tree and you isn't very long, you can easily get back to your place. That way you can strike better and with greater force."

Cándido spat on his hands and struck several good blows. The ax wounded the trunk.

"You see, boy, how everything's easy when you know how it's done?"

Celso started to go back to his own work, but Cándido stopped him. "Tell me, friend, why are you helping me? I hardly know you, and yet you're running the risk of being hanged for taking the time to help me."

"I've already got a few tons cut, and I know that I'll have my quota by the end of the week. And if I do this it's because I'm sorry for you; you're not used to it. Besides, if they hang me once or twice more it will be better, because I need a lot of courage, an immense amount, and if they hang me I'll be able to accumulate it."

"And for what do you need that much courage?"

"To—to catch a wild pig. I'm hungry and I want to eat the fresh, tender meat of wild boar. Soon I'll go hunting."

Celso picked up his machete, put it through the coils of rope around his waist, took a little bag from inside his shirt, and held it out to Cándido.

"Do you know what's in there?"

"Yes, they're arrowheads."

"Exactly. And I've made myself two beautiful bows. When I shoot my first arrow I'll have a wild pig, or at least a pheasant. If I knock down something good I'll invite you and your children and your sister to share my supper. What's your sister's name?"

"Modesta."

"Modesta! I like that name. Once I was in love with a girl. She must be married by now because I couldn't get back. But now not even remembering is good. I prefer to think about hunting."

"Are you still going to do some work?"

"Naturally. I do it without suffering much. Look at my hands."

He held out his hands for Cándido to see. The latter leaned down, examined them, and felt them.

"Man! But they're not of flesh. They seem to be solid bone or iron."

"That's so," said Celso, laughing. "They've peeled more than a hundred times, and each time they come out harder. Now they seem like leather. That's why I can cut up to six tons of mahogany a day if I wish. Usually I cut four—or only three when I'm in a bad humor. But, believe me, when I let one of these hands come down on a foreman's head, it cracks like a nutshell."

"My hands are not like yours," said Cándido, showing his palms, on which the skin was torn away and bits of loose flesh were hanging at some bloody spots.

Celso examined them like an expert.

"Now you'll understand that it's only because of the state of your hands that during the first two weeks they allow you to produce less than four tons without flogging or hanging you. But as soon as your hands have healed, those savages will find another part of your body to make raw."

Celso walked away, but in a few minutes he came back. "Listen, friend. I've just seen the other tree you cut."

"Yes, it's the first I got down."

"All right, old man, but they won't accept it."

"But why?"

"Because you left it half finished. Here they count only logs, not trees. Go back back there and cut the trunk in the right place, calculating how much will make a ton. Then clean the bark off of a piece of it and cut your mark into it with your ax."

"By all the devils," Cándido exclaimed, "doing that I'll lose two hours more!"

"With your lack of training, certainly. But what do you want? That's how you must do it. There are plenty of trees in the forest. What the Montellanos want is logs, not trees. Well, then, you'd better go now. El Faldón will come round here in half an hour on his horse, and if he sees that tree the way you've left it, you'll catch it. He won't admit your ignorance as an excuse, just as lack of strength is no excuse here. Four tons daily—or hang, you lousy, shifty Indian! How are you going to get your four tons? That's your business and has nothing to do with those who give you your grub and a gram of quinine now and then, not to cure you but to prevent you from dying too soon. The other way they'd have to bury you—and then you'd be able to rest."

The month of August came to an end, and Don Severo had decided to roll the logs into the water at the beginning of the next week. Accompanied by four overseers, Don Acacio rode around inspecting the camps on horseback to see if all the logs were collected and ready to be floated off. He was furious when he found that in the west camp more than two hundred trunks were still on the ground exactly where they had been felled. The ox-drivers explained that they had been hauling day and night but that it had been impossible for them to transport all the logs to the dumps. The logs were so deeply bogged down in the mud that to transport more than four of them each day had required inconceivable effort.

Don Acacio called together the west-camp foremen and asked them what they had been doing all during the period of the cutting. They explained that they had had to stand over the cutters to make them produce the necessary wood and as a consequence had not had time to watch the haulers. They could not be everywhere at once, especially as there were only two of them. They begged Don Acacio to take into consideration that the trails and paths were inundated, that the mud-slides were worse every day, and that the hauling was getting more and more difficult now that the rains were at their heaviest. Even the oxen were in a state of exhaustion, and the drivers were finding themselves obliged to haul trunks with their own hands.

"Yes, you bunch of lazy good-for-nothings! Now you tell me this! But during the dry season you do nothing but sleep and get drunk. What else were you doing when it wasn't raining?"

"But, chief, it's been raining in our district for months. And you can't say that we've passed the time in bed and drinking, because here we have no aguardiente and no girls."

"Shut your mouth, you, if you don't want me to shut it with this whip! I'll deduct three months' pay from each of you."

"Just as you wish, chief," replied El Doblado, "but if you hold back our pay for something that's not our fault, El Chapopote and I are leaving. That's what we have agreed."

"That's what you think, but your accounts still show you in debt."

"Quite true," El Chapopote admitted, "we're still in debt. But I'm not having anything taken from me, not even one day."

"Well, then, get going! Get out! Go and tell them in Hucut-sin that I've run you out for laziness and getting drunk! But you'll have to go on foot. The horses will stay here. You'll go through the jungle on your own feet, on all fours if you wish, and one of these days I'll have the pleasure of finding your skeletons well cleaned by the vultures. Come on, now, get moving! Send me some ox-drivers here!"

Half an hour later two drivers appeared at the office.

"At your orders, chief," the men said as they went in.

"Listen well to what I'm going to tell you."

Don Acacio went to the two ox-drivers, caught each one by an ear, and drew them toward him. Then he shook them as if he wished to pull their ears off. The drivers twisted and turned and tried to get hold of Don Acacio by the arm. At last he released them.

"Tomorrow morning all the logs must be taken to the dumps. If not—if they're not, I promise you that you'll have a little fiesta such as you've never had. Get out there and tell that to the others!"

The two drivers replied in unison: "Very good, little chief, it'll be done as you order."

"We're in the state we're in because of your laziness. But you'll see how I'll put an end to your laziness!"

Don Acacio went back into the hut that served as an office and sat down at the table. Outside, it was raining heavily. The ground around the office and the other huts was being rapidly converted into a lake.

Don Acacio sent a servant to fetch him a bottle of mezcal from his kit and, having warmed himself inside, went over the list of workmen. From time to time he got up, strode over to the door, and looked out to watch the lake becoming bigger and bigger.

In the end the water invaded the hut. "Damn the weather!" Don Acacio swore. He took a good swig of alcohol and shouted in the direction of the cookhouse: "Hi! Pedro! When are you going to give me something to eat?"

"At once, chief," answered Pedro. "One second, please. The coffee boiled over and put out the fire—but it's nearly ready."

"Right. But get a move on. I'm dying of hunger."

An hour later the rain stopped. But the lake that had formed had hardly started to recede when another downpour struck the place. Then, night having fallen, the ox-drivers returned to the camp to eat.

The rain had stopped again.

The earth floors of the huts were drenched. Some cutters had hammocks, but most of them had nothing but a sarape.

They were so tired that after having stretched themselves out they lacked the energy to get up when, an hour later, the water again flooded into the huts. The older and most experienced men had put planks on boxes and rolled themselves up on top, managing to sleep dry as long as the water did not soak in through the palm-leaf thatching. As for the others, who were not familiar with the jungle rainfalls, there was nothing for them to do but sleep in the water or decide to make the untold effort of arranging for themselves the sort of places the old hands had.

Only the cutters had lain down.

The ox-drivers, warned of the gigantic task they had to complete in the twenty-four hours to come, quickly ate their supper and rested a moment standing up. Then they lighted their lanterns and went to the camps. After being fed a little, the oxen also were led back to work. The drivers returned early in the morning to eat their rice and beans and go back once again to the camps.

At noon Don Acacio mounted his horse and rode over the region inspecting the camps. Dozens of tree trunks were buried deep in the wet soil. He met ox-drivers sunk in the mud up to their chests and in danger at every moment of falling and being crushed to death under a trunk. They were making superhuman efforts to transport the logs to the dumps. Regularly every two hours the rain fell for twenty minutes, making more and more mud.

"Look, you haven't been able to move even half the logs in spite of the order I gave to move the whole lot. What did I promise you, you herd of swine? A little fiesta, wasn't it? Well, you'll get it—with music and dancing!"

The only answer he got was the creaking, grating, and squeaking of chains against the yokes, the panting of the drivers making the inhuman effort to haul logs out of the swampy earth, the tearing of the roots that held them back, the yells of the men urging the beasts forward, and the smacking sound of the muddy earth as it clung to the legs of the drivers and the oxen, submerging them a little more at every step.

When night fell the drivers and their helpers returned to the camp to eat something. But they were so weary that they could not eat, for when they slumped down on the ground they fell into deep sleep. Only a few of them dragged themselves as far as the cookhouse to drink a little coffee and eat a few beans.

Don Acacio arrived, escorted by his five foremen. Directing his voice toward the shapeless masses made by the bodies of the drivers on the ground and by the small group of men eating in the cookhouse, he shouted: "Get up, you lousy goats! On the way! Now you're going to see who I am. To the dance—everyone!"

The workers, accustomed to obey white men's orders unconditionally, on hearing Don Acacio's voice, stood up immediately.

"Let's go! Down there to the trees!"

The drivers obeyed.

"Hang them by the legs and put salt on their skin," Don Acacio commanded the foremen. "And don't be afraid to draw the ropes tight," he added, turning to El Guapo. "If you pull off a piece of hide it'll grow back on them again. Leave them strung up for an hour until the salt has sunk well into their pig-flesh or they swallow it when their sweat drips down over them. That way they'll remember not to leave logs in the camps overnight!"

The foremen needed at least two hours to rest and recover, but before that they had to be ready to untie and take down the hanging drivers.

The tortured men remained motionless at the feet of the trees on which they had been hanged. There they slept in the mud without the energy to reach their huts, insensible to the cold and the rain.

The next morning two of them did not get up, but went on sleeping. Four hours later they had begun to stink and had to be buried.

7

 Among those who had been able to get up were Urbano and Pascasio, Indians from the same village and friends since childhood. They tended each other's wounds and smeared each other's sores with the grease that the cook distributed among the hanged men.

It was still night when the drivers were called to work. Urbano and Pascasio followed the column, but they had gone only a few yards when Urbano said to his friend: "Now, little brother!"

With catlike movements they left the column and slipped away among the trees, hiding behind trunks. The foreman who led the gang did not see the men disappear in the darkness. Even if he had seen them, he would have thought that they had stopped to look for something they had forgotten.

The two Indians reached their hut, quickly gathered up all the dried meat, tortillas, and bean-meal there, quickly crossed the open space, and disappeared into the jungle.

"We'd better go around so as not to cross the camp," Urbano advised.

"They won't miss us until noon," said Pascasio softly, as though afraid of being overheard. "With a little luck they won't notice until early tomorrow."

The next day, at midmorning when they were wading across an arroyo, they heard their names being called. It was the two foremen sent on horseback to hunt them down. A lasso reached

Urbano in the middle of the arroyo. Pascasio, who was quicker, was able to reach the other bank and make off. He ran to take shelter in the thickets that surrounded a low outcropping of rock. La Mecha sped his horse after the Indian, but the animal stopped at the foot of the obstacle in spite of the rider's efforts to make him climb.

Pascasio was on the summit of the rocks. He realized that he could not escape even if he clambered down the opposite face of the rocks and hid himself in the jungle. The foremen would find some way to make him come out—and then they'd catch him.

La Mecha shouted to him to come down and follow them back to the camp without resisting, but Pascasio did not reply. He remained standing on the rocky platform, watching the movements of his enemy and hoping in spite of everything to find some means of saving himself.

Seeing this, La Mecha got down from his horse and prepared to climb the rock.

The other foreman, El Faldón, who had just returned to the other bank of the arroyo dragging Urbano firmly tied up at the end of his rope, immediately saw the danger: La Mecha was laboriously climbing one side of the rocks while the Indian was getting ready to escape down the other. Pascasio might well succeed, reach the base quickly, take La Mecha's horse, mount it, and escape, abandoning the animal in some distant place because the prints of its hoofs would mark his trail better than those of his own bare feet.

Having guessed the fugitive's intentions, El Faldón acted promptly. He tied Urbano tightly to a tree trunk and then rode around the rocks to cut off Pascasio's retreat. But the Indian understood the maneuver and quickly climbed up again, reaching the summit just as La Mecha did.

All hope of flight vanished. Pascasio picked up a heavy stone and with all his strength flung it at La Mecha's head. The foreman collapsed backwards, followed by the enormous stone. Pascasio, beside himself, picked up the stone, leaped on him, and pounded until his victim's head was a shapeless mass. Then he looked around for his companion. He had lost his machete during the climb, and now he needed it to cut Urbano's bonds, as too much time would be lost trying to untie them. But El Faldón, having lost sight of Pascasio, deduced that the Indian had descended the opposite side of the rocks and was now in the hands of La Mecha. So he retraced his steps and from a distance saw Pascasio at the point of releasing Urbano. But Pascasio also saw the foreman and again made off, running to climb the rock with the intention of hiding and of attacking the foreman from behind. When he reached the rock, his eyes fell on the body of La Mecha, in whose belt was a heavy-caliber revolver. If Pascasio had not wasted time looking for his machete, but had climbed up to hide himself sooner, he would have won the game. But he realized this too late. When he moved back after tearing the gun from the dead man's body, he faced El Faldón pointing a revolver at him.

Pascasio had never before had a revolver in his hand. He knew, and this because he had heard it said, that you had to press the trigger to make the bullet shoot out. Holding the revolver with both hands, he pulled the trigger. The gun fired before he expected it to, and the bullet was lost in the bushes.

El Faldón considered only one thing: the Indian had tried to kill him. So, without hesitating, he in turn fired; and he did not miss. Pascasio doubled up and fell to the ground.

"I ought to drill a hole in your body too," growled El Faldón, looking at Urbano, who, tied up, had been a helpless witness to the scene.

"I ask myself why you're waiting to do it, you stinking coyote," the Indian replied insolently, using the same form of address the foreman used in speaking to him.

"Wait a minute, you mangy cur, and I'll teach you not to be familiar in speaking to me."

El Faldón's whip snapped repeatedly across the prisoner's face.

"So that next time, pig, you'll speak properly to me," said the foreman, replacing the whip in his belt.

But Urbano was determined to incite him. Again using the

familiar form, he said: "Your day will come too. Have patience!"

"Shut up and see to the burying of the bodies!"

"I'll bury my comrade's, but the foreman's can go to hell."

"We'll see about that."

The foreman began to be uneasy, looking in all directions, scanning the horizon as if afraid he would see more fugitive Indians springing from the jungle. Finally he decided to untie Urbano, taking all sorts of precautions and leaving him just able to move but incapable of attack. Before freeing the Indian's body and hands, he tied his legs so that Urbano could just stand up and take short steps. Then he went to Pascasio's corpse, picked up the revolver that had fallen on the ground beside it, and put it in his belt. This done, he drew his own pistol and, aiming it with one hand, untied Urbano's chest and arms. When the ropes fell, he jumped to one side and again pointing his weapon, gave an order to the prisoner: "Pick up that carrion and take it down there among the thickets behind the rock."

While Urbano was carrying out the foreman's order, the latter stood a few paces behind him, lasso in hand, ready to tie him up at the first suspicious movement. Urbano saw that he could neither defend himself nor escape. He carried the body of his companion behind the rock. El Faldón ordered him to do the same with that of La Mecha. Urbano obeyed.

Finally El Faldón made him scoop out a grave. To make a good job of it Urbano should have had his machete, but El Faldón was wise enough to know that at the least sign of carelessness on his part the prisoner would cut his bonds and take to flight. Urbano might easily pick up a stone and smash his skull without giving him time even to shoot.

So he ordered Urbano to cut a strong branch. Using it, the Indian began to dig the ditch. The process was slow and difficult. At last the trench was opened.

El Faldón said: "Put La Mecha in the hole."

Urbano lifted the corpse and threw it into the ditch, using his feet and hands to help.

"Tell me, you bastard, can't you do it like a Christian? As if he were a dog!"

"God will judge better than we can," answered Urbano.

"Come on, get out of there!" roared the foreman.

He went up to the body, took off his hat, crossed himself, and made the sign of the cross over the corpse, all without ever taking his eyes off the prisoner. Now the trench had to be filled in. He was about to order Urbano to do it when he remembered a rite that he had forgotten. He lassoed Urbano suddenly and rolled him over on the ground.

"Stay there and don't move until I tell you to. Understand? If you're unlucky enough to move your head, you know what'll happen to you."

Urbano remained perfectly still.

Then El Faldón, watching the Indian from the corner of his eyes, began to go through the dead man's pockets. He found four pesos and twenty-three centavos. He removed the cartridge belt and examined the body carefully for anything he might find hidden among the clothes. When he did not find anything he regarded this ceremony as completed. El Faldón turned back toward Urbano.

"Get up now, you scum! And fill in the grave."

When the work was finished El Faldón said: "On the way now! We've hardly got time to reach camp tonight."

"But," Urbano protested, "what about Pascasio? Aren't we going to bury him?"

"We'll leave his carrion here. The vultures will take charge of it."

"If I had known that only that dog was going to get a grave, I wouldn't have done anything."

"That's why I made you fetch the two bodies. But what there is of him will stay right here. A pig like him doesn't need a Christian burial. He doesn't deserve it. Now then, get a move on. Let's go."

El Faldón went up to La Mecha's horse, which was tied to a tree.

"I ought to drag you by its tail, but I've got no time. I prefer to hurry and get back to the camp. The devil knows if we can get there tonight."

He jerked the lasso and Urbano fell over on the ground like a bundle. Revolver in hand, El Faldón went and tied his hands.

"Stand up and turn around!"

He secured the Indian's hands behind his back and untied his feet.

"Now mount!"

Stupidly, like anyone who has never been on a horse's back, Urbano tried to heave himself up. El Faldón found himself obliged to put his revolver in his belt in order to help the Indian with both his hands and even his knees and teeth.

During this operation Urbano might have been able to take advantage of the occasion, as of all the other openings offered during the next ten minutes, to try to escape or even to assault the foreman. He knew perfectly well what awaited him on return to the camp. He knew that when night fell he would bitterly regret not having shared the fate of his unhappy companion, who at least no longer suffered. But his strength was beginning to ebb and his energy had left him. The rapid flight and the dash to the arroyo had exhausted him. Then the sight of Pascasio's struggle with the foremen had excited him as if he himself had been the hunted animal. And, finally, Pascasio's death showed him the futility of every attempt at flight. The little strength remaining to him had been expended in digging the trench with the branch. He was in such a depressed physical and moral state that if El Faldón had untied him and left him free on the back of the horse he could not have taken advantage of the occasion to flee, but would have followed El Faldón docilely. In the morning he would doubtless recover his strength and reproach himself for the mistakes he was making. Then he would wish that he had fought to win his freedom or die for it.

"We can't go any farther." These were the first words El Faldón uttered after they started on their way back to the camp. Night had fallen. The sky was covered with clouds. The horses advanced laboriously. El Faldón had lost the way, and it had been the horses that had brought him back to the main trail, but now they were getting lost, and every ten steps they tried to turn to the right or the left, warned by instinct that they were going to get bogged down. El Faldón felt the danger: he was running the risk of getting lost in the jungle. So he decided not to proceed, but to camp where he was. There was no need to fear that Urbano would escape, for to try it at night was impossible. Furthermore, he knew that the Indians had lost their packages of provisions when crossing the arroyo. He and La Mecha had felt so sure that they would catch the Indians and get back to the camp the same night that they had not brought any provisions with them. If Urbano tried to run away, he would die in the jungle. He would not die of hunger, because like every Indian, he would know how to find plants on which to subsist. But he would have to cover great distances without finding even a palm tree, and to cross the jungle it was not enough merely to have sufficient food.

Assisted by Urbano, El Faldón succeeded in lighting a fire for warmth. Their clothes were still went with arroyo water and the drops of rain that fell on them from the trees. El Faldón took the precaution of tying up Urbano before wrapping himself in his sarape and settling to sleep near the fire. It rained heavily during the night. When dawn began to break, both men—the guard and the guarded—felt relieved at being able to continue their journey.

Don Acacio and one of his foremen, El Pechero, had just sat down at the table when El Faldón, leading his prisoner at the end of a rope, stood at the office door.

El Faldón went into the dining room.

"And La Mecha?" asked Don Acacio. "Where's he?"

"The son-of-a-bitch killed him."

"And the son-of-a-bitch?"

"I killed him. He had attacked me from behind."

"Two men lost! A foreman and a peon! The next time you'll pay me for it. This has never happened to me, understand? To lose at the same time a workman and my best overseer. Besides, not one has ever escaped me. I've chased them a day, two days if necessary, but I've always brought them back. Have you at least brought back the other one?"

"Yes, chief."

Urbano appeared in the doorway, his hands still tied.

"Come in, you," shouted Don Acacio without getting up from his chair. "So you wanted to slip away, eh? So you wanted to escape and to rob me?"

Don Acacio tore off a piece of tortilla and dipped it in his soup.

"I didn't want to rob you, little chief."

"You still owe me more than two hundred and fifty pesos, and if you save yourself from paying your debts with your work, you're robbing me! Now I'll add one hundred pesos more to your account."

"It is well, little chief."

"As regards my good co-worker La Mecha, he owed me two hundred and thirty pesos. I ask myself how he came to owe me that much. Anyhow, as he liked to run after the old whores, and as you were the cause of his death, so that now the vultures are eating him, you'll be the one to pay me those two hundred and thirty pesos. Now then, how much do you owe me? Well, whatever it is, I'm not going to bother adding it up, least of all while I'm having a meal. All I can say to you, Urbano—that's your name, isn't it?—is that before you'll be able to pay your debts, you and I will be old men, very old. But that's your business."

"Yes, little chief."

"Go to the cookhouse and get a mouthful to eat. Later, when I've had my siesta, we'll get down to serious explanations, because I'm going to hang you by your thumbs and by something else I know about. We'll see what remains of your skin then. I think that'll make you shed all desire to run away again! Say, cook, what's the matter with my stew?"

"Coming now, chief," replied the cook from the hut that served as a cookhouse.

"Did you understand what I just said to you, or don't you speak Spanish?" he asked Urbano.

"I understand very well," Urbano said in a tone of indifference. "With your permission, little chief," he added, bowing and going out.

"Let the cook untie you," Don Acacio shouted. "I've told you you won't save yourself from this."

"No, little chief," the Indian replied, moving away.

"Winds of rebellion are definitely blowing around here," Don Acacio said to El Pechero and El Faldón, who had just sat down and was beginning to pull himself together. "It's the fault of my brothers. They've been too easygoing with the men and have let them do as they please. Result—less mahogany. If things go on this way until Christmas, we'll all be begging alms from the Indians in the streets of Villahermosa—the Indians we've enriched by our generosity, by filling their hands with money. When those swine arrive here, the only thing they think about is loitering around or stoning to death my best foremen, the ones I've trained myself. But this must change! They'll see what happens when my patience is exhausted. Now, today, I'll begin showing them who I am!"

This discourse, promising energetic measures, had not been delivered in one breath. Between phrases Don Acacio had taken the time necessary to chew and swallow. One after another each of the men around the table took advantage of these pauses to approve the master's words with a servile "Yes, chief."

They wished in this way to bear witness that they shared Don Acacio's opinion. In reality, they were incapable of having any personal opinion, but it satisfied them to put in a word and pretend to take part in the discussion. They felt flattered to be above the peons, who did not have even the right to approve.

All that was asked of a peon was blind obedience, even when he was ordered to throw himself in the water with a rock at his neck. For the slave there is only one virtue and one right: that of considering as gospel whatever his owner says. The slave who neither practices that virtue nor exercises that right contravenes the rules, and in such circumstances to kill him or torture him is a meritorious act that never receives enough praise.

After eating a little, Urbano sat down in the cookhouse. He felt worn out and stupefied. When he had returned to his hut, he had found a few provisions that Pascasio and he had left behind so as not to load themselves too heavily. Among these had been some scraps of tobacco. Now he rolled himself a cigarette and squatted down to smoke in silence. From time to time he replied to remarks directed at him by the cook or the woman who helped him. As time went on, his agony increased. Had Don Acacio and El Faldón battered him to pieces immediately on his arrival back at camp, he would now be stretched out on the ground or perhaps washing his wounds in the arroyo—or he might even be off hauling logs. "It could be," he said to himself, "it could be. . . ." He watched the smoke rising from his cigarette. "It could be. . . ."

He did not know exactly what this "could be" meant. He was trying not to think about Don Acacio's threat. He thought of taking flight again, though he knew that this second time he would have far fewer chances of success. Alone, he could not bring it off, but he clung to the idea of flight as to a life preserver. This time he would defend himself, beat down the overseers with stones or sticks, not so much to avoid his fate (which was settled beforehand) as to make them kill him as Pascasio had been killed. Once he was dead, Don Acacio could not do anything more to him.

As for his body, they could do what they liked with it. Was Pascasio now greatly troubled that a jaguar was eating him, that rats were gnawing at him, or that he was serving as a depository for flies' eggs? With the disappearance of his best comrade, life seemed senseless to Urbano. Why go on living? To stay here in the jungle suffering until his account was worked off? With the single prospect of being beaten to pulp each week or, still worse, hanged? And all because, in spite of all his efforts, he could not produce as much as they demanded. Away in his own village he had always eaten badly, but here the food was much worse. So then?

The office, the bungalows occupied by Don Acacio and the foremen, the cookhouse, and the huts of the workmen were grouped on a sort of open space on one bank of the river. From where he was sitting, Urbano could see the swift current and the opposite shore. The muddy water was carrying branches and roots of trees. Where was it taking them? Urbano did not know. None of the peons had the slightest idea of the course of the river; nobody seemed to give it a thought. He was thinking that the river must end somewhere, in a peaceful region where it passed beautiful villages peopled by men who loved their neighbors. The current rolled precipitously toward such a region—no doubt to reach more quickly that Eden in which peace and goodness reigned.

Two weeks earlier one of the boys had drowned while moving tree trunks with his comrades. Perched on top of a raft made of branches, he was trying to lift up a log when the raft was jerked from its cable and broken apart by the current, which swept the boy away. Because he could not swim, he was flung over three times and then disappeared in the foam. The next day they found his body about one mile down the river among some branches. Urbano had helped to disentangle it. He still remembered the serene expression on the dead man's face. What a contrast the expression on the drowned man's face was to that of boys who had just been flogged or hanged! He must surely have seen, though from far away, the enchanted village toward which the current rushed.

Urbano rose painfully, went to the riverbank, and began looking for a stone. He was so absorbed in his thoughts that he spoke aloud to himself: "If I tie a stone to my feet I'll soon sink to the bottom. Then it'll all be finished and there won't be any more Don Acacio to torture me."

At that exact moment he heard Don Acacio calling him: "Hey, you! Where have you got to? Come here. We still have something to tell each other."

Urbano immediately forgot everything. He was so accustomed to obey that his dreams vanished the moment the voice of his master was heard.

He hurried toward the office. "At your orders, little chief."

Don Acacio ambled out of the office smoking a cigarette and

saw Urbano hurrying toward him. In his hand he held a heavy whip that was beginning to be curved with wear. As he walked he fixed the whiphandle firmly around his wrist. He came to within two steps of Urbano.

"Good, you Indian son of a bitch. We two are going to have a little private talk, you and I. You have to learn once and forever that you're not going to leave here before paying your debts down to the last centavo."

From one of the huts the melody of the waltz *Over the Waves* reached them. Don Acacio turned and looked at his girl in the doorway of the hut, swaying her hips in time with the music and smoking a cigarette.

"Don't go so far away to do what you're going to do, my pet," she shouted. "There's so little entertainment here that I'm dying of boredom."

"Shut your putrid mouth and go inside at once if you don't want me to give you a hiding too," growled Don Acacio.

"Just to think that he refuses to entertain me even when it doesn't cost anything! I think I won't stay very long!" the girl replied in a rage, entering the hut.

"Come," continued Don Acacio to Urbano. "We don't need witnesses for what we're going to say to each other. We'll go a little farther away, to the riverbank. Nobody will hear you there."

From the hut to the river was only a few steps, but the distance was long enough for Urbano to make the most varied plans. He was following a few paces behind Don Acacio. As he went along the lash of the whip, suspended from the handle, was dancing constantly before his eyes. At times Don Acacio's alcoholic breath reached his nostrils. Certainly Urbano himself took a swig of aguardiente whenever he had a chance. In other times, in his village, he had often drunk more than his share when he had money in his pocket. But he had never felt so nauseated by the smell of alcohol as he did now. This fetid odor did not arouse in him any desire for a drink. On the contrary, it disgusted him horribly. He experienced the sensation felt by a smoker who, when he has kissed a pretty girl who smokes a daily pack of cigarettes, swears that he will never smoke again.

They reached the slope and went down it. The enormous whip wavered before Urbano's eyes and at times its tip seemed to strike the agitated water. It seemed to him to cut the current that rushed toward those places he had just been dreaming of. But at the same time there came to him the painful memory of the night when they had hanged him and a dozen of his companions by the feet and had lashed them unmercifully because they had not been able to move their quota of logs to the farthest dump. That had been exactly three days earlier, and it had been that barbarous treatment which had driven him and Pascasio to flee. They had made up their minds never again to suffer such punishment. The welts on his body were still fresh and bloody. Suddenly a terrible fear invaded Urbano. He was afraid of the new blows about to fall on him and reopen his still raw wounds. He feared the pain awaiting him, which he knew he would not survive. One second later his fear was matched by desperation, and the two feelings were transformed into courage, courage such as he had never felt: a fury unknown to him and seeming to possess someone else who was not he.

About a dozen yards from the bank of the river there rose an enormous dried-out tree that seemed to have lost all its sap and its strength either from age or from prolonged contact with water. Not one leaf adorned its branches, which pointed sadly heavenward like the arms of a grotesque scarecrow. It was the only tree to be seen in that place. Along the edge of the river only dwarf vegetation grew, sunk in the sand and so poor and miserable that it seemed certain not to survive the next flood.

"Let's go over there, to that tree," Don Acacio ordered. "We'll settle our accounts there. At least there we'll be left alone without witnesses, away from the chatter of those whores who imagine that for us there's nothing but pleasure and amusement and that we have mountains of money."

Urbano moved on toward the tree.

"Damn and blast it all! May the Devil take me! Why, I've

forgotten the main thing!" shouted Don Acacio in a fury. "You won't be able to stay on your feet if I don't tie you tightly. Quick! Run back and fetch me a rope."

Urbano climbed the slope swiftly, helping himself along with his hands. Two minutes later he returned with the lasso. Halfway down he hesitated a few seconds. The river water was flowing there below him, so free, so independent. Nobody flogged it; nobody tortured it. And that tree trunk looked so miserable, suggested such despair. . . .

Urbano closed his eyes sorrowfully. He remembered the horrible torture of that night, saw in his mind pieces of bleeding flesh that struck the unfortunate wretches in the face and got into their mouths when they opened them to scream or groan. Only the young workers cried out. The older hands simply shrank or collapsed under the blows. It was not their habit to show their sufferings or to ask for mercy. They were too proud for that, however enslaved they might be. They moaned silently, and the only sounds they emitted were of hatred. The more they suffered, the more they hated. The more they hated, the less they felt their pain and the more their spirits were set ablaze by the thought that one day—it might be far ahead, but it would surely come—one day they would be able to return blow for blow, and with interest, even though they might have to pay with their lives for this yearned-for revenge.

Urbano was still hesitating. He thought that ten minutes later that dry trunk would be spattered with his blood. He shut his lips tightly and half closed his eyes.

He was only ten paces from the tree. Don Acacio, leaning against it, was rolling another cigarette. On the ground, two meters from the trunk, Urbano saw a big stone, as big as a man's head. He stared at it for a long time and remembered that his friend Pascasio had armed himself with a stone like that to smash La Mecha's skull. But almost at the same time there came back into his mind the thoughts that had obsessed him half an hour before when he had daydreamed of peaceful places toward which the current must be flowing. His hands shut convulsively as if wanting to weaken his determination. He bent to pick up the stone, thinking to tie it to one of his feet, run toward the river, and wade in until it swallowed him.

"I must do this. Now," he told himself, "at this very moment." He was gasping with excitement. Slowly he approached the shore. Yes, it was necessary to act immediately, because a moment later he would not be able to act. If he decided, the sad tree trunk would not be spattered with his blood.

He let his pent-up breath escape and said: "Yes, now!"

"What are you muttering about there?" asked Don Acacio. "So you've returned with the rope at last. Come on! Stand there with your face to the tree and put your hands up."

Don Acacio was trying to light the cigarette he had just finished rolling. The wind had begun to blow sharply. It blew along the river bank with growing violence. Don Acacio had burned up three matches without being able to light the cigarette. He let out an oath. He tried again. He took two steps back as if to make space for Urbano to pass. In so doing he covered part of his face with his left hand, the rest with the right, in which he held the match he had just struck. His eyes were fixed on the cigarette and on the wavering flame, which seemed to enjoy being buffeted by the wind before fulfilling its mission.

Urbano held out the lasso to Don Acacio. At that instant he saw the whip hanging from his torturer's wrist. With an instinctive reflex movement he struck violently at his enemy's arm and knocked him against the tree. Don Acacio's head slammed against the trunk.

For a fraction of a second Urbano stood stupefied. But immediately he came to and realized that now he could not retreat. He had just rebelled, and he would expiate that involuntary blow with death after terrible sufferings.

He was guided more by terror than by his reflections and his dreams. Terror drove him to carry out to its end what he had begun.

Don Acacio still held his two hands before his face. At last he had been able to light his cigarette. He did not immediately realize that the Indian had struck him; his impression was that Urbano had stumbled in a hole and had caught his arm to prevent himself from falling. If he had realized the truth, perhaps he could have saved himself, but Urbano acted with the swiftness of which only an Indian is capable, his hands and arms being trained from infancy to fight against nature's traps in the jungle and to demolish them with one sure blow.

The day before, Urbano had learned from personal experience how it is possible to secure a man to a tree without the victim's being able to put up the slightest resistance—provided a good lasso is available.

Don Acacio had neither time nor intention to lower his hands when his head struck the tree. In a flash they were made fast to the trunk. Only then did Don Acacio have a clear notion of what was happening. He kicked out at Urbano's legs, but Urbano had foreseen such an attempt, the only form of attack of which Don Acacio was now capable. Rapidly, with catlike agility, Urbano ran round the tree, passing the rope around Don Acacio's thighs, pulling hard on it to make the knots tight and passing another piece of rope around the prisoner's neck, so as to make it impossible for him to move his head.

Then Don Acacio realized that he was lost. Even if he had promised to give Urbano all the camps in exchange for his life, the Indian would not have turned from his purpose. He had had too much experience to believe in a white man's word. In other countries a workman could still trust a policeman's word if the policeman promised to leave him in peace; but the Indian workers had had too bitter experiences with policemen and dictators to have faith in their words or in those of bosses and their agents.

Don Acacio knew well that the Indian would proceed right to the end. Because even in the unlikely event that a foreman were to think of coming to this place, Urbano would have bashed in his skull or strangled him before a foreman could rescue him.

Nevertheless, in spite of his desperate situation Don Acacio did not lose his head. He did not ask for mercy any more than the men did when they were flayed or hanged. Personally he had never struck this man Urbano or kicked him as he usually kicked his inferiors. He had not even noticed the existence of Urbano before this, for the Indian belonged to his brother Severo's camp. It was the first time that Don Acacio had seen him or had anything to do with him, and this merely because the Indian had tried to escape and it was necessary to give him a salutary warning. But he knew that, of the three brothers and the foremen, it was he, Don Acacio, who was hated with most rancor. It would not have surprised Don Acacio if one of his own men, with the hatred felt for him by the Chamula Celso, the driver Santiago, or Fidel, or Andrés (the most intelligent of them all), had waited for him in the jungle and traitorously struck him down. But the fact that this unhappy, scared worm of an Urbano should have him in his power and be about to kill him—that was something he could not bear. His rage was such that, forgetting the situation in which he was, and taking advantage of the circumstance that his mouth was still free, he made use of that freedom, though not to shout for help, for to ask for help against a lousy Indian would have been to lower himself. It would have ended forever his prestige in the camps. The workmen and the foremen would have had a laugh at his expense. The latter especially, and particularly when drunk, would not have hesitated to call him a fairy. In the camps there were only men. Fairies scared of punishments and blows did not exist there.

Don Acacio gave vent to his rage, shouting: "You mangy cur, you son of a whore! What are you going to do? Do you imagine that because you have me tied up I'm going to stay here without giving you what you have coming? Wait a minute, then you'll see how I'll get out of this! . . . But, by the devil, I swear that afterwards you'll pray to the Virgin and all your saints! Now, you idiot, untie me!"

Urbano began to tremble with fear. He knew perfectly well that Don Acacio was tied up firmly, but nevertheless Urbano wondered whether he could not free himself by means of some magic formula or with the Devil's help. Facing him, Urbano felt like a hunter facing a jaguar fallen into a trap and chained, safe, but fearing that by some effort in a desperate rage the animal will break its bonds and spring on him.

For a second Urbano stood there perplexed, his eyes fixed on the river, which flowed a few steps from the sandy bank.

Again Don Acacio shouted: "Are you going to release me, cur? Yes or no?"

Suddenly Urbano moved toward him and took the revolver from his belt. He had never possessed a firearm, and he did not know how to use it. He held it with both his hands and pressed it against Don Acacio's body, but he did not know with which hand or which finger to press the trigger. Finally he pressed it, but no shot resulted because the gun had a safety catch.

"And it's an imbecile like you who's trying to kill me!" exclaimed Don Acacio. And the smile that followed his exclamation was bitter because he was fully conscious of the vanity of his efforts to free himself.

Urbano flung the revolver from him. It described a wide arc before falling on the sand.

The two foremen and Don Acacio's favorite girl were sitting in the office.

The sound of some of Don Acacio's shouts reached them, but indistinctly and muffled.

El Faldón said to El Pechero: "Something must be happening. By my mother, I wouldn't like to be in Urbano's skin. Just listen to Cacho's roars!"

"For the fun of it I'd go down a little closer to see something," the girl said.

"Better not do it, señorita," advised El Faldón, "because if Don Cacho should find out, he wouldn't like it. We don't like to have people looking on. Don Cacho must have told you."

"Then there's no way of having the least bit of fun here?"

"No, señorita, and believe me, for us it's not fun! Damn it all! Now I remember that tomorrow we'll have to get up at three in the morning. . . . I always ask myself why I came to this desert where there's nothing but rats' shit and sometimes a little alcohol and flesh."

He rose and made toward the hut where the foremen slept.

At that moment a sharp cry was heard coming from the riverbank. But it attracted the attention of nobody except Martín Trinidad (one of the ragged men recruited by Don Gabriel on the road), who was just then on his way to the office to exchange his ax for a new one.

He approached the slope and, almost reaching the edge, threw himself to the ground and began to crawl forward, hunching himself together so as not to be seen, for he well knew how bad it was to let oneself be seen where a beating was going on. Hidden behind some bushes, Martín cautiously stretched his neck. From where he was he could see very well a large part of the riverbank.

Urbano picked up the stone again and moved toward Don Acacio.

"You won't do that, you cur!" roared Don Acacio.

"No," replied Urbano, "no. That would be too good for you, too good for a white man without a soul."

He dropped the stone. Don Acacio breathed more freely. But Urbano now turned to look at the river and caught sight of something that Don Acacio could not see because he was facing the slope. He merely observed that Urbano suddenly opened his mouth wide and that a shadow of cruelty crossed his eyes.

Urbano, shrugging his shoulders and walking on tiptoes stepped into the water as though trying to surprise an animal, perhaps a snake.

But no, it was not a snake. It was a branch with thorns as long as a finger and as hard as steel. The branch floated forward and then back again, sometimes getting close to the bank and then moving away. Urbano sprang forward and with a swift motion caught it before the current snatched it away. Then, walking back to the tree, he held the branch before Don Acacio's eyes.

"See these thorns, torturer?" he said, half opening his eyes in a mock smile.

"By the Virgin! When are you going to untie me?"

"In less than a minute you'll be free, torturer," said Urbano, pulling a long thorn from the branch. Then he held it firmly between his fingers and put it so near Don Acacio's face that the latter felt it on his cheek.

"With this thorn I'm going to rip out your savage beast's eyes. That way you'll never again be able to see how they beat and hang the men. That way you'll never see the sun shine again or your mother's face."

"Have you gone crazy, you fool?" Don Acacio asked, going suddenly pale.

"We, the men, have all gone crazy. You and your brothers have driven us crazy."

"You know very well that they'll shoot you or hang you by the neck."

"Nobody will be able to shoot me or hang me or even beat me, because I'll rob you even of that revenge. Because when I've done what I've got to do I'm going to jump into the river, and they can come to look for me there."

"But, in the name of the Virgin, boy, don't do that. Look— you'll go to hell. In the name of all the saints, don't do it."

Don Acacio had changed his tone to one of great gentleness as he uttered these words.

Suddenly Urbano, as though afraid he might weaken, or perhaps thinking that they might come to the rescue of Don Acacio, flung himself at his victim.

Don Acacio uttered a sharp cry—not a cry of pain, but of horror, of mad terror. For the first time in his life he had felt fear.

Without showing any emotion, Urbano leaped on him a second time. Blood began to gush from the sockets of Don Acacio's eyes. He bent his head back so that the blood should not run into his mouth, muttering: "Most holy Mother! Mother of our Lord!"

Urbano looked up the slope and saw the head of a motionless man who was watching him.

Quickly he untied the cord that held up his torn pants, picked up the stone again, dropped it inside the pants, tied a rope around his thighs below his hips so that the stone could not slip out, and then—holding the top of the pants with both hands—stumbled into the water. The current swept him away. He appeared and disappeared several times in the midst of the stream. His head appeared once more. Then he was lost to view.

When Martín Trinidad was sure that Urbano had disappeared, he left his hiding place, went cautiously down to the shore, and with great wariness walked up to Don Acacio and stood looking at him for a time. He discovered the revolver lying in the sand, picked it up, and concealed it in the folds of his shirt. Then he returned to Don Acacio and, always taking the greatest precautions, relieved him of his cartridge belt. Don Acacio did not make the smallest movement or utter the least word. Possibly he was unconscious of the presence of a human being near him.

Martín Trinidad hid the cartridge belt, fastening it underneath his shirt. Then he moved off quickly, following the river's bank until he was out of sight. When he was certain that nobody could see him, he took out the cartridge belt and buried it in the sand. He walked for fifty paces farther along, examined the place well so as to be able to recognize it later, and buried the revolver. Then he climbed the embankment, but at a good distance from the most distant hut of the group. Toward it he walked, on the way picking up the ax, which he had left leaning against a log. At the tool storehouse he asked El Faldón to give him a new ax for the used one.

"Where's the old one?" asked El Faldón.

"Look at it. It's all nicked."

"Damn it! As might be expected—'Made in Germany'! It's not worth a damn and looks like tin plate. God! A German ax. Bah! Here, take this one. It's not new, but it's American, and it will last better. These German tools can't cut even a piece of cheese without the edge turning. They're worthless. They were part of the equipment of the company that was here before we came. They were poor devils who didn't know anything about axes or machetes. They bought any sort of junk. That's why they went broke. Say, how much have you cut today?"

"Well, I don't think it amounts to three tons."

Having made the exchange, El Faldón noted it down carefully in the inventory book. He remained a few minutes longer in the storeroom to tell the caretaker to grease the axes and rub the leathers to prevent the moisture from damaging them.

"This place is a pigsty! What do you do with yourself all day long? Look around! Mushrooms are growing in every corner. The climbing-irons have pounds of rust. I've half a mind to put a pair on you and make you climb a tree with them. Then you'd see how you'd break your thick head, but at least you wouldn't forget that they have to be greased."

"But, little chief, how do you expect me to prevent the mushrooms from growing when it's always raining? Nothing can get dry, and, besides, to grease these tools I have to have grease. . . ."

"Shut your mouth if you don't want me to smash it in for you."

El Faldón went outside, looked at the sky, and saw that another downpour was on the way. He was quite pleased to find himself on guard in the camp that day instead of out watching the cutters. He retraced his way quickly toward the hut, but stopped halfway.

"Christ!" he said aloud. "It seems to me that Cacho is prolonging this thing too much. It's more than an hour and a half since he began."

He turned in the direction of the river and was about to go to the edge of the slope to see what was happening. But he stopped.

"After all, it's of no importance to me if he burns the hide of that guy a bit more or less. That's his business. I'm happy that he didn't give me the job of doing it. I'm worn out. I feel as if I can't do anything more. . . ."

Heavy drops began to fall, and then immediately it rained fiercely. Although not more than twenty paces from the hut,

El Faldón reached it wet to the bone. He stood in the doorway and shook the water from his hat.

"Serves me right for meddling in what doesn't concern me."

The rain fell with increasing violence. Suddenly El Faldón felt himself gripped by a sense of uneasiness. Without leaving the doorway he faced the river and listened intently, his eyes fixed on the slope, hoping to see Don Acacio at any moment.

"The devil!" he murmured. "I guess I'll have to see what they're doing." He put on his rubber cape and pulled down his sopping hat. When he reached the edge of the slope he saw at once that it was not Urbano but Don Acacio who was tied to the tree. He recognized him by his clothes, which left no room for doubt. Don Acacio's head had dropped forward. His chin rested on his chest, and his long black hair had fallen over his forehead. He was making futile attempts to free himself from the ropes but visibly lacked the strength to struggle.

El Faldón heard him calling: "Pechero! Faldón! By all the devils, where is that pair of lazy mules?"

It was evident that the distance and the noise of the rain had prevented his cries from being heard in the office.

The foreman ran down the incline.

"Christ! At last somebody comes! Gang of thieves! While I was in the claws of that savage you were scratching your bellies."

El Faldón untied the ropes and held him by the shoulders to help him straighten up. When Don Acacio lifted his head the hair that had been covering his forehead fell back and disclosed his face.

"By our most holy Mother, chief! What happened to you?" Crazed with terror, El Faldón crossed himself several times.

"Now it occurs to you to come and ask what has happened to me! The bandit ripped my two eyes out! And naturally he has escaped. But we'll catch him, and then he'll learn what it will cost him. Come on, now! Let all the foremen get their horses! He must not get away from us. He fixed me, finished me beyond repair!"

He felt uselessly for his pistol. He felt at his waist, searching for the cartridge belt.

"That bastard has taken everything, even my cartridge belt —unless it has fallen somewhere." He felt for it in the sand with his feet.

"No, chief," said El Faldón, "there's no gun or belt anywhere."

"Then that damned swine has taken them."

"Probably, chief, that's most likely it. Never mind. He sure will cause us trouble before we can catch him. He won't stop to think before firing at us."

"So! Now you're all of a tremble because of a lousy Indian! Only bring him to me, and you'll see how I'll strangle him with my own hands."

"He can't be far off, chief. In this rain he can't make headway, and he's very likely to get bogged down in the jungle."

During this conversation El Faldón had led Don Acacio toward the office and had helped him sit down. The girl, seeing her lover in such a state, rushed toward him, shouting: "Ay! My poor man! Savages! They're not Christians, they're wild animals. But I'll never leave you!"

Don Acacio flung the girl from him violently.

"You shut your whore's face! Leave me in peace from your goodness. I've many other things to think of!"

"But, my love, I only want to console you," the girl sighed tearfully.

"I don't need your consolation, you sow! What I want is for you to get out of here and not be bothering me."

The girl threw herself on the bed and began to howl and lament in a voice loud enough for Don Acacio to hear.

"Faldón!" shouted Don Acacio.

"Coming, chief. I'm preparing a dressing."

"Throw that bitch out of here! I don't want to hear her howls. Throw her in the river or do whatever you like, but get rid of her quickly."

He got up and gropingly took some steps with his hands stretched out in search of a bottle. When he did not find one, he thought they had maliciously moved everything in the place.

"The devil! Where have you put the bottle of mezcal?"

"Here it is, chief."

El Faldón held out the bottle, which Don Acacio took and emptied in one long swallow. Then he threw it with all his force, not heeding those around him.

"What I can't stomach, what I'll never be able to stomach, is that a lousy pig of that sort caught me, Acacio! No! That, no! Never!"

He beat his head against the wall, stumbled a little, tripped on a chair, and fell full length on the floor. In rising he struck the corner of the table. His rage passed all limits. Beside himself, he shouted: "I'm no good for anything now, not for anything!"

"Take it easy, chief," said El Faldón, going up to him with the makeshift bandages he had cut from a white shirt and dipped in a washbasin full of hot water in which he had put a few drops of alcohol.

"Sit down here on that chair, chief, the one just behind you, and let me treat you."

Don Acacio turned, seized the chair, and beat it so violently on the floor that it smashed.

"What good to me are your treatments? It would have been better if you had arrived in time. I don't need anything now. You can stick your treatments up your ass!"

He went up to the bed where the Indian girl was lying. He heard her weeping softly.

"So it's you, still there, you sow! I gave them orders to throw you in the river. Go on! Get up!" he added, moving toward her with his fist raised. But the girl dodged. When he realized that she had escaped him he had a clear idea of his helplessness.

"To think that I can't even break the skull of this whore who so well deserves it. To think that from now on I'll have to go on living like this, letting even the dogs piss on me! And all because of that God-damned son of a bitch!"

He tried to find the door.

"What are you whispering about?" he asked El Faldón and the girl, who were in a corner discussing the best means to calm him and get him to lie down.

The Indian girl understood his state and had decided not to abandon him.

"God damn it! Something between you so soon? Now I'm in a fine position! You no sooner learn that I'm no good for anything than two steps away from me, right in my face, you're acting like rutting swine!"

"But, Cacho, my little love," protested the girl in a tone of tenderness, "I love you and I'll always stay with you, if you'll let me."

"You'll stay out of pity, bitch! I don't want your pity! Understand? Where's that bottle?"

"My life, you've drunk enough already. Be reasonable. Come and lie down. I'm going to help you."

"Don't come near me or I'll strangle you, you wretch."

"Good. Here I am. Strangle me if you like!"

Don Acacio heard her get up. He struck her in the face. Then, violently shutting the door that separated the two tiny rooms of the bungalow, he let down the crossbar to lock it and remain alone in the bedroom.

El Faldón and the girl pressed their ears against the door and heard him lie down.

"Thanks, most holy Mother! At last he has settled down. When he gets up he'll be calmer and will see things differently."

El Faldón laughed sarcastically.

The girl commented: "He'll be quieter and will realize that he can go on living blind and even be happy."

The two turned to bringing a little order into the room.

"It would be good to saddle a horse, Faldón, and go and tell Don Félix. Unless it would be better to tell Don Severo."

"Don Severo is in the main camp, which is nearer—but it's already very late. I'll go the first thing tomorrow morning."

At that moment they heard a shot. They both rushed forward, bursting open the door that Don Acacio had closed. They found him with a bullet in his head.

"Holy God!" the girl shouted, horrified. "But where did he find the pistol? I took care not to leave one within his reach in the office."

El Faldón went up to an iron-bound wooden trunk that stood open near the body. It contained letters, documents, some books, a number of little sacks full of coins, two loaded revolvers, and six boxes of cartridges.

"Now I know why he wanted to lie down," said the girl. "Just for that! Unfortunately, I didn't know that he had a pistol there. I never stuck my nose into his affairs during the two years that I've been with him. Believe me, Faldón, I loved him a lot."

She knelt down, caressed the dead man's face, and with the foreman's help straightened the body out decently on the bed.

"Yes, I loved him very much," she repeated. "I loved him from the first day."

She wept disconsolately and remained kneeling, holding one of Don Acacio's hands between hers.

El Faldón left. Then she went to look for a jar of water and a towel and began to lay out the corpse. She crossed the hands on the chest. She took the crucifix that was suspended from his neck and put it on the body. Finally she pulled the bed toward the middle of the room and put candles around it on chairs and boxes. She covered the face with a black shawl and sat down, weeping and mechanically passing through her fingers the beads of her rosary.

8

Don Severo and Don Félix arrived to assist at the burial of their brother. They interred him in the cemetery intended for workers who died in the camps. The graves were all the same, except that for a personage as important as Don Acacio it was necessary to raise a cross of more impressive dimensions and to enclose the grave in a sort of cage sufficiently strong to prevent the vultures from coming in search of the body. For greater security, the spot was covered with stones.

The moment they got back to the office, Don Severo asked: "Did the men see what happened to Don Acacio?"

"Nobody saw it, and we have not said a thing," replied El Pechero, El Faldón, and the girl.

The men learned of the boss's death that evening in the cookhouse from the mouths of the cook and the woman with him. But the cook was unaware of the circumstances of Don Acacio's death. That same night a rumor began to spread about the camp that Don Acacio had had a terrible row with his woman, that she had picked up a pistol, and that when he had tried to tear it away from her hands, it had gone off.

When night came Don Severo said to the girl, the foremen, and Don Félix: "Keep this thing to yourselves. If the men get a smell of the truth behind this story, it will be dangerous for all of us. Tricks like this are contagious. If the men get to know, it's possible—one can go so far as to say that it's certain—that they'll imitate Urbano. Furthermore, I ought to tell you that I've received letters with news that's far from reassuring. The newspapers that come remain silent. They say nothing because they can publish only what the old chief likes. He's not only the soul of the country—he also rules the periodicals and books. But letters are less prudent, and they provide plenty to think about. And in the newspapers themselves you can read between the lines. In one place it says that they have arrested three schoolmasters and sent them to Vera Cruz or Yucatán. Another deals with two teachers sent to jail of whom no further news has been heard. Or again it deals with all the men of a small village in Morelos whom the old man's rural police have taken God knows where—and twenty of whom were found later hanged along the road. There's mention also of derailed trains and of bombs exploded in the main Puebla police station. In Monterrey they caught a whole traveling coachful of men who were going about inciting rebellion. The driver, who perhaps was innocent, was shot there and then. That's the latest news. There's no need to be a great prophet to be able to say that everything's on the verge of bursting. If the old president's throne shakes and falls, the whole of this republic will go up in flames. And, as for long years nobody has learned to think, because thinking is forbidden, things will go on burning until we have all been consumed."

Don Félix coughed and said: "All that's correct, brother, but we knew it when we first went to Villahermosa to buy this property."

"Quite so," replied Don Severo, "but now things seem more serious. They're moving rapidly toward real trouble. That's why I advise you all, and particularly you, Félix, you Pícaro, and you too, Gusano and Pulpo, to slacken the reins a bit. Treat the men a little better. There's something in the air that I just don't like. Pascasio's attack on La Mecha and the crime committed by Urbano against Don Acacio are far from encouraging. Six months ago nobody would have dared to raise his little finger, and now they have the audacity to attack and to kill. To speak quite frankly, friends, I think we're sitting on a barrel of dynamite. Let one spark touch it, and up we'll go.

Then there'll be nothing left of us, not a hair of our beards. If sometime the disturbance should start on one of the nearby fincas, and if one of the men from there should get over here, we could consider ourselves lucky if we had time to do what Don Cacho did yesterday."

"That's so, chief," said El Pícaro. "But then, what do we do? Run away?"

"Certainly not, burro-head! Do you think that we're going to lose our investment here like that? We still have many thousands of tons of wood ready to toss into the water. It's not exactly to pay out advances to those Indian pigs that we've worked."

"Then give us your instructions, Don Severo," answered El Faldón.

"But I've already told you what to do. For a few weeks move softly—slacken the reins. If the men can't give us four tons, be content with three or even with two if it's necessary. You'll go on threatening them as before, but no whippings or useless hangings for the time being. The days will return, you can rest assured, when we'll be able to insist again on the four tons daily, but not until after the floods. Meanwhile, we'll let the atmosphere of the whole country clear up. It's even possible that that little man Madero may see the light. He's a dwarf who scarcely reaches the edge of a table. But perhaps for that very reason he's had some success in lighting a fire on the seat of the old man's chair until the old man's on the point of leaping out of it and falling down with his ass scorched."

"Why haven't they put Madero in jail?" asked Don Félix.

"Why? Why? They did lock him up for six months, and naturally the dwarf got hundreds of supporters and adorers at one stroke that way! The old man had to order his release because if he hadn't done so, Madero's friends would have battered the gates down, spilled oil, and started a fire that would have spread everywhere. What could the old man do when in every corner there's somebody with a dynamite bomb—a thing easy to get from the miners? I don't know what would happen here if we needed dynamite in our work too."

"Oh, you're nervous, Don Severo, because of what's just

happened to your brother, but that doesn't easily scare us."

"Sure, Chapopote, say what you like, but in the end you have nothing to lose except your torn pants. But it's different with my brother and myself. We've put all our money into this business, everything we've been able to make in fifteen years of hard work. In any case, all you have to do is what I tell you to. For the time being, go easy. That's all. Understand?"

Don Félix got two bottles and filled the glasses to give the session a more pleasant aspect.

Don Severo got up and went into Don Acacio's bedroom.

"What are you going to do now, Aurea?" he asked of Don Acacio's "widow." "During these rains you can't leave. You'd sink in the swamps, horse and all. And even if you got through, it would be impossible to cross the rivers. They're swollen tremendously, and they'd sweep you off like a wisp of straw."

The woman was stretched on the bed crying uncontrolledly. Her eyes were red. On hearing Don Severo she pulled herself together and sat on the edge of the bed.

"I don't know what to do. It doesn't make any difference. It's all the same to me." She fell back and began sobbing again.

"No need to make such a fuss," said Don Severo, consoling her in his own way. "There wasn't a day that he didn't drag you around by the hair or beat you black and blue. Isn't that true?"

"Yes, it's true," replied Aurea between sobs, "it's true that we were always fighting—but I loved him and he loved me. He had promised to take me to Spain and marry me when he had enough money."

Don Severo moved his chair toward her.

"What do you know about that! More likely he'd have sent you packing when you reached Villahermosa. Besides, what's the use of talking about it now? Now he's under the ground and we have no time to waste remembering him. That's why I want to tell you something."

The girl stopped sobbing. She felt comforted by the thought that, after all, someone was disposed to help her.

"Yes, Aurea, I must tell you something," Don Severo repeated. "You can't stay here alone. You'd fall into the paws of some pig of a foreman. Unless there's one of them you like?"

"There's not even one of them I'd honor by spitting in his face."

For a few seconds Aurea forgot her grief when she heard Don Severo say: "In that case, Aurea, there's only one thing for you to do. You come with me."

"But, Don Severo, you've already got two women in your house."

"That's so, but if I can take care of two women, I don't see why I can't take care of a third."

"Maybe. But the two girls who're with you will tear out my hair."

"That's my business. Do you think I'm going to let them do it?"

"Of course not, Don Severo. You're the master, and when you speak we all must obey."

She gave vent to two or three sobs more, but it was plain that she was disposed to accept her fate. Moreover, what point would there have been in prolonging her mourning? Life is too short to go on weeping forever for a man who will never return. A man dies and, the same day, nobody thinks any more about him. What's lost is lost, and there's nothing that can be done about it. The next day it will be harder to find than it was today, and so on day after day. Happiness must be enjoyed when it's here. The next time it appears, it will be less beautiful and less fresh. Aurea had had more than enough experience to know that women can devote less time than men to the past and to the dead. Because it's sure that women's attractions, though more numerous, last for a shorter time.

Aurea replied in the doleful voice of a martyr: "If you order it I'll go to your house and do whatever you wish."

"I don't give orders, Aurea," protested Don Severo in a fatherly voice.

The girl moved away from him, sat on the edge of the bed again, and began to comb her disheveled hair. This occupation enabled her to consider the advantages of Don Severo's proposal without showing it.

"I know very well you don't order it, Don Severo," she said, sobbing again. Definitely she could not throw off her widow's weeds for Don Severo so abruptly without cheapening herself in his eyes. And she had been considering her own value from the moment Don Severo had entered the room to speak to her. Although this price was not conceived in figures, it nevertheless existed. A woman who does not value herself or know how much she is worth is generally held cheap by men.

"You don't give orders, Don Severo, that's true, but I have no choice. I can't go away because I'd get drowned in the swamps. So I must stay and take advantage of your kindness. But I do hope that you won't treat me like a servant, because, you see, in spite of our eternal fighting your brother treated me respectfully. I come from a good family. My father was a merchant and a businessman."

"You know I never thought of treating you like that. Your education is not to be compared with that of the two women I have in my house. I can't send them away, because they can't travel just now either. Otherwise I'd send them to the devil right now. For you must know, Aurea, that you attracted me from the first time I saw you with Cacho. You always pleased me more than any other girl. But it was difficult to tell you once you were with Cacho, and I wanted no disputes. Now you know it, and you'll come with me."

"Very well, Don Severo. I'll go with you."

Her tears had almost completely disappeared. She carefully wiped her face with her damp handkerchief and did what every woman tries in order to appear fresh and pretty when she has just won the man who can keep her from dying of hunger.

Don Severo half opened the door and called: "Faldón! Help the señorita get her bundles ready. We'll leave very early tomorrow morning. Have them get the mules ready and send me one of the men to help me."

El Faldón made a significant gesture to the other foremen, pointing at the room where Aurea and Don Severo were. Unfortunately, Don Félix was sitting at the table with them, for otherwise their tongues would have been wagging. A moment later Don Severo joined them, shutting the bedroom door behind him.

"She could have come with me too," Don Félix said.

"Sure. But with that woman of yours things would have turned out very badly. Tomorrow we would have had another funeral, perhaps two. And well you know it, little brother."

Don Félix filled a glass, drank the contents, slammed his fist on the table, and exclaimed: "You're right, Severo. It's better that things should be as you've decided."

All the foremen, or at least the principal ones—the majordomos—had been called to headquarters to be informed of the new division of districts, necessary because of Don Acacio's death, and also to learn about the areas they would have under their charge.

Don Severo had been managing the north region. Now he took over the west and a part of the south, so as not to overburden Don Félix, who would continue to carry on the general administration of the camps. The regions allocated to Don Severo were still poorly cleared off and they demanded the full attention and all the effort of an experienced man.

Furthermore, the central office was relatively free of work for the time being. As a consequence of the floods, no mail was arriving. Don Félix therefore could manage the north, south, and east regions, the ones nearest the clump of buildings around the office. He also took over the districts on the other side of the river, where cutting was to be started the next week. It was unnecessary for Don Félix to give all his time to them—the operations there would not be important enough to keep him away from administrative tasks, which could not possibly be entrusted to underlings, being of basic importance in a sensibly administered camp. The "village" was on the bank of the river. All the tree trunks brought in by the smaller streams passed that point, which was the counting station. The rainy season, which, though it had been raining sporadically for some time, was actually just beginning, would soon bring with it constant activity.

The village was also the meeting place of the boatmen in charge of the floating logs. Their job was to prevent the logs from piling up at certain places and thus slowing down or stopping their forward movement, or even diverting the river. It was absolutely necessary to prevent the forming of such jams. This was dangerous work—much more dangerous than in temperate zones. The men had to slither in among the trunks to discover what was causing the jam—it might well be just one log—move it into a good position, and get it into the current again. But often while the men were balancing themselves among the logs, trying to get them in order and to even up the movement, enormous masses of water that had accumulated somewhere upstream as the result of a torrential downpour swept down upon them with a roar and the irresistible power of an avalanche, thundering against the log jams and sucking up the men at work on them. The men could see the flood coming, but they had to be exceptionally agile to escape in time to prevent the logs from pounding against their bodies and turning them into shapeless pulp. Most often their skulls were bashed in before they could make the first jump toward safety, and moments later only some blood-tinted spume showed for a fraction of a second the spot where their bodies had been torn to pieces. The more fortunate among them, those able to reach the water and try to get to the bank by swimming underwater, generally drowned. It was not uncommon for twenty men in a gang of fifty to perish.

Downstream, in the populated regions, little motorboats were in use, and watching the log movement could even be fun, but that pleasure was unknown to the men in the camps.

In the downstream villages free peasants or professional boatmen were employed to haul in the logs and stack them in safe places.

The village nearest to the camps lay a long distance downstream. Ten leagues below the camps, nevertheless, on each side of the river, a mounted armed gang was posted, watching to prevent any of the men from slipping by astride a floating log, reaching some village, and fleeing. It was impossible to escape at night. The watchers knew this well and contented themselves with keeping a lookout during the day. At night the gloomy banks of the river, matted with underbrush, concealed too many dangers.

When Don Severo arrived at the principal camp, there were about four weeks to go until the date fixed by him and Don Félix for completing the launching of the logs. It was raining heavily nearly all day, but the arroyos and streams that cut through the region still were not high enough for logs to be launched on them from the distant corners of the camp. It was necessary to wait until the beds of the streams were so saturated that they had become impermeable, making the streams overflow and thus permitting the launching.

On the other hand, the longer Don Severo waited to launch the logs, the more tons of wood he would have, for the cutting did not stop. To obtain the maximum number of tons was his sole preoccupation, as it was of his brother Don Félix.

Three days after the famous conference everybody had forgotten the resolution about treating the men with more consideration. The foremen, who received a handsome commission for every ton delivered, as well as Don Félix and Don Severo (who were interested only in accumulating all the wood possible), loosed themselves again on the ox-drivers and cutters with the same harshness as before. What had happened to Don Acacio had been forgotten before the worms began to enjoy his remains.

Besides, they were far from certain that Don Acacio had fallen under the blows of one of the men. At the best, some rat of a foreman might have had it in for him for bad treatment in the past or because Don Acacio had taken his woman while he was away at work. For Don Acacio had never despised the forbidden pleasures, and Don Félix and Don Severo had known what to expect of him.

9

 For a whole week Celso had sacrificed two hours each day to help Cándido produce his four tons the same as the others.

"You don't need to help me any more, my friend," Cándido often said to him. "You're using up your own time, and they'll whip you because of me."

"Don't worry, brother. Aren't we both from the same village?"

"That's true, we're both Chamulas, and we're neighbors."

"You see! That's reason enough. And maybe I'll have another reason soon."

Cándido smiled, put down his ax, and lighted a cigarette. "Don't get impatient, little brother. She hasn't any sweetheart. We were talking again last night, and she told me that she likes you. But you know that among us these things aren't arranged overnight. What I can tell you is that you don't displease Modesta."

"How her name pleases me! I don't think there's a prettier one."

"You've told me so many times. But even before you had spoken to me about her, I had already understood everything."

Cándido picked up his ax and again set to work.

That night after he had finished his supper Celso rolled some cigarettes, put them in his shirt pocket, and went down to the river. He sat on the sandy bottom and moved forward into the water until only his head stuck out. That way he could smoke. This was the only way to kill the ticks that had penetrated beneath his skin and were too small to be pulled out. Too, the water was like a balm: it soothed the bites of the mosquitoes and horseflies that had harassed him during the day. The insects were particularly voracious during the rainy season, and there were far more of them then. While he was submerged, the smoke of his cigarette protected his face and head from the mosquitoes that swarmed in clouds over the riverbanks. Celso was not the only one refreshing himself like this. Near both banks he saw other men resting, some of them squatting in groups, some by themselves. After five minutes he saw a man come and take up a spot near him. It was Martín Trinidad.

"Hey, Celso, pass me your cigarette. I want to light mine."

"Why didn't you get it going before you came into the water?"

"I did, but it went out."

"All right. But tell me—where do you hail from? Who are you?"

"I'm going to tell you, Celso, and you'll be the only one to know it. I'm from Pachuca, where the silver mines are. I used to be a schoolmaster there."

"Hah! A schoolmaster, and now a cutter in the camps?"

"Yes indeed. What of it? I've never known how to keep my mouth shut. I always told the truth to the miners, who, for the most part, were fathers of the little ones I taught in the school."

"You told them the truth? What truth?" Celso asked suspiciously.

"I told them the truth about the dictator and about the people's rights. I told them that no man, however clever he may be, however convinced that he has the right to rule a whole people, has the right to take away freedom of thought and expression or to crush other men's wills. For every man has the right to say what he thinks, and every man also has the duty to teach, to explain to the rest that they are being badly governed and wronged. And even though a man is wrong in the eyes of others, he has a perfect right to say what he thinks and how he believes things can be made to work well."

"Is that what you said to the Pachuca miners?" asked Celso, looking at him sidewise. But it was now too dark for him to make out the expression on Martín Trinidad's face.

"I told them that and many other things besides. I advised them to stop going down into the mines, not to go on working for the profit of the owners and of nobody else. I advised them to ask for an increase in wages and for permission to form a union to help them make collective bargains, because a man by himself can't do anything. You know. One is shot, another is dragged off to jail, a third is beaten to death. But if they all join together to fight for their rights, they won't be shot, because then there would be nobody left to work and to extract the precious metal from the ground. And if the mine owners want silver, they'll have to pay the miners' demands in silver."

"And what did the miners say to your advice?"

"When they heard it they refused to work. The soldiers came and shot ten of them. The others went back to work because there was no union to get the miners together."

"And you? Why didn't they shoot you? That's very strange, don't you think?" Celso asked, his suspicions again aroused.

"No, after beating a miner until they made him tell who had put those ideas in his head, they locked me in the jail and told me that I wouldn't be as lucky as the ten men I had misled, who had been shot. For three days they tortured me. When one of the sergeants torturing me got tired, another one took his place, and so on. Tomorrow I'll show you the hundreds of welts on my body. They wanted to make me shout 'Long live Don Porfirio!' I refused because I hate him and don't want anything but his death. Every time I could open my mouth it was to shout: 'Down with Porfirio! Death to the tyrant! Down with the exploiters! Long live the people's revolution!' And each time I shouted they lashed my face."

Celso asked: "And how were you able to escape?"

"I didn't escape. How could I have escaped when I was half dead? They took me to the railroad station with a hundred other men, all young students, teachers, workers, and peasants.

They locked us all into one freight car, stacked one on top of another, without ventilation or light. For food they threw us a handful of moldy tortillas, which we rushed for, because we were all ravenous. A few times they emptied a potful of frijoles over us, which we picked off of our clothes and scraped up from the floor all mixed with other filth, which we ate without noticing the difference. Instead of water they emptied pots of piss over us. Finally one day, after having traveled forever in a boat in worse conditions than those I've told you we suffered on the train, we reached Yucatán. We were supposed to work on the plantations or at roadmending. They tied forty of us together to pull a heavy roller that even twenty horses might not have been able to drag. To make us advance, they whipped us. We had to pull under a sun a hundred times hotter than it is here. There were women among us too, and they were treated the same way. Many of those men and women were textile workers from Orizaba who had refused to go on working unless their wages were raised. They had escaped the massacre. Those who gave in were punished by being made to work for still lower pay."

"And how were you able to escape from Yucatán?" Celso asked.

"One day we assaulted four policemen. After killing them as we'd have killed mad dogs, we fled as fast as we could. There were thirty of us. The other men hadn't dared—they were too terrified. Many of the thirty were caught again. Others were shot in the back by the rural police who pursued us. Others drowned while crossing a river. But we three—Juan Méndez, Lucio Ortiz, and myself—were shrewd enough to keep well away from the main roads. By taking shortcuts we reached Campeche and then your region. There we met Don Gabriel, the contractor, who seemed to us like the Saviour Himself, and who brought us to the camps. Here, at least, they won't look for us."

Celso laughed silently.

"What a lot of lies you can tell, my friend! Certainly they won't look for you here. You'll soon find out that all you've done is to change prisons. Unless you see a difference—"

"Yes, for me there is a difference, which is that this is worse than Yucatán. There each one had to work, sick or well, as much as he could. The work was hard. They beat us, and they fed us badly. But here we all must produce our four tons, and, besides, in Yucatán they hadn't discovered the trick of hanging."

"And the two companions who escaped with you—who are they?"

"Juan Méndez was an infantry sergeant in Mérida. Now he's a deserter."

"Why did he desert?"

"A drunken captain entered the barracks one night. Juan had a brother serving in the same company with him. It was his first year's service. That night he was on sentry duty near the stables of the artillery mules. The captain had no reason to be in the stables, but he went in staggering, cursing. He stumbled and fell down in the mule's filth. Then he shouted for the sentry—Juan's brother—struck him a blow, and, with all the strength that marijuana-smokers can muster, dragged him to the water trough and held him under water until he drowned. The captain was tried by a court-martial, and all he got in the way of punishment was the forfeit of one month's pay. That was all. Two days later, when the captain was passing in front of the stable door, Juan Méndez jumped on him, shouting: 'Murderer! You murdered my brother, and they didn't punish you, but I'm going to punish you with my own hands to show you that there is still justice in the world!' And before the captain could put up any defense, Juan slit his throat. Lucio was corporal of the same battalion and a close friend of Méndez. The two had enlisted at the same time and they had been together through good times and bad. When Juan found himself driven to desert, Lucio didn't want to abandon him. 'If I'd had the chance I'd have done the same thing to the captain. I'm as guilty as you, and, that being the case, I'm going with you.' They ran away together and since then have stayed as inseparable as Christ and the cross. We met in Tabasco and, finding that we share the same ideas, decided to travel and try our luck together."

"But," Celso asked, "but why do you tell me all this? How the devil does it concern me?"

"It's quite simple. I tell you because it's a thing of interest to all of us. I know perfectly well that you have the same idea we have—and that we're not very far from what you've been thinking of."

"And what is that?"

"We're not far from the day when all this must end, from the day when we'll begin to hang so as not to be hanged ourselves ever again. Don't think I was the only one in Pachuca. In Yucatán I met others, even though you always had to be afraid that your bedmate was a spy for the rural police. But when there are thousands of men in the prisons, in the dungeons, on the prison islands, because of the same idea, it's because the country is on the point of blazing up, and the blaze is ready to devour everything, despite the lies spread by the newspapers. In the north, blood has begun to run, and the dictator, the old baboon who has the audacity to call himself the protector and savior of the country, doesn't dare step out without a guard of fifty. Who can say but at this moment, while we're talking about him—the Irreplaceable Man, as he calls himself—he hasn't been kicked out of the palace and isn't hiding under his bed, wetting his pants because he's scared to death? The crueler a tyrant is, the more cowardly he shows himself at the first reverse. I've read a lot of books, Celso, you can't imagine how many, and I know an endless number of things about revolutions and insurrections. The same thing always happens. Tyranny lasts for a time, but only for a time."

"It's a shame that I don't know how to read, Martín," said Celso. "I can only sign my name, and that very badly."

"Perhaps I can teach you and the other men to read and write."

"If we had time, even just a little time, we could learn lots of useful things, lots of things that could bring satisfaction into life. My comrade Andrés, the ox-driver, can read and write, and he often tells me that in books you can read wonderful stories that very few men know how to tell. But books only have life in the hands of those who can read; for those of us who can't, they're only so many sheets of paper put together. It was Andrés who taught me to write my name. Unfortunately, he sleeps in the other camp so as to be near his oxen. When he's able to come here it's always late at night when we're very tired. We need to have more time and, above all, to work less so that we can think a bit about ourselves and things instead of looking at each other like oxen that carry the yoke, chew the cud, and frighten flies with their tails. Sometimes I think that we're more unfortunate than the oxen. They don't know anything about a better life. But we do know about it because we've seen other places, and we know other men who are less miserable and less ignorant than ourselves."

"I'm going to tell you something you don't know yet, Celso, something only I know."

Celso strained again to see the face of the man seated at his side on the sandy bottom of the river, but it was too dark. He sucked sharply at his cigarette. When the burning tip revived, a glow illuminated Martín Trinidad's face. The latter looked around him to make sure that nobody was close enough to hear what he was going to say. He inched closer to Celso and spoke in a half voice.

"What they say in the office about Don Acacio's accident is a lie."

"What are you calling a lie?"

"The story is entirely different, but they don't want the truth to be known. They're terrified that we'll do the same."

"The same what? Speak up! Nobody's listening to us, and if anyone should stick his ear in, I'd give him such a wallop that it would be a week before he could talk!"

"Pascasio and Urbano ran away. You know that. But what you don't know is that when Pascasio was about to be captured he smashed La Mecha's skull with a stone. El Faldón shot him immediately. Urbano told the cook's woman all about it while he was waiting for Don Acacio to get ready to give him the usual beating. But what Urbano did down here on the river-bank only I was able to see. Urbano took advantage of a moment's carelessness on the part of Don Acacio, jumped on him, tied him to that tree you see over there, and gouged out his eyes with a thorn."

"Are you sure?"

"I saw it with my own eyes. I was on my way to change my ax in the store when I happened on that scene. I hid behind some bushes and saw everything that happened. After doing what I told you, Urbano tied a stone to his belt between his pants and his skin and jumped into the river, drowning himself. Nobody knows that. They all think that Urbano fled again and they've sent two men to follow him. Later Don Acacio, crazed with the idea of never seeing again, put a bullet in his own head."

"Did you see that too?"

"No. But Epifanio, the boy in the store, saw it all through a crack. He saw Don Acacio commit suicide."

Celso hissed softly and said: "Do you know, Martín Trinidad, all this is very pleasant!"

"Yes? Well, I know still something else," said Martín, getting even closer to Celso and lowering his voice further. "The others up there think that Urbano escaped with Don Acacio's pistol and cartridge belt. The fact is that he threw the pistol aside because he didn't know how to use it. The poor fellow was very stupid. When he walked into the river I came out of my hiding place, picked up the revolver, and took the cartridge belt from Don Acacio, who was by then blind and unable to take in anything that happened."

"Then you have the revolver and the bullets?" asked Celso in a low, very excited voice.

"Yes. I buried them in the sand. You're the first one who knows this. As you can see, we could save ourselves easily."

"I've thought a lot about that. But no purpose would be served if I were to save only myself or you only yourself. We must all of us flee on the same day, and it's essential for us to swear that we'll never allow them to capture us and that we'll die rather than let them bring us back here. The best thing to do would be to do away with everybody who isn't one of ourselves. If we let them go on living, everything will go on as it was before, and some day or other they'll have their feet on our necks again. Only a complete and well-directed operation will do. One man by himself can't change anything or do anything. We must all work together and at the same time. Otherwise everything would be useless. I could have fled a hundred times, alone, or with Andrés or Santiago or Fidel—who are also to be trusted. But we have told ourselves again and again that all these camps must be wiped out, completely destroyed, and the bosses liquidated and overseers exterminated. Otherwise it's not worth the effort."

"You're more intelligent than I thought, Celso."

"Don't think that I've worked out all these ideas by myself. I'm strong and can stand a lot, but reasoning is a different thing. We've been discussing it together—Andrés, Pedro, Santiago, and all those of us who during their lives have seen something beyond the village or finca where we were born. And look, a schoolmaster and two soldiers who think exactly on the same lines come to join us! We needed exactly such help. Now we must think about how and when. It's a pity that Urbano drowned himself. He was a true rebel, the sort of man we want. Because up to now nobody had dared to attack a boss and tear his eyes out. I don't know if I myself would have had the guts to do it. Maybe so, it all depends. It's a matter of the moment when a man has to say to himself: 'This is the end. This is all I can endure. Anything more would be too much. Now I attack, cost what it may, for all that matters now is to end this, once and forever.' "

Martín Trinidad took a last puff of his cigarette, threw it away, and stepped out of the water, shaking himself.

Celso put his head under water, made great bubbles, spat, wiped his wet face with his hands, tossed back his long hair, and with his arms outstretched propelled himself like an arrow onto the sandy bank. "I feel like a sponge," he said to Martín Trinidad. "But at least I think I got rid of all the ticks. The mosquito bites have disappeared and even the marks of my last hanging don't show up now."

When they reached the top of the embankment Martín

Trinidad said quietly: "It's understood that you won't say anything about what I've just told you, Celso. Not even to Andrés. Nor will I say anything to Méndez and Ortiz. Only you yourself know it. Let the men go on thinking that we're three tramps, three escaped convicts. Let them think whatever they like. I wanted you to know who we are and that we think and want the same things as you and your friends. You go your own way and we'll go ours. But when it's time to break loose you must know that if you take the lead, I'll form the rear guard or that I'll take the vanguard if you decide on the rear. We may have to wait two months, maybe six, but I know we won't have to wait a year. Over the whole country the fire is spreading, the first flames are rising everywhere. What mattered was for me to tell you what I have told you. Our war cry will be 'Land and liberty!' and 'Down with the dictatorship!' "

"Not in such a hurry, little brother," Celso replied. "Not yet. When with all our strength we cry 'Liberty!' not a single man must fail to respond to the call."

"We don't need banners or standards," Martín Trinidad said. "All we need is blood in our veins. 'Land and liberty!' "

And instead of "Good night," Celso answered: "Land and liberty!"

10

The following night Don Félix walked into the lean-to where the workers ate their meals. Six tree trunks held up a thatched roof, and that was all. When it rained, the men had to huddle as closely as possible together in the center of the lean-to to avoid getting wet. Of course there were neither tables nor benches: the eating men squatted on the ground with the pots and tortillas within reach. The bosses had never stopped to consider whether their workers might have wanted a little comfort for eating.

Don Félix penetrated a few steps inside, looked at the men, and spoke: "You Cándido, you Tomás, you Cástolo, and you," he said, pointing to a number of the men, "get your packs ready immediately to go across the river. From now on, you will work in the new camps about four leagues from here. Get a move on, quick now! Finish eating and get on the way. The boatmen can't wait all night."

The men who had been picked hurriedly finished their supper and ran to their huts to get ready.

Cándido sent his two boys to look for the little pigs, which wandered freely about the camp, feeding on whatever they could find. Don Félix had often said that he would have them killed and then would eat one after another because, seeing that they had grown fat on his property, he had a perfect right to them.

Modesta helped her brother to tie up his bundles.

Don Félix made his way to the hut where Cándido and Modesta were.

"Hey, girl," he called out, "why don't you stay here in the main camp? Down there in the new camps there's nothing but jungle. You won't find anything but jaguars and snakes there, not one cabin built. Today and tomorrow they'll have to sleep in the open, unless they set about making lean-tos when they arrive in the middle of the night. And as it's going to rain, that won't be any fun. I know what I'm saying. Better remain here, little one."

"Many thanks, little chief, but I prefer to go along with my brother."

"Just as you like, girl. What I'm telling you is for your own good. If you change your mind tomorrow, you know that you can come back. I'll wait for you until tomorrow, but no longer."

Returning to his own hut, Don Félix passed the cook. "When a man wants to help these pigs, they refuse. They prefer to live in their pigsties. That's all they know."

"That's true," replied the cook approvingly.

He had learned that it is always better to agree with the powerful ones in this world. That way one runs no risk of making a mistake, and one's daily bread is assured. The cook had never been beaten or hanged. From time to time Don Félix would give him a few slaps, but these he accepted as if they were friendly gestures.

When Celso returned to the camp from work, he went to the eating lean-to. Seeing no sign of Cándido, he went to the latter's hut to look for him. "Then the boss is sending you to the other side of the river?"

"Yes," replied Cándido wearily. "What can we do?"

"It's real jungle there. You'll have to start by cleaning out underbrush. The first night you'll have to sleep in the thickets. At least wrap yourselves up well in the mosquito nets. Wait, Modesta, I'm going to help you."

Just then the youngsters returned with the little pigs, which were squealing desperately, thinking that the day had come on which they must be converted into hams and sausages.

"I'll come over there and help you both," said Celso.

"That'll put you way behind with your own work," replied Cándido, pleased, in spite of everything, by this promise.

"Perhaps I'll be sent there too after the logs have been launched on the water. It would be nice for all of us to get together every night as we do here."

"Sure, I'd feel very happy. And you, little sister—what do you think?"

Modesta did not reply.

Celso, taking courage said: "Would you be glad if I should join you there, Modesta?"

"Yes, very glad."

"I like to hear you say that," replied Celso, laughing happily.

The first convoy of workers had been put off on the other bank. The two canoes that had carried them across were returning. The trip downstream was child's play by comparison with the upstream return, for the river was turbulent and its current extremely violent.

The canoes were nothing more than simple dugouts, long, hollowed-out tree trunks. Only the canoeman stood up during the crossings. All the others huddled in the bottom. The canoe constantly rocked back and forth dangerously, leaning far to each side. A canoeman had to be well trained and very skillful to guide such a skiff over those tumultuous waters without upsetting it and tossing all his passengers into the water.

Cándido, Modesta, the two little boys, and Celso were waiting on the shore for the return of the canoe that would take them. Their bundles and packs were on the ground beside them. The boys had the pigs firmly tied up.

The little animals had become so fat that Cándido could no longer carry them easily on his back. He did not know what to do with them, but he kept them, thinking of them as friends, because for him they were the only links to the home for which he had bought them.

He had recently had a conversation about the pigs with the

camp cook, who wanted to buy them. The cook had assured him that with the money he would get for them he could pay up his debt and go free. But a workman whom Cándido had consulted had said that the thing wasn't that easy: even if he cleared up the debt he would not be free, because his contract was for a certain period of time. If, at the end of that period he had paid up all his obligations, he would certainly be able to go home with some money in his pack. That could happen. But for the immediate future Cándido would not consider getting rid of the animals. His one fear was that Don Félix would simply take them without deducting more than a few miserable pesos from his debt account.

Cándido and Celso were waiting right at the water's edge with lanterns in their hands to show the canoeman the exact spot where he should come in. The lanterns were full of moisture and gave very little light. The moon was full, but its beams were hidden behind thick clouds. A fine rain had begun to fall, and it was impossible to see even two yards into the darkness.

Suddenly, as unexpected as a ghost, the first canoeman emerged from the mist and rain. Cándido jumped into the canoe and called to Celso and the boys to pass him the packs and bundles. But the canoeman said: "You're not going in my canoe. You're going with Felipe, who'll be along in a minute. He's just a few yards behind me. He's soused, that's sure, and can barely stand up. But even when he's asleep or has both eyes blindfolded he can manage the canoe better than I can. I have to take some of the other men over and also carry a load of tools, axes, whetstones, and God knows what else, besides El Faldón. Here comes Felipe now."

Felipe was even more drunk than Celso had supposed from the words of the first canoeman. He reeled about in his canoe, which he had not even succeeded in bringing to rest on the sand.

"God Almighty!" the canoeman shouted, "what stinking weather! Wet from head to feet, without a dry hair!"

He was accompanied by a small boy, who he took along to

help him and whose job it was to jump out and haul the prow of the canoe up the sand.

"Run up there and get me the bottle," he ordered. "I need to throw a little fuel into my body."

"You can't take us to the other side in your drunken state," Celso protested. "You can't even stay on your feet."

"Who's drunk? Me? And it's you, you greasy Chamula, who's daring to tell an old canoeman that he's drunk? Me—drunk? Tell me just this: who's running this boat—you or I?"

"You," replied Celso.

"Exactly! So you shut your trap. Do you people want to get into this canoe or not?"

Cándido collected all his courage and said to Celso: "Wait for me here. I'm going to look for the boss and ask him to let us go in another canoe."

"You'll go in the canoe that you've been assigned to," decreed Don Félix in reply to the request of the wretched man, who stood in the doorway of the hut and explained that Felipe was in such a state of drunkenness that his legs would not support him. "Who gives orders here, Chamula?"

"You do, little chief."

"In that case you have nothing to fear. Felipe can be as drunk as he likes, but that doesn't prevent him from being the best canoeman in the camps. Pablo drinks less, but when it comes to knowing the river he can't touch the points of Felipe's shoes."

"Little chief, if you'd like, we could cross the river very early tomorrow morning."

"Don't even think about that. We'd lose half a day. You're crossing the river right now—and you're leaving me in peace this instant. Pablo has to transport the tools, the axes, and the other men. Besides, with all the stuff you carry around, to transport you and your drove takes a whole canoe. Now then, get going! Tomorrow very early I'll come over to see how things are going. Here, have a drink."

Cándido accepted the cup and at one gulp swallowed its contents, which cheered him up a little. He said: "Thanks," and left after a courteous "With your permission."

He went back to the riverbank where Celso was waiting. "Nothing doing."

"I knew that beforehand, and I've loaded everything into the canoe. Sit in the back. Up front everything is soaked. The kids have been bailing it out, but with this rain there's no way of keeping anything dry."

Celso had arranged the bundles in the canoe. Modesta was seated in the middle with the children on either side of her. They kept the pigs in place by holding fast to the lasso with which they were tied. On her knees Modesta had the bundle containing her things.

Cándido jumped into the boat, stepped over the pigs and bundles, and huddled himself down in the bottom holding up a lantern. Near him Felipe stood with a long paddle in his hands. He was in a rage—first because his small assistant had stumbled and spilled half a bottle of aguardiente, and second because his passengers were so slow in getting settled. This was his last trip across the river for the night, and he was in a hurry to get to sleep.

Celso handed the lantern to the boy assistant. "Get into the canoe. With this load it would be too much for you."

Celso put his shoulders to the prow, lifted the canoe a little, and made it slide along the sand until it floated. Felipe began to paddle. Celso climbed into the primitive craft, which began to move out into the enveloping darkness.

Felipe gave two vigorous strokes with the paddle, which carried the canoe to the middle of the river and into the foam. He straightened it out quickly to avoid getting caught in the current, working with such skill that Celso and Cándido recognized that their fear of the water had been foolish.

The canoe sped like an arrow. From time to time Felipe pushed the long paddle into the river's bed to steer the canoe toward a spot where it would move more swiftly. He wanted to finish his task as quickly as possible. Generally, when the current was as strong as it was now, the canoemen did exactly the opposite of what Felipe was doing, keeping away from midstream so as to avoid the risk of being swept away by the current. In fact, if a pilot were to lose control of his craft even for a second, it would be swept off its course, and the current, catching it broadside, would capsize it, throwing all it held, men and things, into the water. For this reason the canoemen preferred to keep well in toward the banks, searching out calmer spots. But the calm areas were not always on the same side. Sometimes they were near the right bank, sometimes toward the left, depending on the course of the current. Therefore a canoeman's real work consisted in steering his craft from one bank to the other, looking for the least rough surfaces. Crossing the river demanded not only consummate skill but also a thorough knowledge of its course, of the whirlpools, sandbanks, and rapids. The canoemen began their careers in childhood, accompanying older canoemen who served as their teachers.

The trip was difficult by day; at night the difficulties doubled. The old hands knew the stream so well that by merely touching the bottom with their paddles they could tell on which side they were. And even when completely intoxicated they maneuvered to perfection. Nevertheless, drunkenness not being a normal state, it was difficult to say beforehand how a drunken man would react to an unforeseen occurrence.

In his alcoholic cloud Felipe felt daring in the extreme. Moreover, he was a mestizo and felt an unbounded contempt for the Indians. He was as dark as Cándido. His hair was as black, thick, and straight as Celso's. But he regarded himself as the equal of the white men. They never beat him, and his skill as an experienced canoeman, his merits as a builder and owner of two canoes, made him an independent workman who had the right to get drunk as often as he wished or when he had the money for liquor. The whinings of the cowardly Cándido, who had dared to ask Don Félix to delay the trip so they wouldn't have to cross by night, made him even more reckless. He was going to demonstrate to that lousy Chamula what a real canoeman was capable of, and how he could guide his craft at full speed in the middle of the night even on a river broken loose.

So he continued to keep the canoe in the heart of the current. They shot forward as though they were in a motorboat. About fifteen minutes were required for the crossing, but Felipe wanted to show that he could make it in ten. Unfortunately the canoe moved so fast that he could not keep it in the full current with a few paddle strokes. That crazy speed lasted only two or three minutes, at the end of which the prow struck the stones at the edge of a rapid so violently that it became lodged among them. With a marvelously skillful stroke of the paddle Felipe swung the stern about. But his second stroke went wrong. The craft veered too far to the left and was out of control.

Felipe took in the situation instantly, knew what was inevitably going to happen. Nevertheless, he made a tremendous effort with his paddle, but stuck it into the bed of the stream a fraction of a second too late. The current struck the canoe broadside, swamping it. Felipe, unsteady on his legs, stumbled and fell over the right side into the water. The craft was dashed against a gigantic tree trunk. It sank.

"Make for the bank!" was all that Felipe shouted.

Cándido, Celso, Modesta, the children, the assistant, and the pigs—all were struggling in the water. The profound darkness prevented them from seeing the banks, but luckily, foreseeing the inevitable, Cándido and Celso, thanks to the lanterns, had been able, just as the accident was about to happen, to see that they were nearer the right bank than the left. They had also noticed that near the right bank the paddle had hit bottom at half its length, which made them think that they were near a sandbank and stones used as a ford.

Cándido stuck his head out of the water to call the children. The younger one, floundering near by, answered him. Cándido quickly grabbed him by the shirt.

Celso was calling Modesta and Cándido. He groped for Modesta, caught hold of her clothes, and began to pull her along.

Cándido shouted: "Make for the right bank!"

The region of which Cándido and Celso were natives offered few opportunities for learning to swim, there being neither lakes nor rivers near by. But when Indians fall into water they get out like dogs, by instinct. Moreover, they wear no shoes, and their cotton clothes are loose and light enough not to hinder them.

They managed to reach a foothold. They were separated from one another, and they called out in order to get together. Felipe and his assistant also joined in. Freed suddenly of his drunkenness, Felipe did not understand exactly what had happened.

"By the most holy Virgin!" he exclaimed, "such a thing has never happened to me. I've capsized once or twice, but in some rapids. It's never happened to me here. It's impossible! Somebody must have played a dirty trick on me. Perhaps it was one of you, you damned Chamulas!"

They were all together. Even the little pigs, tied to the lasso, were there. The dog that had followed Cándido from his village was barking contentedly and shaking himself to get dry.

The packs and bundles had all been lost. Modesta, wringing out her underskirt, turned suddenly and asked: "Celso! Is Ángel with you?"

"No! He isn't here. He must be with Cándido."

In anguish Cándido replied: "No. Not here. I thought he was with you, Modesta, or with Celso."

They all began to shout: "Angelito, Angelito, where are you?"

But the only reply they got was the furious shout of the water as it roared on.

When he noticed that Felipe was late in returning, Don Félix realized that something out of the ordinary had happened. Very early the next morning he sent Pablo with his canoe. Pablo discovered the shipwrecked group squatting on the shore. He took them into the canoe and to the new camp, where the other men had begun to erect their huts.

Celso returned to the main camp with Pablo. Don Félix received him abusively: "What have you been doing over there? You arrive now after losing half a day's work! Perhaps *I* sent you to the new camp?"

"I wanted to help Cándido move his things, little chief. He has his family with him."

"And meanwhile your work stays undone! Cándido is old enough now to travel alone."

"He lost one of his children," Celso answered.

"Through carelessness, I'm sure. He should have watched him more closely. Besides, nobody told him to take the kids. They're not good for anything here. Now then, get along to your work and hack out your four tons as usual. If you want to have a good time again, don't have it at my expense. I pay you for your work, and your work is to cut four tons."

"Very well, little chief."

Don Félix went on with his breakfast, saying to the two foremen who were with him: "You see? I was right again when I picked Pablo to transport the tools and axes. Had I ordered that drunken Felipe to take them, we'd have lost them all. That would have been at least one hundred and fifty pesos thrown in the water. Just what we needed! For two weeks there's been no mail and not even a bunch of Turks has turned up here! But where's that swine Felipe now?"

"He went with Pablo," replied one of the foremen. "He wants to try to find his canoe."

"Yes? That'll take three weeks or more!"

Cándido went on working, eating, sleeping, getting up, going back to work, returning to eat, sleeping again, rising again, felling his trees, coming back to his hut, squatting in a corner, and looking fixedly before him. Scarcely speaking at all, he was living like an automaton. Every morning and every evening he went down to the riverbank and watched the rushing of the convulsive waters that had snatched away his Angelito. And every time he returned from work he walked around the hut and looked at Modesta in silence.

When he returned, weary and crushed, Modesta well knew what he had hoped to find.

Four identical days passed. One evening he said to his sister in a suppressed voice: "Modesta, Pablo's canoe is tied to the riverbank. When it gets completely dark we'll set out."

"Where will we go, little brother?" she asked in surprise. She seemed to doubt that he was in his right mind.

"I can't stay here. They killed my Angelito, murdered Marcelina's firstborn son. We're going to go back to our village, because I can't stand it here. Modesta, I must go back there to my land, to cultivate my corn, to see how the house is that I built with my own hands. I can't stay here. I must go back."

"Will we take the pigs, little brother?"

"Sure we'll take them. How could you think we'd leave them here? They can't stand it either—nor the dog, nor you. . . ."

"And Celso?" she asked.

"Celso knows where we're from and he'll come to look for you. He told me so, only he asked me not to tell you. He said that if, as he thinks, the girl he loved has married someone else, he will ask you to be his wife. He'll follow us, little sister, you can be sure about that."

Modesta finished stacking the pots in a corner and said: "They'll catch us."

"Maybe so. What about it? I can't stay here. I must leave, and if they catch me, I'll leave again and keep on leaving. I can't stay here. They killed my Angelito."

"No, little brother, by terrible fortune he fell into the water."

"Yes, but not by the will of our most holy Mother—by the will of that evil man, of the boss. Why didn't he want to let us cross in the daytime? Why didn't he let us go in Pablo's canoe? Simply because he hated the children and wanted to kill them. I know it well. A hundred times he told me that they must work, because otherwise they had no right to be with me. He wanted to make them work, the children of my poor Marcelina, my poor woman, who was murdered too, by that doctor, murdered because I couldn't pay in time."

"We'll do what you want, brother."

"We'll wait until the other men have fallen asleep. But you can start taking Pedrito and the little pigs down to the bank now. The others will think that you're taking them to bathe."

That same night Cándido, Modesta, little Pedro, the pigs, and the dog embarked in Pablo's canoe. For two days there had been less rain. The level of the river had gone down somewhat, and the current had lost its violence.

Late that night the waning moon shone out. There were only a few clouds running, and things could be seen rather clearly.

Pablo had taken away the pole-paddle with which he maneuvered the canoe. But Cándido knew perfectly well that he himself would never have been able to handle it, because to do that required a long apprenticeship. To use in its stead he had cut three boards, one of which was long and flat, and which he intended to use as a paddle.

He did not risk the middle of the current, but kept near the banks so that he could always touch the bottom with his paddle, which was only eight feet long. Thus he could steer the canoe as he had planned.

No bundles or packs increased the weight of the load. In a piece of his only shirt they had wrapped tortillas, bean paste, and a small piece of dried meat. One of the men had lent him a flint and some tinder for making fire. Unfortunately he had lost the knife that he had always carried in his belt in a leather sheath, but he intended to make some spears to catch fish that he could roast. He would also be able to bring down a few birds with his sling. All things considered, the prospects were not entirely bad.

The canoe glided along smoothly. For some time the moon lighted up the watery road. Later the underbrush on the banks of the river began to form two impenetrable barriers. From the land the murmuring of the forest reached them, filling the night with life. From time to time the croaking of frogs or the song of some bird blanketed the jungle's murmuring. Constantly overhead the bats and nocturnal birds crossed, beating their black wings. Pedrito had fallen asleep on Modesta's lap with one of the little pigs resting against him and warming his body.

"Brother," asked Modesta softly, "how long will our journey last?"

"I don't know. Far, very far ahead we'll come to the great rapids. Then we'll have to take the canoe ashore. We'll go on down the river and reach new falls, but then we won't be able to carry the canoe overland because of the rocks. We'll have to walk toward the sunset until we reach our village. One of the men told me that, one who knows the river well, because last year he was in the gang that kept watch over the floating of the logs."

"There's something I don't understand, little brother. If it's so easy to escape in a canoe, why do all those peons stay in the camps instead of running away?"

"Because they don't all find canoes handy, or because they're afraid of the water, or because they're afraid that they couldn't steer a boat."

"Maybe you're right, brother," said Modesta. In her heart she did not believe it, but she kept silent.

On the following morning Don Félix called El Chapopote and El Guapo.

"Drink up your coffee quickly. Then take your horses and go to Las Champas, the new camp. Ride over it and count the trunks and mark them. Felipe will take you down."

The overseers took what they needed and went aboard the canoe. El Guapo carried his gun with him, because, he said, he was sure they would surely find much better hunting over there, especially as it was still virgin forest. The cutters had not begun to chop or to frighten away the animals by their shouting. Thus they would be able to collect some fine prizes that it would have been a pity to let escape, especially as, since the floods had started, the meals had begun to be extremely sparse.

They were about fifty yards from the landing place of the new camp when, from a distance, they caught sight of Pablo, with his arms held skyward, who was swearing. "They've stolen my canoe. God damn them! Just let me get my hands on that son of a bitch!"

Felipe brought his craft in to the sandy shore and said: "You just forgot to tie the canoe up securely. You left it slack, and the water carried it away. It's your fault."

"My fault! Don't talk rubbish! What do you know? I

moored it there last night, see? The river is quite low, and you won't tell me that the canoe started off by itself?" Addressing the foremen, he shouted: "And by all the devils, I know who took it! That swine of a Chamula, the one who goes about with his whole family and a drove of pigs."

"Now you're the one who's talking rubbish! How could that stupid animal of a Chamula manage to steer your canoe?"

"All right! Since you know so much, look for the Chamula. Locate the bastard and his family. They're not here. They're not at the camp. They've even taken the pigs with them! Hurry after him—and when you get your hands on him, I'll get my canoe back."

The two foremen climbed the embankment, pulling their horses after them. They ran into El Faldón, who was waiting for them.

"It's true," he said. "The Chamula took the canoe. Believe it or not, but he's cleared out, and you fell like rain from heaven to go and look for him."

"That's the only thing left for us to do," El Chapopote said, nudging his companion. "What do you say, Guapo? We'll count the trees later. But first, let's go and toss something into our bellies. What with nothing but a swallow of coffee this morning, I'm dying of hunger. Don Félix is worse every day. How does he expect us to count tons of wood in a place where there are no trees? I don't know the trick of making them grow. If I did, I'd make myself a millionaire, and it'd be a long time before I'd be taking care of those Chamula bastards as if I were their wet nurse."

"Let's begin by having a shot to lubricate our throats!"

El Faldón produced a bottle and they all had good swigs to renew their energy.

"You follow us with your other canoe, Felipe," said El Chapopote. "El Guapo and I will go along the bank on horseback."

"No, not like that, no," replied Felipe. "None of that. We'll never catch them with the canoe. Just think, they've got a night's head start, and even if we caught up with them, they'd jump into the water as soon as they saw us and the canoe'd be carried away by the current, and we'd never be able to get it back. On horseback you'll go a hundred times faster than I could go in the canoe. The river twists and turns constantly. I ought to know! You can take some short cuts without having to follow the river and you can get way ahead of the Chamula, who doesn't know the river. You can be easy in your minds. Before five minutes are up he'll have smashed into some rocks or run up on some sandbar. And besides, there's no reason for me to go so far away. I must get back because Don Félix wants me to go upriver and help to get the logs into the water."

It was true. Don Félix had ordered him to return immediately to go with him on an inspection tour of the dumps. But in a case like this, a matter of pursuing a fugitive, Felipe could have disregarded Don Félix's orders. The real reason for his refusal was his fear of finding himself alone with Cándido before the foremen had appeared to help him. He knew that Cándido, like others who had taken flight, would not hesitate before killing him to avoid being captured.

Cándido seemed to have the gods on his side: in three days not a single drop of rain had fallen. The river was low and quiet. On turbulent water Cándido would not have been able to get far. But if the weather was favorable for him, it would also be so for his pursuers. For if the rain had been as steady and violent as during the preceding week, the jungle tracks would have been impassable, the horses would have sunk to their knees in the mud, and the foremen would often have been obliged to lead their mounts by the bridle. They would have had to make long detours to avoid the flooded places and the swamps near the banks.

Instead, the surface of the ground was dry enough to permit fairly rapid progress on horseback. The waters had gone down and for many miles it was possible to gallop along the sand or even on the uncovered stony bed of the river. In some places, as is usual with rivers running through tropical forests, this one widened out for a mile or more, becoming shallow except for short stretches that were usually possible to jump. The more twists and turns in the river, the more his pursuers gained on the Chamula, especially as the peaceful current bore him forward slowly, and for mile after mile the horsemen progressed three times as fast as the fleeing man.

If Cándido had not been given advice by his comrades, he would have been dashed to pieces with his family at the first cataract. It was not so easy an operation as he had imagined to haul the heavy canoe out of the water by himself and transport it across steep rocks in order to get round the rapids. He would have been able to cut down branches and work at them until he could use them as rollers—but he had no machete.

On the other hand, he could not abandon the canoe and go on through the jungle, because his pursuers knew the trail he would have to follow so as to avoid the swamps. The foremen would merely have had to wait patiently for him at some open place. Cándido did not know any of this, and it was precisely his ignorance that made his escape from the camps difficult. Celso, who, with all his heart, wished that Cándido and Modesta would get away to freedom, would have done everything possible to dissuade them from this expedition. He had had enough experience to know that such an attempt at flight could not succeed.

The day was well advanced. In about two hours more the sun would have set. El Guapo said to his companion: "Look. There's a little arroyo and we can take shelter under that tree with the thick foliage. It's up high enough so that we can watch the river. Let's sit down here for half an hour, eat a bite, and smoke a cigarette."

"Besides, the horses must have a rest," replied El Chapopote. "They must have a breather."

El Chapopote ("Tarface") had been given his nickname because his dark skin was nearly covered with black spots that betrayed his racial background. He had been born on the Pacific coast.

They were carefully wrapping beans in tortillas when El Chapopote, who was scanning the horizon, uttered a cry of joy: "Hurrah! Look! The Holy Family sailing along in their transatlantic liner!"

It was, in fact, the canoe approaching them, moving slowly. Clumsily managed, the prow was turning to right and left as if the pilot were in a state of hesitation about the direction he ought to take.

Cándido, Modesta, and the boy were seated in the bottom of the canoe, above the edge of which only their heads and necks could be seen. El Chapopote and El Guapo put down their tortillas carefully so as not to spill any of the beans. Then El Guapo unfastened the shotgun from his saddle.

While El Chapopote was taking out his revolver to load it, one of the horses for some unknown reason let out a neigh. Immediately the occupants of the canoe became aware of the presence of the two foremen. Cándido tried vainly to steer his canoe toward the opposite bank, but the current bore it irresistibly toward where the two foremen were. Before it had come up to them, El Guapo shouted: "Bring the boat in close, Chamula, or I'll shoot."

The foremen could not judge whether Cándido had any intention of disobeying or whether he simply could not steer the canoe, which, instead of coming nearer, was continuing on its way. So El Guapo fired. His intention was simply to scare the Indians, but the whole load of shot sprayed the canoe. Pedrito groaned and screamed, shouting that he had been hurt. Then he stood up in the canoe, pressing one hand against the other little arm. El Chapopote fired his revolver while El Guapo reloaded his shotgun and, aiming toward the canoe, shouted: "Come on in here, Chamula, or by our holy Mother today you'll die!"

El Guapo went down the embankment and with his feet in the water pointed his revolver at the canoe, ready to shoot.

On seeing his son's bleeding arm, Cándido lost all his courage. He no longer even thought of escape. He realized the seriousness of the foremen's threat. They were surely going to fire again and to go on shooting until all of them were wounded or killed—his son, Modesta, and himself. He shouted: "I'm coming, little chiefs! By the most holy Virgin, don't shoot any more!"

By desperate efforts he succeeded in getting the canoe to a sandbank, on which it grounded. He got out of the canoe, picked the child up in his arms, and went toward the bank followed by Modesta, the water reaching their waists. The little pigs followed excitedly after him, grunting. When they reached the bank they began to root about. The dog shook himself and leaped about happily in front of the group.

11

 "Well, then, swine of a Chamula, you not only tried to get away, but also to rob me of my canoe," Don Félix bellowed at Cándido, whom he had summoned to appear before him.

Don Félix had ordered them to bring him the Indian, Modesta, the child, and everything that Cándido had with him. He wanted to give a punishment that would teach a lesson, and thus demonstrate how he treated those who dared to break their contract.

"Yes! It's becoming a habit here, this leaving the camps when anyone feels like it!" Don Félix thundered. "Rebellion! Mutiny! Here in the camps!"

Near him were four overseers. The workers of the encampment had come out of their huts, and from the doorways the boys and some women looked at the scene, though nobody dared go near.

"And you too, you ungrateful bitch, you also wanted to run away from me," said Don Félix to Modesta, catching her by the chin. "But this time you won't get away, because I need a really young girl."

"Forgive us, little chief," Cándido pleaded. "Forgive us. We'll never do it again. I was very sad. I needed to go back to my village. I couldn't stay here after my son was drowned in the river. I had hopes of finding him. It could be that he managed to save himself. But I won't find him. Forgive us, little chief!"

Peditro, with his arm in a sling tied with a piece torn from Modesta's underskirt, began to cry when he heard his father pleading. Then he knelt down and, joining his hands as his mother had taught him to join them before the image of the Virgin, said: "Forgive us, little chief. We promise never to do it again. We miss my little brother so much!" He tried to say something more, but he only got his words confused, a mixture of Tsotsil and very bad Spanish.

"Shut your mouth, brat," said Don Félix, giving him a cut with the whip, which immediately left a red streak on the child's small face.

Bowing his head, Cándido in turn got down on his knees with his hands joined as Pedrito had done. He was not thinking of himself; his only thought was of protecting his son.

Modesta also fell on her knees, lowered her head, and pressed her forehead between her palms as if silently, passionately, to invoke the image of some saint. At last she was able to speak, and she muttered: "Have mercy on us, little chief!" But her voice was so weak that Cándido scarcely could hear it. The girl was barefooted. Her wool skirt was torn and covered with clay, her white underskirt in shreds, baring her legs to the knees. Her cotton blouse no longer covered her arms.

"So you still have the gall to ask for pardon, you lousy swine!" Don Félix answered, giving Cándido a violent blow across his bent back.

Cándido took it without moving, awaiting the blows to come.

"Every day, rebellions, mutinies," continued Don Félix, his face ablaze with rage as he struck Cándido again. "Every day you get more insolent. At night behind my back you sing revolutionary songs. But you'll learn that I'm still the master, and I assure you that I'll go on being boss, you bunch of pigs! I'm going to teach you the price of running away from the camps. That's finished! I'll not be a Montellano if anyone manages to run away again!"

Turning toward the foremen, he shouted: "Hey, Gusano!"

"At your orders, chief."

"Get your knife out."

El Gusano drew a hunting knife from his belt.

"Cut the ears off of that dog of a Chamula!" Don Félix ordered.

El Gusano looked at his master with inquiry and fright.

"Can't you hear me, you ass? I've just given you an order. Do you want me to give you, too, what you deserve?"

Don Félix underlined his words by making his whip whistle in the air.

El Gusano leaped on Cándido, grabbed him by the ears, and —not without an expression of disgust—sliced them off. Cándido, still on his knees, did not try to defend himself.

"Now you can eat your own flesh!" shouted Don Félix, "instead of getting fat swallowing lice, you swine of a Chamula!"

He kicked Cándido, who fell sidewise, then righted himself, got up, and made as if to leave.

"Gusano!" said Don Félix again. "Where did that fool go?"

"Here I am, chief, at your orders," said Gusano, going up to him.

"Don't be in such a hurry. Don't put your knife away yet. You still have to cut the ears off the brat. They'll soon see how I re-establish order here. Come on, now, cut the mule's ears off the little bastard!"

Cándido leaped forward like a jaguar and shielded the boy with his body.

"You, you swine, get away from there! Get down on your knees as quick as you can if you don't want to lose your nose and your fingers too!"

Cándido continued to clasp the child closely to him.

"For the love of God, little chief, don't hurt him! Cut off my nose and hands if you wish, but the boy—let him go!"

"Cut off your hands? You're smart, eh? So that you could watch the others work while you rested? No, I need your paws, whereas the ears of your brat are no good to me. Go ahead, Gusano, or you'll be the one to get fixed up!"

El Gusano rained blows and kicks on Cándido. Then, taking advantage of the surprise, he snatched the boy away. At once Modesta intervened. In one movement she grabbed the child and put herself in front of him. But El Pulpo, one of the cruelest of the overseers, took him from her and pushed him toward El Gusano. The boy stumbled and fell. At the same time Modesta flung herself down, covering him with her body.

Don Félix leaned down and, taking hold of her braids, pulled her up.

"Don't be afraid. I won't cut off either your nose or your ears. I like very much to look at them. I'll only separate your legs."

"Do whatever you want to me, little chief, anything you want! I'm here to serve you, little chief. But don't touch the boy, I pray you!"

She had fallen on her knees in supplication before Don Félix.

"Why didn't you say that sooner, you whore? It's too late now. And whatever I want from you I'll take by force."

On hearing Don Félix say that it was too late, Modesta turned suddenly and sprang to the spot where the child was. She caught her skirts up to her thighs and tried to staunch the rivulets of blood running down both of Pedrito's cheeks.

"And now that's what will happen to everybody who tries to escape or rebel, or who simply sings insolent songs during the night. Here I am the boss—and I'll go on being the boss! You'll all work. That's what you're here for. Don't forget it!"

He took in his cartridge belt a hole, turned around, and strutted toward his hut, stopping a moment to light a cigarette.

That night he called the cook and said to him: "Do you know that Chamula, the one whose ears we cut off? The one who tried to get away and to steal my canoe? Well, go and tell him to give you the pigs, that you're going to kill them for me as the best way to balance the cost of chasing him. What could he need pigs for? Isn't he a pig himself?"

"So at last, chief, I'm going to be able to serve you a nice piece of meat," replied the cook, laughing.

"Come in and have a swig, meanwhile."

"Thanks, boss."

On the following day Cándido was sent to the new camp. But, by order of Don Félix, Modesta and the child had to stay in the main camp. Don Félix was convinced that it was Modesta who had incited her brother to flee. If he separated them, they would not think of leaving, or at least, if the temptation came to them again, they would have to go looking for each other to make plans. He had also decreed that Modesta should help in the cookhouse and clean the hut in which he lived. For wages she would receive fifty centavos a day and her food. Nobody in the camps had a right to live unless he earned his meals. As for the boy, he was big enough, Don Félix thought, to earn his bread as an ox-driver. "He'll learn very soon," Don Félix said. "And all the better because we've cut off his ears— he has the advantage that now nobody can pull them."

The camp where Celso had been sent lay about an hour and a half's walk from the main camp. To avoid a great loss of time, he and his companions had chosen to build some tiny shelters in which to spend the nights on the spot where work was. They returned to the main camp twice a week to get their rations and change or sharpen their axes.

The heavy September rains were drawing near. In three weeks' time it would be possible to throw the logs into the water. This work always began in the regions farthest away from the river, where the flood waters lasted only three or four days. The other districts, nearer the river, could wait, because there the high waters lasted two or three weeks.

The heat had become unbearable. In the jungle that Celso and his companions were clearing of undergrowth, the air was charged with stifling humidity. As the sun rose higher in the sky, the workers found the work more painful.

On the open plains the rainy season is agreeable and refreshing, but in the jungle, where the rains last longer, the three or four weeks during which at least half a dozen times daily the ground is covered as though by a lake three feet deep, man's existence and that of domestic animals become a hellish torture. The ground is carpeted thickly with mosses that make it impermeable, preventing it from absorbing one drop of water. Also, evaporation is slow because the hot rays of the sun do not penetrate to the pools and swamps. The tops of the towering trees are so packed together and their foliage is so dense that the sun does not get through them except when by chance a gust of wind stirs and separates them for an instant. The previous days' rains have created such vitality in the soil that it is practically carpeted by thick, light-green vegetation. In a few days the undergrowth has covered trails and paths, and the opaque arches of foliage form an almost unbreakable barrier against light and air. Heat is the jungle tyrant. It makes sweat run in streams from man, and the steaming air does not permit it to evaporate.

This unbreaking humidity under the arch of impenetrable foliage, together with constant standing in water up to the thighs, leaves a man in a heavy stupor. Whatever way he turns he sees only the green arch and closed walls of foliage, and the asphyxiating humidity is everywhere. The atmosphere alone is enough to debilitate a man, blunt his senses, and make him lose his judgment. At each stroke of his ax against the mahogany trunks, which are as hard as steel, the cutter thinks that he is at the end of his strength. He feels that he will be unable to go on and that before attacking the next tree he will fall, indifferent to the fate awaiting him.

But his torment must still increase. As the rainy season is prolonged, the wild animals, snakes, and insects multiply. The mosquitoes swoop down in huge, dense clouds. In the jungle their violence lasts throughout the year, but during the rainy season hundredfold swarms contain them by millions. For these voracious armies blood is a gift, the most coveted of gifts. They arrive in inconceivable numbers, no doubt vomited up by hell to poison the existence of man on the earth and to make him sigh for the peace of paradise. Little black flies, whose bite leaves a painful red dot, appear in incredibly numerous squadrons that in half an hour can turn a man's skin into a mass of coagulated blood. The bigger varieties of mosquitoes also arrive, as voracious as rats, and with them giant and dwarf spiders, scorpions, centipedes, and snakes that seem to be waiting patiently for the naked foot of an Indian to be placed on their ambush of moss and vines. Jaguars, pumas, and wildcats spy on their victims from sloping tree trunks, ready to spring on a passing cutter absorbed in his work and not even thinking of looking up.

During the rainy season working becomes atrocious toward noon. The men made a habit of drinking a little coffee and eating some warmed-over tortillas on waking, before starting to work, and of eating more substantially at noon. In this way they avoided the torture of working during the hottest hours.

In the little camp that they called Fallen Log some of the workers were squatting around a fire, raised up on a dry spot. They were Celso, Martín Trinidad, Juan Méndez, Lucio Ortiz, Casimiro, Paciano, Encarnación, and Román.

They were all cutters. Two of them were leaning over the fire and watching the pots of coffee and the bowls in which rice and beans were heating. The others, a little distance away, were smoking, half-asleep, waiting for the food to be ready.

Early that morning Celso had killed an iguana with stones. Lucio had cleaned it and was cooking it on the hearth. That day their fare would be a little less frugal.

For a long time Celso had been smoking less for pleasure than to drive away the mosquitoes. Seated quietly, he finally dozed off with his knees apart, his arms at his sides, and his head resting against a tree.

Suddenly he woke up in fright and exclaimed: "Somebody just called me from over there! Who can it be?"

"Who'd be calling you? I haven't heard anything. You're dreaming, old man. El Pasto was here half an hour ago to mark the trees, but he won't be back, at least not before night. You've certainly been dreaming."

"Go on snoring," said Lucio, laughing. "You've still got to be patient for half an hour. The iguana is getting soft, but it's not yet cooked. I'll wake you when it's ready."

Celso did not seem satisfied with this explanation. He tried to stare through the underbrush and said: "I'd have sworn that somebody called me by name. By God, I heard a voice as clearly as though somebody was speaking into my ear."

Once again he stared into the surroundings. Then again he tried to sleep. He had hardly shut his eyes when he jumped to his feet. "You can say what you like, but somebody just called me again. I heard someone say: 'Celso! Celso! Where are you?' I assure you that I'm not crazy. It was a woman's voice."

Lucio and Paciano laughed heartily. "A woman! Look at him. A woman calling him by name! Certainly you need a woman, and that's why you're hearing them call you even in your dreams. Go take a leak so that you can snooze in peace."

Celso remained standing. His companions' words could not convince him that he was mistaken. He picked up the cigarette he had dropped in his sleep and relighted it at the fire. He walked around a little and then went into the underbrush. Suddenly he took the cigarette from his mouth and cocked his ear.

"Boys!" he shouted. "This time I'm sure. Somebody's calling over there. And I'm sure that it's a woman."

Paciano stood up, also cocked his ear, and said: "You're right, Celso! Somebody's calling, and it's a woman's voice."

"Listen! She's calling again! The voice seems to be coming from that dense thicket," said Celso, who was scrutinizing the jungle walls with impassioned curiosity. "Come with me, Paciano. Let's go and see what it's all about."

They had not moved two steps when they both began to tremble. This time there was no room for doubt. They had heard a woman's voice.

"Celso! Celso! Where are you?"

"Here I am!" Celso shouted at the top of his lungs.

"Where?"

The men pressed forward in the direction from which the voice came, moving as rapidly as obstacles permitted. All at once among the thickets they saw Modesta's face.

"Modesta!" Celso shouted in astonishment. "What has happened to you?"

As the girl saw the men approaching, she hid herself behind some bushes and said: "I am naked. I've only some branches to cover me!"

Celso took off his shirt, which he wore only during periods of rest to protect himself from mosquitoes, and threw it to Modesta. The shirt was all torn, but it covered the girl enough to allow her to show herself before masculine eyes.

"Give me your shirt, Pachi," Celso said to his comrade, pulling it off him without waiting for a reply.

Celso led the girl to the little clearing where the men were preparing their meal.

"How long have you been wandering around in the jungle like this?" Celso asked Modesta when the girl had sat down.

"For a long time. I didn't know where to find you, Celso. I met one of the men near a dump. He told me you were working in Fallen Log, but he couldn't tell me exactly where it was. He could only indicate the direction. I walked a long way without meeting a soul. In the end I saw some recently cut trees and thought that perhaps you wouldn't be far away. So then I walked on a little farther, calling you. What are we going to do now, Celso?"

"But explain what has happened to you. Has Cándido run away again?"

Celso insisted on learning what had driven the girl to run naked through the jungle. A dark presentiment of what had occurred, or of what had threatened her, began to take constantly clearer shape in Celso's mind, but he wanted Modesta to tell him the truth, not because of useless curiosity, but in order to know whence the danger might be coming and how he could protect her.

"This morning very early Don Félix sent them to call me from the kitchen, where I've been helping the chief cook and his woman." Modesta hesitated a little, not knowing where to begin her story.

"Was it the cook who threw you out?"

"No. The cook was very good to me. He gave me two straw mats to sleep on. You know I have nothing. We lost everything we had in the river."

"Then it was his woman?"

"No, not the woman either. Let me think, so that I can explain it to you. The little chief sent for me to come and make his bed. When I got there, he grabbed me as hard as he could and threw me on the bed. I defended myself and scratched his whole face. Then I saw a bottle right there. As he had hold of me by the neck and legs, I had only one hand free. We struggled. I was able to pick up the bottle, and with all my strength I hit him with it on the forehead. Then I got free, stood up, and ran to the door. But my clothes were so old that they had been ripped off in his hands. All I had left was a little piece of blouse. I got away with just that."

"But," interrupted Román, "doesn't he still have his two women?"

"They had gone out. . . . I ran and the chief ran after me, shouting: 'Stop where you are or I'll shoot.' And he fired two or three shots without hitting me. Then he began to shriek like a crazy man, saying: 'I'll catch you, you dirty bitch! I'll tie you to my bed, and then we'll see if you'll get away from me. And when I've had enough of you I'll cut off your ears and your nose too!' "

"And he'd certainly do it!" Juan Méndez affirmed.

"Then I got so frightened that I felt like going back to stop him from cutting off my ears. Then he went to the foremen's hut and ordered El Gusano to catch me. Luckily El Gusano was very busy with the horses. Then the chief began screaming again: 'I'll not only cut your ears off, witch, but I'll tie you for three days and nights to that tree down there. Maybe that'll take away your wanting to hit me with a bottle.' Just then the cook came out of his hut and said to me: 'Run, girl! Run for all you're worth and don't let them catch you!' I asked him quickly where I could go. 'It doesn't matter where,' he said. 'It would be better to be caught by a jaguar than by Don Félix.' And then I came this way."

The men remained silent.

"Celso, you're going to help me, aren't you?" asked Modesta, noticing the indecision of the cutters.

"We could hide her," suggested Encarnación.

"Fool! Where could we hide her?" replied Lucio.

"Oh, Celso!" said Román in an agonized voice. "Look! There comes El Gusano on his horse!"

"He must have seen us."

"Celso! Celso! Help me!" Modesta begged him. Then, without waiting for the help she had begged for, she sprang like a mad girl to hide in the underbrush.

El Gusano was in fact very near them and could see the girl run. Don Félix had ordered him to bring her back. His horse could progress only very slowly through the undergrowth, but he had followed her tracks. All the men stood up and anxiously watched the pursuit.

In her bewilderment Modesta suddenly fell. A second later El Gusano had seized her by her hair and tied her with his lasso. Exhausted, the girl gave up the struggle. Undoubtedly her fate was to be captured by Don Félix. She would not escape.

El Gusano dragged her after him and approached the group of cutters. He pulled up his horse, took a pouch of tobacco from his shirt, rolled a cigarette, and said to Celso, who was nearest him: "Give me a light."

Celso held out a burning stick. El Gusano inhaled a few puffs of smoke and said: "What have you got to eat?"

"Iguana, chief," answered Lucio.

"Pigs! How can any Christian eat iguana without vomiting from disgust! Hogs! That's what you are."

He blew out more clouds of smoke. Then, smiling disagreeably, he nodded his head toward the tied girl, adding: "So! On the other hand I'm taking a very tasty dish back for Don Félix. What the chief is going to eat tonight will taste much better than iguana. And when he's tasted it thoroughly, he'll leave it for me so that I can try it. He's promised me the leftovers. As for me, I'll eat it even if it's without a nose."

He roared with laughter menacingly, smacked the flanks of his horse to get it moving, and at the same time pulled violently on the rope to make Modesta follow along.

Modesta, surprised by the unforeseen pull on the rope, fell flat. El Gusano only went on pulling more violently.

The girl half stood up and then fell at once to her knees. She exchanged a glance with Celso. There was no reproach in her eyes. She knew that Celso, like all his companions in misery, was helpless. But the infinite sadness that he saw in her eyes hurt him more than the most bitter reproach, more than the greatest insult. He looked at her fixedly a moment and then turned to look at his companions. He saw Martín Trinidad close his lips and breathe heavily through his nostrils as if to relieve himself of a great oppression.

All this did not last more than two or three seconds.

Celso swallowed his saliva with effort and gathered himself as if for a big jump. Then he straightened up and let out a scream of such force that the foreman's horse reared up and tried to dash away as though in the presence of a jaguar. But in the attempt the animal stuck its hoofs into a pool of mud, from which it tried helplessly to pull them out. El Gusano lashed at the animal, pulling vigorously on the reins. The horse's legs stretched taut in a useless effort to get out of the swampy spot. But while it was struggling and its rider was trying to find a way to force it up and out, Celso, in a prodigious leap, landed on the horse's rump and clasped the foreman in his arms from behind, by this unexpected shock making him let go of the stirrups. El Gusano had hardly fallen to the ground before Celso jumped on him, pounding his face with clenched fists. El Gusano defended himself, trying to drive Celso off by kicking him in the stomach. But the man dodged the kicks without losing his grip. They fought desperately on the ground. El Gusano's face was becoming purple.

"Are you going to get off me, you dog?" he said, gasping and choking on the words.

With one hand Celso felt around on the ground for something to use as a weapon. Juan realized what Celso wanted. He picked up a thick piece of branch and smashed it down on El

Gusano's skull. The foreman's hands relaxed, releasing his enemy.

Juan went on beating El Gusano's head. The blows fell with such violence that in an instant Celso was able to step away from his victim. El Gusano's skull was nothing but a bloody mass.

"I warned you some time ago, Gusano," he said, getting up. "I sang you the same song more than a hundred times. Now you see how I keep my promises and do what I sing."

With the back of one huge hand he wiped away the sweat and blood running down his face. Then he went over to Modesta, cut her bonds, and asked her tenderly: "Are you hurt, Modesta?"

"No," she replied in a scarcely audible voice. "No, the thorns in the forest made these bloody spots on my arms and legs. But I was so frightened, Celso!"

"Don't be afraid, Modesta. We can't turn back now. We've got to go ahead from now on. We'll all run away together. What do you say, boys?"

"Yes, all of us," Román interposed.

"The ones from the fincas? And the peons too?" asked Paciano, who himself came from a finca whose owners had sold it to the Montellano brothers.

"Yes. All the peons on the fincas too!" Martín Trinidad affirmed. And to underline what he had said, he shouted what had become his war cry: "Land and liberty!"

Like a single voice all the men answered: "Land and liberty!"

Celso turned over the foreman's body, taking hold of it by one of its bare feet, leaned over the corpse, and removed the cartridge belt and the revolver.

"Martín," he shouted, "you already have a pistol and cartridges. This one is for me. Come and tell me how to load it and fire it."

"In five minutes you'll know as well as I do."

"We ought to bury the body of this dog before going back to the camp," Román suggested.

"Nothing of the sort! Let the wild hogs take care of it if they like that dead meat!"

Celso said to Martín Trinidad: "Are you taking the horse or do you want me to ride it?"

"You'll be the leader. Well, then, get up! When we have other animals, then we'll ride."

"Hey!" Celso shouted. "Come on, everybody. We have to think. We must make plans."

"Yes, that's right," the men replied.

"But not here," Celso answered. "Because that filth will begin stinking before long. Let us go on a little way. And you, Modesta, come with us. We need to have you around."

Modesta made a gesture of assent, held together as well as she could the rags that covered her, and followed the cutters.

The men sat in a circle, as Indians do, and Celso spoke: "This is just the beginning, but now we can't turn back. We've done for that sickening worm, who's had it coming to him for a long time. But if we don't keep on now, we all know the risk we'd be running. That Félix will hang the lot of us after cutting off our ears. Since Cacho got his from Urbano, they've all gone crazy. The truth is, men, that they all go around pissing from fright. And out of pure fear they're capable of striking out blindly without seeing whom they're hitting. Would you like them to cut all our ears off? Or would you prefer to lose our noses or our fingers?"

"Don't be stupid," Lucio interrupted, laughing. "Why are you asking us such questions?"

All the men laughed with Lucio. Celso himself laughed with them.

"Good! But you must tell me if you want to return to your homes, to your women, your parents, to cultivate your land."

"Sure we do!"

Then Martín Trinidad rose and, waving his arms vigorously, said: "No, you drove of oxen! Animals! We won't do that. There'll be a time for you to sleep with your women and to cultivate your land—which will always stay in the same place. While I'm able to stand on my feet none of you will run off home! We must raise all the men suffering in the camps, we must go to the fincas and do away with the finqueros and the majordomos and then with the rural police and the federal soldiers. The peons must be free—all of them, absolutely all. Do you understand? All of them must have their patches of land that they can cultivate in peace, and the harvests must be for them only and for nobody else. That is land and liberty! The land must belong to them. Because without land there is no liberty, neither for you nor for anyone else. And if we don't start by ridding ourselves of finqueros, majordomos, overseers, rural police, federals, political chiefs, and municipal bosses, we'll never have liberty. Now you'll see them, when they see us coming, throw themselves down before us in supplication. But for them, war without quarter! If we don't exterminate them they'll soon put us in chains again. And this time they'll have forged them heavier than those we carry now. The enemy must be killed, and we must kill all who can become our enemies. If you have pity on them, you'll be betraying yourselves, your women, your sisters, your parents, your children, and even those not yet born."

"Bravo, Martín! That's the way to talk," cried Celso and Paciano.

"Bravo!" the rest called out in chorus. "That's what we all think!"

"In that case, forward! Don't let the flame go out. Long live the rebellion! Long live the rebels!"

All the men repeated: "Long live the rebellion! Long live all the rebels!"

They collected their tools, their axes and machetes, and proposed to march immediately and attack the camp headquarters.

"Not so fast, men," said Celso. "First we're going to think what we must do and how to do it. If we rush in crazily it won't cost us anything to take over the office. But then? You know very well that there are overseers in every corner of the jungle and that the other men don't yet know anything about our plans. The overseers can all get together and finish us off easily. They're all well mounted and armed. They can gallop to outside camps for reinforcements, and we can't win against them. Listen to what Martín Trinidad told you—he speaks the language of reason. Let's stay here and talk it over. If we make useful decisions now, we won't have to regret them later."

"Celso, tell us, what do you think?"

Celso proposed that some men should go to alert the ox-drivers who were hauling logs to the Mono arroyo.

"I know them well," he said, "and I know they're real men. Among them are Andrés and Fidel, the one who some time back broke El Gusano's jaw; and Santiago, who doesn't fear the Devil himself; and Matías, who's only waiting for the right opportunity to wring the neck of El Doblado for stealing his woman. Also there are Cirilo, Sixto, and Prócoro. With those guys we don't need to be afraid. With them we can conquer the whole jungle and clean up the fincas. If all the cutters were like the drivers, nobody could stand up against us, and we'd get a long, long way!"

"Good, go first and find the drivers!" Martín Trinidad ordered. "You, Juan, get on the horse and go ahead. Talk to the first driver you meet and send him to the Mono arroyo."

"But," said Juan, "supposing I run into a foreman on the way and he sees me riding a horse—what shall I tell him?"

"Tell him that the chief sent you urgently to fetch Andrés and Santiago. But why give excuses? Take the revolver. Carry it on the saddle, and if a foreman tries to stop you, just shoot him quietly. You know how to shoot. If the first bullet doesn't kill him, fire a second. Take the cartridge belt too—and don't be afraid. We're going to carry this through. The comedy has lasted long enough! It's either them or us! If we want to live, we must destroy them. Get going, Juan! In half an hour we'll all be with you at the arroyo."

12

 When the men reached the arroyo they found the ox-drivers already alerted by Juan Méndez. Their young assistants seemed to be in a state of terror. They bustled around the beasts, trying to give the impression, if a foreman should appear, that they had no part in the blow being prepared. They knew what awaited them if the affair turned out badly.

Not counting these youngsters, more than twenty men had gathered together, and every quarter of an hour another ox-team arrived with its driver, who was immediately informed of what was happening.

The men decided to march first on the main office, but by a roundabout route to recruit as many drivers and cutters as possible.

The cutters carried their axes. Others had machetes as well. They all took hooks from the hauling chains and whatever other iron utensils could be used as weapons.

"Besides," said Juan Méndez, "everyone must understand that for the first assault stones and clubs will be enough for us. When the thing has really broken loose we'll do like the peons of Morelos, the first who dared to attack the sugar refineries. The rural police and federals sent to put them down were welcomed by a wonderful ambush."

"And why the ambush?" asked Celso.

"What a thick head you have! What a question! The more soldiers that came after them, the more arms they could pick up later. Don't you know that every policeman and every soldier has a rifle, and every officer a revolver? It's very simple: you surprise a soldier or policeman, knock him down, and seize his carbine or pistol—and the cartridges. Now you see that it's not complicated. That's the way a revolt is made."

"And did the rebels of Morelos win?" asked Santiago.

"They certainly did not. For the moment it was impossible. But they, along with the peasants of Tlaxcala under the command of their chief, Juan Camatzi, have started the thing and have taken the most difficult step. Because now the peons and the peasants all over the country know what they have to do and are convinced that the dictatorship and the tyranny are neither invulnerable nor invincible. Before, they believed that nobody could do anything against the tyranny because it had been established by God Himself and because all the priests predicted that it would last for at least a thousand years. Patience! Next time the men of Morelos will win. And those of Tlaxcala too. Who knows but that right now, while we talk about it, they've succeeded in raising the whole state of Morelos? Unfortunately, we don't know anything about what's happening in the rest of the country."

"The devil! What are you all doing here together?" asked El Doblado furiously as he rode up on horseback accompanied by El Tornillo.

On seeing them, the men, or at least most of them, felt wild panic; but not one among them moved or showed a sign of returning to work.

"Didn't you understand me, you swine? Tell me—what's the meaning of this meeting? Lounging around in the middle of the day—when next week we'll have to begin throwing the logs in the water. Come on, now, get to work!"

The terribly frightened young drivers' assistants and two or three drivers with less experience than the others returned to their teams.

"Stay here, cowards! Don't move!" shouted Celso.

The deserters stood still.

"But what's happening?" screamed El Doblado, brandishing his whip. "Is this a strike or a mutiny?"

"That's just what it is, coyote!" replied Santiago Rocha. "You guessed it perfectly: it's a mutiny, a meeting of rebels. Now you know it, dog!"

El Doblado went pale, dug his spurs into the flanks of his horse, and tried to retreat. But the horse only half obeyed and for a few seconds pranced where he stood. El Doblado felt a mortal uneasiness creeping over him. He looked at the men, who, in a threatening attitude, seemed to be waiting only for a signal.

El Tornillo, the other foreman, was a little farther off. He could have tried to escape, but on reflection he told himself that it would be better to remain at El Doblado's side, not so much to protect El Doblado as to save himself. In fact, to abandon his companion in order to save his own skin could have grave consequences for him if the other foremen should learn the truth later. And he saw no great difference between dying immediately and being killed later by his comrades.

While El Doblado's horse continued to hesitate and prance, the man on his back suddenly lost his head. He wanted to draw his revolver, but he was carrying the whip in his right hand, and its handle got stuck in the gun.

Matías, taking advantage of the moment, struck the horse's hind legs with a branch, at which the animal reared. Fidel jumped onto its rump and grabbled with the foreman, twisting the hand with which he was reaching for the revolver. El Tornillo, realizing how serious the situation had become, turned his horse to make off. But Cirilo was watching him and struck the horse's hind quarters with an iron chainhook. The animal reared and pranced in confusion, but El Tornillo remained firmly in the saddle. Then Sixto stooped to look for a stone. He did not find one, but found instead a piece of a yoke, and with this improvised weapon struck the rider a vigorous blow on the back, at which El Tornillo turned to defend himself. But at the same moment Pedro attacked him from the other side, tearing the reins from him and dragging him to the ground. A few seconds later the two foremen were dead.

Fidel, who had his own special reasons for hating El Doblado, had finished him off furiously with blows of his club. He was like a madman and shouted as he laid on each blow: "Take this one! And this one! That'll teach you to leave our women in peace!"

When Fidel straightened up after striking his enemy a final blow, Martín Trinidad said to him: "His pistol and cartridges belong to you. You've earned them."

Then he turned to the other men and, pointing with his finger to the corpses of the two foremen, shouted to them with conviction in his voice: "Look! Just look at them! That's the way we get arms, men. Every pistol you get this way has a double value, because your enemies will be without it, and you'll have it. Attack from the front or behind, in broad daylight or in darkness. Attack any way you like, but attack, by God! If you want to make a revolution, then carry it through to the end, because otherwise it will turn against you and tear you to shreds."

"Well, I'll be damned," exclaimed Andrés, who at that moment arrived, goading his oxen and knowing nothing of what had happened. "Man, how well you can make speeches! Who are you?"

"I've already told Celso. He knows my name and who I am. I'm a schoolmaster, a fellow who doesn't know how to crawl or to lick anybody's boots. I'm a schoolmaster, a simple schoolmaster. But later, when peace reigns in the country, when at last we've freed ourselves from the dictator, when every man has his piece of land and enjoys freedom, then I'll teach the new generations in the university. Now you know why I'm with you—because I don't know how to bow down or salute those who despise me. Liberty doesn't exist when the expression of thought is forbidden. For you freedom will be the land you cultivate. I don't want land. I want only the freedom to teach what I believe is sensible and true."

"But, man," replied Andrés enthusiastically, approaching Martín Trinidad with his hand held out, "that's exactly what I want. Only until now I couldn't put it in words. I'm very glad that you've made it clear."

"We'll be friends, Andrés, though you're very young. I'm exactly twice your age, but we'll be good friends."

"I hope so, professor!"

"Yes, we'll be friends, very good friends as long as you like, son. But now we don't have time for declarations of friendship. We're right in the middle of a battle. We mustn't lose the game. To go on living in our shameful state is a crime against the country. You're a soldier now and I'm a soldier, soldiers of the revolution. We have no chiefs or officers; we're all soldiers. Let's embrace one another before we set out again!"

Then Celso spoke: "We're not here for embraces! They'll come later. Let's go! On to the main office! And you, Modesta, come here! You'll always march in front at my side. You'll be my faithful *soldadera*."

"That's the way it will be, Celso."

"I'll take the prettiest clothes we find there for you. And when we've made a clean sweep, we'll go find Cándido and the boy."

"Let's really clean up that office," Martín Trinidad said, going up to Celso. "But first I ought to go ahead and dig up my pistol and cartridges. It's the best automatic I've seen."

Whistling, singing, and shouting, the rebels advanced, making a long detour. Three men now had horses. Two of the horsemen marched at the head of the column, and the third followed at the end, to protect the rear. But they had not thought of laying plans for the attack on the office. They were relying on the force of revolutionary action, which, when not sidetracked by politicians, never loses its impulse toward self-renewal.

The rebels were sixty resolute men. They arrived within shouting distance of the main office an hour before sunset. All the camp dogs began to bark in chorus.

Don Félix had returned scarcely half an hour earlier from an inspection of the camp. At the office he had met Don Severo, who had come to make arrangements with him and the foremen regarding final details for launching the logs on the river.

Hearing the incessant barking, Don Félix said to himself: "Blast those devils! What's happening? Can't we ever have peace here? The whole camp must be drunk, the lot of useless bastards!"

The dogs continued their concert. Don Félix went out to the portico, picked up a stick, and beat the first animals that crossed his path. The dogs yelped with pain and ran off, but did not stop their howling.

"Probably the Turk is arriving with his caravan," said Don Severo, seeing his brother return.

"Impossible!" El Chapopote commented. "He'd have drowned before getting here, because everything is flooded. It's more likely oxen that have broken loose and wandered this way to get away from the flies."

"That's possible," Don Félix said hoarsely.

"Did you tell all the foremen that they must come here tonight, Chapopote?"

"Sure I did, chief."

Don Severo and Don Félix bent over their lists and tried to work out the approximate number of logs piled up at every launching place.

"By the way, Severo," said Don Félix, "tomorrow you're going to have some pork chops."

"Where did you get pigs?"

"I confiscated the Chamula's."

"The one who brought the woman and some kids with him?"

"That's the one. I have them in the new camp now. The girl escaped from between my hands this morning, the sow! But I'll catch her."

Don Severo sighed, saying: "Those women! God damn them! The messes they get one into! Those three of mine fight at least five times a day. There's hardly a hair left on the head of one, the other two have torn out so much. I think that before long I'll have to bury one of them. And all because I'm a good fellow and don't dare to throw them out because of the floods."

"You a good fellow! Don't make me laugh! Get off your high horse! You'll make me die laughing."

"That's what I said! Do you imagine that I'm a savage, that I don't know how to behave? I could give you lessons! But let's not discuss that. Pass me the bottle. You've been hanging onto it for a long time, and I'm dying of thirst."

The first huts of the village around the office appeared through the foliage. The men halted. Some of the dogs, more suspicious than the others, ran toward the workers. Although they knew nearly all the men, they felt instinctively that something out of the ordinary was happening.

"Wait for me here," Martín Trinidad told the men around him. "I'm going to dig up my pistol and my cartridges. We'll have use for that little toy pretty soon."

He was not gone long. He returned proudly flourishing his weapon. "I could kiss this little pistol as though it were a pretty girl."

And in fact he kissed the pistol several times.

"I'd like to know if all the foremen are there," said Celso. "The cook told me this morning that Don Severo had arrived with his men to organize the launching of the logs."

Andrés replied: "They can't all have arrived. At least those from the new camp can't be here."

"Look over there. That looks like them. From the top of the slope I saw a canoe coming upstream, and if my eyes didn't deceive me, it was the men from the new camp arriving. There's no mistaking them—the foremen don't dress like us."

Andrés said to one of the men: "Vicente, you run well. Go up there ahead and keep your eyes on the foremen as they arrive. As soon as they've gone into the office, tell us."

The man obeyed at once. Martín proposed that they discuss a plan of action.

"You, Juan and Lucio, you've been soldiers, accustomed to command. You take ten of the men, each of you. When

Vicente gives the signal, you'll attack the office from the river side so that nobody can escape by jumping into a canoe. If you see anyone trying to do so, fire—and be sure not to miss. We'll occupy the open space in front of the office. There are no more than three paths leading to the jungle. Where each one leads off we'll hide two men, whose job it will be to finish off with their machetes any foremen who venture that way. Arrange things so that if any of them should try to get away, they can run only toward the office, where, if they hope to find refuge, they'll get the surprise of their lives. As for the men returning from work, send them immediately to join us outside the office."

Vicente came back running.

"The foremen have arrived. They're making for the office."

"Then forward!" Martín Trinidad ordered the little group of men who had been given the task of cutting off the retreat of those about to be besieged.

The dogs had ceased their barking. Some were following the rebels.

The men spread out along the slope up to the level of the main office. Soon they crept up the slope and dispersed, concealing themselves in the thickets so that they could observe what was happening without being seen. As soon as they were in position, Secundino let out the mournful howl of the coyote, imitating the sound so well that the dogs dashed off to hunt their natural enemy.

"They're ready," Celso said quietly. But his eyes and quivering nostrils betrayed his anxiety.

Neither he nor any one of those men had ever rebelled before. They had not even ventured to cover their faces when they were lashed with a whip. The masters, whether Spaniards, white Mexicans, or the Germans of the coffee plantations (whom they called "white Chinamen"), were gods against whom an Indian peon had never dared to rebel. It was not because of cowardice or any hope of obtaining mercy that they behaved so. They knew that there are gods and slaves, and that whoever is not a god can only be a humble and submissive slave. Between these two classes there was no other except, perhaps, that of a fine horse. But when the slave begins to be conscious that his life has become like that of animals, that it is in no way better than theirs, it is because the limits have been reached. Then man loses all sense of reason and acts like an animal, like a brute, trying to recover his human dignity.

What was happening in the lumber camps, like what was happening on all sides, could not be considered a crime of the men, but only of those who had created the conditions in which things had developed.

Every blow given to a human being is a bell-stroke announcing the decline of the punisher's power. Unhappy he who forgets a blow received! Thrice unhappy those who, shrinking from the struggle, fail to return blow for blow!

13

 All the men felt their legs grow heavy when they realized that the moment for the assault had come. But they knew that it was impossible to retreat. They had burned their boats. The death of three foremen left them no alternative but to advance. Nobody asked whether they were marching to victory or to defeat. They had to march, that was all, and the rest did not matter. For that reason the strange feeling of apprehension did not last more than a moment.

When Celso shouted: "Forward, men! Land and liberty!" they did not march—they leaped forward like wild horses galloping toward a water hole.

Without knowing it, scarcely even wishing for it, they had already won half the battle.

Had they advanced slowly, Don Félix and Don Severo would have imagined that the men were coming because of some happening out of the ordinary—perhaps a landslide causing the death of some men, or the shifting of a pile of logs with the same result, or the appearance of jaguars. The Montellanos would have begun by speaking to them, by asking questions, and the men, unable to express themselves, and especially to discuss anything with the bosses, would have become confused and would not have been able to make their grievances known or to make demands.

Don Severo was standing in the office doorway talking with

his brother, his back to the open space. When he heard the tumultuous noise made by the onrushing men, he turned toward them, but he could not understand what they were shouting because most of them were shouting in their own Indian dialects.

"The devil! What's the matter with them?"

It was not to the men that he addressed this question but to his brother and the foremen, who had just begun to wolf down their supper and who had glasses in their hands.

Don Félix and the foremen jumped up and rushed to join him on the porch.

Don Severo went a few steps forward and shouted to the men: "What's wrong? Why have you all come? You could have worked another hour. There's enough light yet."

"Dog!" was the reply.

"Bastard! Son of a bitch!" cried another.

The insults poured out. All the men were yelling, but it was impossible to determine what they were talking about. All that could be clearly distinguished were oaths and obscene phrases.

Don Severo half turned toward the foremen and asked again: "But what do they want?"

A new rain of insults and oaths came from the group of rebels standing a few steps from the office.

"God only knows what new stupidity you have committed!" said Don Severo to his brother.

"Me? But what do you think I've done? Lately I haven't beaten or hanged a single man. Since we buried Cacho, since you said we should hold the reins loosely, we haven't touched anybody."

"Pardon me, chief," El Faldón said. "Don't forget the Chamula and his son. Cándido—isn't that his name?"

"Yes. But he ran away, and despite that we didn't hang him or beat him. He was simply sent to the new camp."

"Yes, but his sister was kept here," insisted El Faldón.

"And what do I care about his sow of a sister? I didn't do anything to her, and anyway she ran away this morning."

"Then by all the saints I don't know what's the matter with the men," said Don Severo.

He stopped for an instant and looked around. "God help us! We've got a whole army on our backs."

He had just seen the men who had come out of the forest and now threatened to cut off all retreat.

"It seems to me, chief, there's something very nasty about all this," El Chato said.

"Shut up, you idiot! Do you think I have to be told that? I only wish those swine would shout less and say clearly what it is they want. I can only get a few words of what they're saying."

"That's what seems so strange to me," interrupted Don Félix. "I suppose they're referring to two or three foremen, because they wouldn't dare speak to us like that."

Don Félix turned toward the foremen: "Speak up, you! What have you done now? I've got tired of telling you to leave the guys' women in peace. Haven't you got your own?"

El Faldón looked around the group of foremen. "I don't see El Doblado," he said. "What's happened to him?"

"Nothing," replied El Chato. "It just isn't time yet for him to come back."

"Hell!" said Don Félix. "You must have something in your mind about El Doblado. . . ."

"He's been in a mess with a girl one of the men brought here."

"In that case he'll deserve whatever happens to him. He knows perfectly well that he mustn't get mixed up with the women. There are enough whores at hand to satisfy everybody."

Don Severo raised his arm above his head, expecting the men to quiet down and let him speak. But his lordly gesture had no doubt already lost the magic it had formerly had, because the clamor increased: "Sons of bitches! Swine! Bastards!"

Don Severo realized that he was making himself ridiculous. Changing his position, he stood with arms akimbo, stuck out his chest, and tried to look as though he believed in his own authority. The response to this was a great roar, as though from one man with two thousand lungs: "Down with the Spaniards! Down with the white men!"

For the first time in his life Don Severo went pale. He watched his brother going back into the office and saw the foremen making for the door with feigned casualness. He did not move. He remained as though rooted to the porch. Several times he opened his mouth to speak and then, suddenly, he felt clumsy, not knowing what to do with his hands and arms. Finally he let them fall with a grotesque gesture, leaving them hanging in front of him as though trying to protect his lower belly, in the attitude of a schoolboy caught trying to satisfy an unhealthy desire. He did not realize how comic his position looked until the men shouted at him: "Hold the little bird tight! Don't let it fly away!"

There was a burst of laughter from the group. Another of the men shouted: "You can't save it, Spaniard! You won't be able to use it tonight!"

Don Severo, taking advantage of a second's silence, shouted: "But, men, what is it you want?"

"We want to go back to our people. We don't want to work now! We want our freedom! We're going to set free all the men on the fincas and in the lumber camps! Land and liberty!"

Don Severo went still paler, took a step backwards, and turned toward Don Félix. "Now I know what it's all about. That's the cry of the rebels: 'Land and liberty!' It said so in the last letters I got."

"God Almighty! Who could have come here and brought all this? It can't be one of our men. The few of them who can read don't receive letters or newspapers."

"Perhaps it was Andrés," said El Chato in an undertone.

"No. He's not capable of that. I think more likely it's that one who's got the Chamula's sister with him, the one called Celso. He's the most barefaced and hardened of the lot. Even beatings don't stop him. El Gusano told me that it was Celso who sang songs about rebellion at night. And El Gusano? El Gusano's not here either."

The other foremen turned and Don Félix observed: "Two foremen are missing."

"Three," corrected El Faldón.

"Listen, men," said Don Severo, finally finding courage to speak, "once we've put the logs in the water, when the work's completed, you all can go back to your homes. On my word of honor!"

"Stick your word of honor up your ass, you bastard!" Celso replied, his powerful voice rising above the tumult.

It was like a bugle call. He recovered his breath and roared: "Shit on your damned logs! They'll help us make a good fire in hell. Savage! Hyena! Four tons! Now cut them yourself with your own hands, you Spanish son of a bitch!"

This was too much for Don Severo, who thought he was about to burst. From white his face turned to crimson: "And you, swine of a Chamula, how dare you speak like that to your boss! On your knees, dog, get down on your knees at once!" He had drawn his revolver, and fired at Celso, underlining each of his last words with a shot. Celso fell as if hit. But as the men had foreseen how Don Severo's speech would end, a real rain of stones had fallen on him before he could aim carefully. Struck by the stones, he had fallen on the porch floor. But he kept his head and was far from being knocked out of the fight. He fired again, but could not tell whether he had hit any of his enemies. He had fired seven times, and that was the only thing he could be sure of, because the chamber of his pistol was empty when the men burst into the office. They swarmed in a mass from the open space and the slope. Not one of those who had arms fired a shot. They attacked the foremen with sticks and rocks. When a foreman went down, they flung themselves on him, smashing his face, breaking his ribs, and battering his body until it gave no more signs of life.

When the men invaded the office, Don Félix was the only one to draw his revolver. The foremen had immediately chosen prudence. Like confused rats they had run into the office and shut the doors, trying to escape without recourse to their weapons. They tried to reach the horses, but in vain. Not one could escape. The men did not let them. Nobody had the smallest intention of helping them. All were battered to pulp, torn to pieces. Their remains were brought back into the office by the workers, who immediately started to round up the pigs and dogs to shut them in with the corpses. Thus the carrion was devoured by the animals.

Don Félix had drawn his revolver. He succeeded in firing once and wounding one of the men in the leg. But the man leaped on him, pulling him down. Don Félix fired a second time, but the bullet lost itself in the porch roof. An instant later the weapon was torn from his grasp. The conqueror stood up, brandishing the pistol above his head, and shouted: "Now I've got a pretty little pistol too!"

Don Félix tried to pull himself up and to hide in a corner of the porch. But the workman who had taken his revolver leaped at him, smashing him into that corner. Seizing him by the throat with one hand, the man hammered his skull, with the revolver held in the other. Don Félix warded off the first blows with an arm. The man was about to strike again when a voice suddenly held him back:

"Brother, little brother, don't kill him!"

14

 Turning, the man saw Modesta standing a few paces away. Celso arrived at the same moment. He came from locking the office doors after driving the pigs and dogs in. He drew close to Modesta. His face did not show the least astonishment, for he had understood. He knew that Modesta was of the same blood, the same race, as himself. He knew that she was obeying an ancestral instinct, the instinct for justice and harmony.

"Brother, little brother, do not kill that man!"

Modesta still stood motionless in the spot from which she had uttered her first cry, in the exact center of the porch that ran the length of the office. Between her and the corner in which Don Félix was pinned down, there was nobody except the young cutter ready to kill him. All the workmen had gathered behind her. . . . Less than twenty minutes had elapsed since Celso had given the signal. They still had half an hour of daylight left, but the sky was covered with clouds. And the night would bring another downpour.

Modesta was still wearing only the torn shirt that Celso had given her. She was barefooted. Her legs were exposed to the thighs, which were bloody and raw from the wounds she had received in the underbrush during her desperate flight through the jungle.

Her thick black hair hung in disorder around her shoulders and down her back. After the unlucky canoe trip she had lost her wooden comb and the ribbons from her braids. That morning she had intended to ask the cook's woman to lend her a comb, but just at that moment she had fallen into the paws of Don Félix.

Modesta was very small, like most of the women of her race, but her body was well formed and harmoniously proportioned, so that she seemed to be taller than she really was. Among all those muscular men she looked a mere child, but she seemed to grow bigger when she called out for the third time to the man who was about to punish Don Félix: "Don't kill that man! I want him alive. I must hold him alive between my hands! Only that way will I be able to go on living!"

Then the Indian who had Don Félix under his knee got up, drew away from him, and slowly went to take his place near Modesta. He looked long at her, but she did not notice his stare. Her eyes were unblinkingly fixed on Don Félix, who, apparently fearing an attack by the girl, shrank more and more, trying to hide himself in his corner, leaving visible only his head and his broad shoulders.

Modesta raised her right arm and pointed her forefinger at the face of the conquered monster, Don Félix. "Listen to me carefully, you, you who compelled my brother and the little boys to set out in the canoe with a drunken boatman, you who despite his protests made them cross the river at night, so that the child was drowned—this I forgive you."

An anguished silence gripped the men, because they did not approve of what the girl was suggesting. Some were restless and muttered: "No! Why forgive him? We must kill him!" But those nearest Modesta imposed silence on them. From the girl's tone they had sensed that her words were no more than the beginning of what she had to say.

Still pointing at Don Félix with her extended arm, Modesta took a deep breath and continued: "That the boy was drowned through your fault I forgive you because you are the master. You command, we obey. . . ."

"Finish off the masters!" some of the more excited men shouted, but others silenced them.

Modesta did not hear anything of what was happening behind her. She stared fixedly at Don Félix as if trying to hypnotize him. One could see clearly how terror little by little was contorting the man's face. Perhaps he remembered having heard it said that the most terrible thing that could happen to a prisoner was to fall into the hands of the women of the tribe. For men usually work quickly, whereas women perform their duties without haste, with the deliberateness of work in their kitchens.

Modesta raised her voice: "That you wanted to rape me, to take me by force against my will, that you forced me to flee naked before the eyes of the men, this also I forgive you, for you are a man, and I am a woman . . ."

Celso, who knew more about Modesta's misfortune than anybody else, began to understand. Something like a smile lighted his face, and within himself he felt proud that the girl had chosen him as her protector. He made a quick sign to the other men and said: "Let her speak. She knows what she's about."

Still rigid in her attitude, Modesta continued: "That you cut off the ears of Cándido, my beloved brother, that you mutilated him because he was lacking in respect toward you, this also I forgive you, because when he fled he broke his contract, and you, his master, had the right to punish him cruelly, horribly. . . ."

The men realized that Modesta's charge had reached its culminating point.

Putting all the strength she possessed into her final words, the girl continued: "But for the boy, the little boy, the baby who could do you no harm with his tiny hands, with his innocent thoughts, for whom I implored you, kneeling on the earth, for whom I begged you in the name of the holy Mother of God with all the agony of my heart . . . You, Satan, savage beast, before whom the little one clasped his hands and fell on his knees, beseeching you as he might God Himself, you, Spaniard, white man, to take revenge for a mistake committed by the boy's unfortunate father, you, lacking even a dog's heart, cut off his little ears, leaving him mutilated for the rest of his days. And that—that I do not forgive you! If in heaven there is a just God, and if He condescends to spread a little of His grace over His forgotten children, if He hears the words that rise to Him from the bottom of my soul, I entreat Him never to forgive you, that among all sinners you be condemned for all eternity. For that I ask help of the most holy Virgin, who knows my sufferings, because she saw her own son suffer as I saw the little boy suffer who regards me as his mother. For him, to give him my protection and my love, I followed his father here. I do not spit my contempt in your face, for you have fallen too low to deserve a woman's contempt. I do not touch you because I don't want to make my hands filthy. I do not curse you because my curse could not bring you lower than you are. I leave you to hell, to the condemnation and just punishment of God. Because to you, such as you are, our Mother in heaven, however great her loving kindness may be, will refuse her pity."

Modesta fell silent. She felt herself standing on the solid earth again as she came out of the ecstasy in which she had lived as she spoke. She looked around her and for the first time seemed to realize where she was. She dropped her arm and felt her strength ebbing. She shuddered. Up to that moment she had spoken in a strong, vibrant voice, agreeable to hear. But now, as she came to herself again, her words became harsh, and her mouth was distorted in an ominous grimace: "Now, men, you can do what you like with the tiger of the camps. The beast belongs to you! Take him. He has no soul, no heart. He is not a human being, he's a wild animal. Make him pay for the little ears of my poor little boy. Make him pay for the little ears he stole! He must pay, pay, pay!"

Modesta ran around the circle formed by the men, shouting her last words as if trying to incite them to action, as if calling them to arms.

The workers were carried away. They shouted: "Bravo, girl! Long live Modesta! Long live the little Chamula! Long live the brave little Chamula! Long live the rebellion! Land and liberty!"

The wild clamor shook the girl out of her state. She tottered and had to reach for support. Hands were held out to help her. She covered her face with her hands, fell to the floor, and began to weep.

The men suddenly felt a shock. They talked and squirmed about, but stayed where they were.

15

The fact that the men remained where they were did not surprise Don Félix. Moving suddenly and supporting himself against the porch railing, he reached the best stretch of it and then, leaning on it, raised himself up. He had acted with such speed that the man who had been on his right felt himself brutally pushed back by the tremendous force of Don Félix's head striking his chest. But at the moment when Don Félix was about to drop over the railing to the ground, Celso, in a great leap, fell on him, spilling him on his back. The two men rolled about on the floor, never for a moment letting go. Celso had hold of his adversary by the collar of his shirt, and with his iron fist was punching his face, which seemed about to burst under the blows. Don Félix succeeded in freeing himself and backing against the wall again. Celso grabbed him and, punching him again and again, in a few instants turned his face into a bloody mass. Never interrupting the blows, Celso uttered cries of pleasure. When he had had enough, he said, wiping one hand with the other: "I'll have to wash them with holy water so that none of your carrion sticks to them. Look! They look as if I had just felled four tons of mahogany. That's the way hands look after cutting four tons. That's what I wanted to show you just once, you pig!"

Don Félix had been thrown into the corner. With a hopeless

gesture he was wiping away the blood that was flooding his face.

"Well, men, you heard what Modesta told us. Let's cut off his ears! Then we'll hang him for a little while. A short hanging won't be bad for him. We've had lots of experience in the matter. . . ."

He turned toward Modesta, who was still lying on the floor and weeping. "Don't cry any more, my dear. This very night we'll go to look for Cándido and the boy. If the canoemen don't want to, we'll know how to make them."

While Celso and some of the young cutters went off toward the huts of the workers and canoemen, the others drove and shoved Don Félix to a tree, one with strong branches. No one had to give instructions to the men. They knew what had to be done. Every man had been strung up at least once and had had enough experience. They disentangled some strands from a rope and tied one end of them around Don Félix's right ear, the other end to a branch. Then three of the men, after trussing Don Félix's body, pulled it up until his head hung a few inches from the branch. They held him there while the others adjusted the rope. At a cry of "Ready, now," they let the body drop in such a way that it remained suspended mostly from the right ear. The cheek, the whole face of Don Félix was pulled entirely out of shape.

"No, no, not this!" he cried while he could speak. "Kill me! Finish with me!"

Very soon, in spite of his wish not to betray his agony, he began to scream piercingly. The more the hanging was prolonged, the more his throat was squeezed, because his skin was stretched more and more tightly, pulling taut that on his neck and shoulders.

"Now, mad dog, you know what it is to be hanged!" shouted one of the men.

"We know how to do it as well as your brother pigs, whom we've already sent to hell," another said. "And we won't ask you to be ready to cut your four tons tomorrow. We'll be satisfied with just hanging you. But because you've beaten and hanged hundreds of us, you must pay for at least one hundred. . . ."

"Let me down, men! I'll give you all the mahogany, everything in the storehouse!"

Although he had often sworn that he would never ask for pity from the workmen, even if they put a knife at his throat, Don Félix began to beg.

"The storehouse? The shop? We don't need your permission to take them. And the mahogany? We don't need it. You can do what you like with that. You can let it rot!"

"Release me!" he implored again. "Do what you like with me, but take me down."

One of the peons replied: "Listen, Spaniard! We haven't the least desire to stay here listening to you scream. We're hungry. We've worked all day for you without a bite. Now we're going to the shop and open a few cans. Sardines, preserves, soups, ham, bacon, butter, chocolate, coffee—that will let us forget a little the moldly tortillas that you seemed to think good enough for us."

"And in an hour," another added, "we'll be back to see if your cheek is still holding out or if the rotten meat of your face has fallen away from your bones. Then we'll change you over to the left ear!"

Another interposed: "It all depends on the quality of your hide, my dear Félix. If the hide is good and resistant—and we hope it is—the pleasure can last six hours or even ten. . . . Oh, how all of you took it easy in your houses, swinging in your hammocks while we were sweating at work! Now it's your turn to sweat blood while we eat your provisions, smoke your cigars, and go to bed with your women—if they should happen to please us, which remains to be seen."

"Have a good time, my good friend Félix!" shouted one of them as they started for the shop.

Darkness was beginning to fall. In a quarter of an hour it would be completely dark.

New groups of ox-drivers and cutters were arriving at the

main camp. Many of them had been told what was happening, but they stopped to rest around their huts as though everything was normal.

Andrés and Santiago mounted guard at the shop to see that there was no pillaging—a useless precaution, as it seemed that nobody had thought of taking anything. Soon, however, they began to gather around. After a discussion with Celso and Martín Trinidad, it was agreed among them that Andrés should make an equitable division of the provisions among the workmen. Andrés was selected because he was the only one who could read and write.

When he arrived at the shop, he found it locked, the employee who took care of it had run away to hide himself.

Andrés left Santiago as sentry and went off to a group of huts where he felt certain he would find the storekeeper. His intention was to ask him for the key, so that he would not have to break open the door. On the way he met Celso, who, with a few other men, was looking for the canoemen. They wanted to be taken to the various encampments in search of Cándido.

The blacksmiths, carpenters, ropemakers, cooks, and canoemen were the privileged workers. They constituted a sort of middle class. They earned one peso or one and one half pesos a day. They lived in the camps with their families and formed a real little village. Among them were mestizos and white men.

They looked down on the laborers as much as the bosses did, or more so, and considered themselves to belong to the upper classes They spoke a fairly correct Spanish, had their own little chapel, and could read and write. They never mingled with the other workers except when they wanted to sell something or when they saw that the men had some money they might get. They felt proud to be able to speak to the bosses almost as equals and were disposed to do whatever the bosses required of them. They all but regarded themselves as aristocrats, and though in fact their material circumstances were very similar to those of the workmen, they did not wish to admit it. Although they sometimes earned less than the cutters, they considered themselves richly rewarded if the boss made a small friendly gesture or invited them occasionally to have a drink, though not to sit down. They were always ready to take his side against the lazy Indian pigs and to do them harm when that suited him.

All these workers, the canoemen, the supply-keepers, and their families, had witnessed the assault on the office from the shadow of their huts. A large number of them had pistols. If the Montellanos or the foremen had called on them at the moment of the attack, they would have rushed forward, perhaps much against their will. But Don Severo had not had time to call on them, even if the idea had occurred to him. Apart from anything else, he had not taken the mutiny seriously, and when he had taken its magnitude in, it was too late.

All these artisans were congratulating themselves on being forgotten. They deemed it wiser and less dangerous to witness the battle through peepholes, watching the development of events from a distance, having made up their minds to congratulate whoever won and to join that side immediately. If the men triumphed, they would make common cause with them. If the bosses won, they would be ready at once to perform their duty and to lend themselves to the task of crushing the rebellion.

Now, the rebels having won the day, the artisans, seeing the victors approach their huts, hurried out to greet them, saying: "We said that this had to happen some day. 'If the men aren't better treated, some day they'll rebel.' You can't go on all the time ill-treating a horse, much less a man, who, in spite of everything, is a human being."

Celso, Andrés, Santiago, Fidel, Martín Trinidad, Lucio Ortiz, and most of the others knew what value to put on these protestations of friendship from their new friends. They therefore declined the services now pressed upon them with so much enthusiasm. The more intelligent among them, not rebels of the moment, but permanent revolutionaries, understood those invertebrates well and knew better than to trust them. Experience told them that if the situation changed, thanks to help from the federal army, those puppets would go over to the side of the bosses with the same obsequious air they now employed. And not only that. They would immediately become the most bloodthirsty informers, the most ardent assistants to the bloodhounds. The men therefore remained unmoved by the abject attitude of the artisans.

"I said it all along," the blacksmith repeated, "isn't that so, comrades? I always maintained that this couldn't go on."

"Sure, you always said that."

"Shut your mouth!" Celso said brutally. "Shut it before I knock it shut. Tell us, you swine, which is the canoemen's hut?"

"Over there, Chamulito. If you wish I'll take you. See that hut where the lantern's shining? That's Pablo's, and Felipe's comes next."

Celso went to Pablo's hut and called him from outside: "Pablo, come here."

The canoeman came out trembling with fright.

"How many children have you?" Celso asked.

"Three."

"Bring them out."

"But I implore you, Chamulito, you're not going to do anything to them!" the canoeman pleaded in terror.

"Come on, now, get your children out here."

"They're asleep, fellows."

"Do you want me to get them with this machete?"

At that moment the children appeared in the doorway, drawn by curiosity about the voices. Their mother was in the little lean-to kitchen preparing the supper. She seemed not to have heard anything of what happened, but in reality she had taken shelter there on orders from her husband, who feared that the workers might wish to avenge themselves on the women for the many humiliations suffered at their hands.

One of the men seized the children, who began to scream. Then the mother rushed out and threw herself on her knees.

"Don't squeal like that, you old sow," said one of the men, "we're not going to do anything to your kids."

Celso ordered: "Take the two older ones to the embankment. And you, Pablo, come with me."

The woman began crying again, and one of the men in irritation said: "Shut your trap if you want your rats to come back!"

On reaching the slope Celso had the two children, one of seven and one of ten, tied up. The children struggled and wept, but Celso told them: "Be quiet now! We don't eat children. We won't hurt you if your father obeys our orders. Vicente, run to the shop and tell Andrés to give you a piece of chocolate for the children. Then you stay here and watch out that a snake doesn't bite them or a scorpion sting them while they're tied up here."

Vicente ran off toward the shop.

"You, Pedro, listen to me. You know well all the camps up and down the river. You're going to go right now to the new camp and fetch Cándido and his little son and all the men you find there. Call Felipe to get his canoe and go with you and help you bring them back as fast as possible."

"But don't you see that it's already night? How do you expect me to steer the canoe in the darkness?"

"Tell me, you pig, when your boss ordered you to go out at night did it seem dark to you? Now we're the bosses, and you'll do as we tell you. I'll keep the kids so that neither you nor Felipe will run away in the canoes. I'll hand over your children when you've brought all the men from the camps on both sides of the river. The sooner you bring them, the sooner your children will be free. If one of you makes off, I'll keep the kids tied up for four weeks. As you see, we are using exactly the methods the bosses used on us. You invented these systems, and it would be a mistake for you to complain if we apply them. So you'd do well to get going at once. You know quite well that the red ants like to amuse themselves at night, and I don't think your kids would enjoy being eaten by them. We've known about this torture for some time. . . . Come on, now, get a move on. Go and find Felipe and whoever else can guide a canoe, and bring those men to me here. Tell them to bring their belongings and their machetes—to bring everything they own."

Celso turned to some of the men near him. "Each one of you

will take his place in a canoe to keep watch on the canoeman. I don't want these swine to play any tricks."

Two minutes later four canoes were on their way downstream.

"Forget that nightmare!" Celso said to Modesta. "Do you know what we're going to do?"

"How can I know if you haven't told me?"

"That's right! Look, then—we're going over to the store, and you're going to pick out the best clothes and the shoes you like best."

When they reached the store, they found Andrés, Santiago, and some of the others there. Andrés was having a heated discussion with the storekeeper.

"Don't waste my time. Give me your pistol and the cartridges. And do it right now!"

"But this pistol is mine. It never belonged to the Montellanos."

"It's all the same. Give it to me!"

"How do you expect me to live without a pistol in this wild place?"

"Exactly the way we've lived up to now. Coming and going at the mercy of the jaguars. And now—get out!"

It was Santiago who said these last words, pointing them up by kicking the storekeeper in the ass.

"Andrés," said Celso, "give Modesta a dress—the prettiest there is."

"With pleasure," Andrés said, laughing. "How many do you want, muchacha? Three, six, ten, twenty—as many as you want! In any case there'll be enough left over even after we dress up all the girls. You'll find everything here—blouses, drawers, slippers. We even have watch chains and earrings. Holy God, you should see what things they had piled up here! And all for those old whores of theirs."

But the storekeeper returned to the charge: "Please, men, you must give me my inventory and my stockbooks. Without them they'll think I've been dishonest."

"Listen to this idiot!" Celso said. "Inventory, stockbooks?

And what else? All the books and inventories will be burned, and all the contracts, too. Accounts, debts, and everything are finished! We've started to clean up, and we'll clean thoroughly. Do you understand? Isn't that right, fellows?"

"We've waited long enough for this moment," Santiago answered, picking up a carton of cigarettes. "To win our freedom we must burn everything. And now that you know it, get out! But get out and stay out, and don't let us catch you hanging around here or I'll tear your hide off!"

"Don't worry, Modesta," Andrés said to the girl. "Pick the best dresses and go behind the counter and get dressed in peace. Don't be afraid. All this belongs to us. We've paid far too much for it. Tomorrow we'll divide it all, and only God knows how many things there are to divide."

"Celso," Santiago broke in, "do you know what we could do? Let's have a look around the huts of all those bastards of artisans. We'll requisition their guns and the ammunition they have. If one of them tries to hide anything, we'll tie a rock around his neck and throw him in the water."

"Agreed. Take a dozen of the fellows with you and collect all the guns you can find. And don't be gentle with those pigs or waste your time arguing with them. If one of them opens his mouth, shut it up right away with your fist."

Juan Méndez, who arrived just then, interrupted: "Right. Because you can be sure that if the bosses were able to take revenge, nobody would lend himself to repression with more cruelty than these artisans, who now smile at us idiotically and offer us whatever they can to save their skins. I know it from experience. When I was a sergeant I saw them take part in suppressing strikes and punishing runaway peons. So let me go with you, Santiago, I'm very fond of pistols."

The group of searchers had just left when Modesta heard herself being called by name. Cándido, the little boy, and the workers from the new camp had just arrived.

"You see, Andrucho!" Celso exclaimed in a triumphant voice. "The canoemen have never traveled so quickly and safely as now. I'm sure that before midnight all our men will be collected here. See how the canoemen push ahead with the torches in their hands so as to arrive more quickly. Now they're really moving!"

"All the men from all the camps are here now," said Pablo, the canoeman, who had come to give an account of his mission. The workman who had been detailed to watch him confirmed what he said.

"Andrés!" Celso called out. "Andrés! I name you supply man. Have you the keys of the shop?"

"Yes."

"Good. Go to the tree where Pablo's children are tied. Untie them, take them to the shop, and give them a piece of chocolate or whatever they want. Also give the little girl a pair of earrings and the boy a jackknife. Then send them to their hut."

"Many thanks, my friend," Pablo said effusively.

"Keep your thanks!" Celso replied dryly. "Take your children and go and look for your wife and the other sneaks like yourself. We're not going to do anything to them, I give you my word. We're getting out of here and we'll leave you the whole encampment for yourselves alone. We'll even leave you provisions in the shop. You'll find enough corn there. And you can keep the oxen. That way there'll be no danger that you'll die of hunger. And fifteen days after we're gone, you can start out too."

Pablo thanked Celso. Martín Trinidad interrupted him: "What our comrade here has just told you concerns your future, canoeman. But I have two words to say about your present. That it must not occur to any of you to try to escape and carry the alarm to Hucutsin or to denounce us to the military authorities. Be clear about what I'm saying! Celso has made you one promise and I'll make you another. If one of you leaves the camp today or tomorrow or even one day before the fifteen days set by Celso, we'll cut the throats of all of you, men, women, and children. I swear it. As for me, I'd drown you right now like sick cats, because you and we aren't and never will be friends. I know exactly what you'd do if things turned out differently. For that reason we'd do well to get rid of you once and for all. Nevertheless, for the time being we'll leave you in peace. Go back to your pals and tell them what you've heard. Explain it to them carefully. Above all, don't forget to tell them what's waiting for them if they don't obey. From now on you're the watchdog of the pack."

16

 "When we leave we must see to it that none of the men is left behind," said Martín Trinidad.

Dawn was breaking, and they had gathered together for a council of war.

"We won't leave a single one of us in the camps. Even if someone resists, we'll take him along by force. Everyone must respond to our call."

It was still very early. The sun was now on the horizon, but its rays did not yet reach them. The embankment was enveloped in a thick mist. The clouds were so low that the river could not be seen even from the slope.

Cándido exclaimed happily: "The devil, but my pigs are pretty!"

"Listen, Cándido, for the moment there are other things more important than that to worry about. Leave your pigs in peace."

"Why, little brother?"

"Don't bother with them. Leave them to the sons of bitches of canoemen."

"But the animals have grown so fat! It would be a pity."

"Then sell them to the artisans. They like fat pigs."

"That's what I'm going to do! It would be impossible to take them with me the whole way back. We'll have to cross the swollen river several times. I don't know how we're going to get home."

Meanwhile the council of war went on deliberating. In the end it was decided that Juan Méndez and Lucio Ortiz should leave with twenty armed men on horseback to visit all the camps within a radius of twelve miles to requisition all arms and bring back all the men—as had been done the preceding evening in the Montellano camps—and that the men and arms should be pooled at the general headquarters, where they would form an imposing rebel force of three or four hundred men. Then they would be able to march on Hucutsin.

On the way to Hucutsin they would destroy every form of authority they met. They would kill all the finqueros, bosses, aristocrats, and white men and would enlist all the peons and workers being held as slaves. They would take Hucutsin by assault, and then all the villages as far as Balún-Canán and Jovel so as to take control of the highway to the state capital, and, once there, the railroad station.

Nobody seemed to ask himself what would happen once everything had been destroyed. Even Martín Trinidad had only a vague picture of what might happen later.

He and the most intelligent of the men—Andrés, Celso, Santiago, Fidel, Matías, and two or three others—explained that if land and liberty were to be won for everybody, they would have, in the first place, to carry the revolution to the farthest corner of the republic.

Only half the men would remain under arms, while the other half would return to the villages to cultivate the fields. Then the ones who had been working on the land would relieve the combatants, who in turn would go back to continue the work at home. The women, children, and old people would take in the harvests.

The first task was to kill off the finqueros, the bosses, and their relatives and children, to sack their strongly fortified domains, to prevent all possibility of a counterrevolution when the rebels should finally have laid down their arms. The difficulty was that the fincas and haciendas were a long distance from the jungle and near the towns and garrisons. To conquer them it was necessary, before anything else, to defeat the rural police, the federal army, and all the defenders of the dictator.

And to win against these it was essential to destroy everything that could be useful to them.

The rebels were not to blame for their ideas of death and destruction. They had never been allowed freedom of expression; every possibility of communication and discussion had been denied them. Nobody had ever come to them to talk about economics or politics. No newspaper had dared criticize the acts of the dictator. They never saw a book that might have given them any conception of how to improve their condition without recourse to destruction and killing.

Those who were not on the side of the dictator had had to listen and keep quiet. The workers, the peasants, all the humble people, had been deprived of every right, and had only one duty: to obey. Blind obedience was inculcated in them by lashings until it became their second nature. Wherever all the rights are in the hands of a few people and the mass has nothing but obligations, not even the right to criticize, the result will inevitably be a reign of chaos.

It was not only the dictator who ruled. The big industrialists, the bankers, the feudal lords, and landowners had the well-defined duty of assuring the dictator's domination. But these lofty personages at times also had something to decree on their own account. They did not do it themselves, but forced their leader, the dictator, to decide in their favor. In this way they could enchain the people, supporting their acts with laws. If they had taken it on themselves to make decisions openly, the people would have soon seen that the leader served only to fill the pockets of the powerful. Dictating to the dictator what he should decree, however, they had their wishes published as being in the interests of the State, and thus they deceived many sincere patriots.

If the workmen had proposed to the bosses an amicable discussion of their differences, the bosses' reply would have been wrapped in lead, for the mere fact of a wage-earner's proposing the examination and discussion of his situation was considered a crime against the State. And it was also a crime to permit workers to submit any proposal. The workers had the sole right to work hard and to obey. That was all. The rest was the business of the dictator and his cronies, to whom the right to give orders and to criticize belonged exclusively.

Thus it was not savagery that drove the Indians to assassination and pillage. Their acts could not be taken as proofs of cruelty, because their adversaries and oppressors were a hundred times more savage and cruel than they when safeguarding their interests.

Fifteen days after the mutiny, the troop was ready to march. In the meantime they had captured two batches of mail. The letters and newspapers that the less ignorant men were able to read brought news that in the north of the republic four regiments had rebelled against the old decoration-covered dictator, always disposed to sing his own heroism. The soldiers were tired of hearing him call himself "the God and savior of the Mexican people."

The newspapers proclaimed that the old man would not be dethroned so easily, because thousands of creatures favored by him and enthusiasts of his reign would prevent it. These enthusiastic creatures would not be defending the old leader but merely their own beans, and when it's a matter of defending one's daily beans one's zeal is greater than when one is fighting in the defense of a dictator. And when a dictator looks for his friends, he often finds empty the corners where his songbirds used to be.

After reading the newspapers Martín Trinidad commented: "All in all, this doesn't interest us. Nobody bothers about us, and nobody's at our side helping us. If we want our land and liberty, then we must fight alone. If when the accounts are totted up, only one of us should remain, and if he should be able to cultivate his field in peace, our struggle will not have been useless. We haven't come into the world to obey, to be submissive and badly treated. No, men, we live on the earth to be free. But if we want to be free, we must win our freedom every day. He who rests on his freedom for one moment will lose it in less than a week. I know what I'm saying, comrades, liberty can be lost the very day you're celebrating it. Don't believe that you'll be free just because your liberty is written in bronze letters and consecrated by law, by the constitution, by whatever you like. Nothing is established for eternity in this world, and all that you can count on is what is renewed and struggled for every day. Never be confident of a chief, no matter who he is, what his promises may be, or where he appears from. Those of you will be free who fight every day for their freedom and entrust it to nobody. We'll all be free if we really have the will to be so, and we'll be slaves if we allow ourselves to be ordered about. Don't worry about your neighbor's freedom; begin by looking after your own first. And if each one of us is a free man, then we'll all be free, and there won't be any more finqueros, politicians, or government toadies able to send us back to the lumber camps."

"You're right, comrade!" exclaimed Celso. "Come. Now we'll march, and there won't be any federal soldiers or rural police who can stop us. We'll set out day after tomorrow."

"Day after tomorrow! Day after tomorrow!" hundreds of voices repeated.

Through the jungle sounded the roar of "Land and liberty!" —words that expressed the unanimous will of the men.

"There's still a lot of work to do before we leave," said Andrés as they were having a meal. "Lots of work, and very important too."

"Ah, and what's that?" asked Celso. "We'll do whatever must be done. We could even finish off that filth we're thinking of leaving here. That way we'd be sure those sons of bitches wouldn't attack us from behind at any moment."

"No, I wasn't thinking of that," said Andrés, and with a nod he indicated the main office. "That's where there's something to be done. We must burn all the papers in there and then scatter the ashes to the wind."

"By my mother, that's a good idea, Andresillo! Just to think we were forgetting about that! We certainly must burn all the account books, contracts, papers, and lists of debts. And as we go through the villages on the way to Hucutsin we must always burn the town records, the civil registry, and all."

"Why?" asked Pedro. "We don't owe anybody anything there."

"Because there's some doubt, and because there may be papers there saying that one of the men owes something. What's more, you ought to know that if you want us to win and stay winners we'll have to burn all the papers. Many revolutions have started and then failed simply because papers weren't burned as they should have been. You can kill all the finqueros you like, but later, one fine day, their sons, their daughters, their cousins, or their uncles will come back to confound us with their documents, registries, and account books. You'll be cultivating your cornfield peacefully with no more thought of the rebellion, and they'll come out of their hiding places, their caves, and they'll come with their police, their rural police and federal troops, carrying thick lawbooks and endless documents to prove to you that the cornfield doesn't belong to you, but to Don Aurelio or Don Cornelio or Doña Rosalía or Doña Regina or to the Devil. And then they'll say: 'Boys, the revolution is over at last! Now we live in order and in peace, now we've returned to civilization. You must respect all these documents, with their signatures and seals, for without seals and signatures civilization is impossible.' "

"By twenty thousand devils! That's how they talk!" Matías exclaimed. "Why, we'd have been working for nothing, and we'd have to begin all over again."

"I'm glad you see the point. Now you know. We must find all those papers, pile them up, and make a bonfire. And when we go into the fincas or the villages, into Hucutsin, Jovel, Balún-Canán, Oschuc and Canancu, Nihich and Achlumal, the first thing we must do is attack the registry and burn the papers, all the papers with seals and signatures—deeds, birth and death and marriage certificates, tax records, everything. . . . Then the heirs won't ever come and stick their papers under our noses. Then nobody will know who he is, what he's called, who was his father, and what his father had. We'll be the only heirs because nobody will be able to prove the contrary. What do we want with birth certificates? We live with a woman we love, we give her our children. That's being married. Do we need papers to prove it? Papers only serve to let someone come along and take away the lands we cultivate. Land belongs to the man who cultivates it, and if it's granted that we cultivate it, that's more than enough proof that it belongs to us."

The men seemed bewitched. They had forgotten their meal and were paying attention only to what Martín Trinidad was saying. They had collected near the group formed by him, Celso, Andrés, Pedro, and Matías. Martín Trinidad's words had a novel sound for them, but they understood easily because the words were simple. They were fully familiar with the omnipotence of documents. It had always been by means of papers covered with writing and seals that it had been proved to them that they had nothing to say, that they must submit and pay.

"What fools we are!" said Santiago. "I never thought a thing about all this, but you're quite right, Martín. We must burn all the papers we can get hold of."

"What I should like to know," said Gabino, one of the cutters, "is where you learned all this. The truth is that you know more than a priest."

"I've read a mountain of books. I've read all that's been written about revolutions, uprisings, and mutinies. I've read all that the people in other countries have done when they became fed up with their exploiters. But with regard to burning papers I have read nothing. That's not written in any book. I discovered that in my own head."

"Man, you're the best of us all!" exclaimed Pedro. "If it's true that you found that in your head, you by yourself know much more than the books!"

"Damn it!" said Celso. "Don't be an idiot! Sure he knows more than can be read in all the books. Don't you know that he's a teacher, a real professor? He has taught hundreds of children in big schools."

Martín Trinidad continued to talk to the men for some time, telling them that the moment had come for them to exchange their life as beasts of burden for an existence befitting their dignity as men.

"It's better to die rebelling than to go on living on one's knees! Land and liberty! Long live the revolution!"

The defiant cry resounded once more through the encampment around the office, and its echoes were heard in every corner of the impenetrable jungle.

All the papers the men found in the main office were burned in the open space outside in the presence of Martín Trinidad and Celso. After that the artisans were forced to turn in the little account books and notebooks, every piece of paper they had, even to pictures of saints, calendars, and snapshots. Not one letter, not one written word, was left in the principal camp. All went up in smoke. Even the ashes were scattered carefully.

Santiago directed this operation. When it was all completed, Martín Trinidad, now referred to by everyone as Professor, expressed his satisfaction.

"Very well done, little brother. Now you know how to set about it in Hucutsin, in the fincas, and in the administrative offices. Our comrades in the paper factories of San Rafael will give us all the paper we want, to write and print all we wish and when we wish."

At nightfall Andrés and two of the other men went around to the various groups telling them to think over well what they intended to carry with them. For the next day there would be a dividing up of everything in the camp store: suits, pants, shirts, jackets, bedclothes, machetes, watch chains, earrings, rings, spools of thread, ribbon, hats, bolts of cloth, huaraches, rope, tobacco, cigarettes, matches, and lanterns. Having enumerated the treasures in the store, Andrés gave them this warning: "Let nobody ask for more than is absolutely indispensable to him. Once our real needs are satisfied, we'll talk about what's left over. Very likely it won't be possible to please everybody. And besides, you must realize that everything we distribute will have to be carried on your backs—the horses, the burros, and the mules will already be overloaded. Don't forget that we must take with us a dozen women and more than twenty children."

Martín Trinidad, "the Professor," added: "Later we'll hold a meeting to settle the order of departure. But seeing that we're talking about things from the store, I'll tell you that the provisions won't be distributed individually. They will be divided among groups, and the groups will take charge of provisions and of preparing food. We'll form the groups at the meeting, but if any of you want to be in a different group from the one you get assigned to, you can arrange to change places with men in another group. Obviously each man will have to carry his share of the provisions for his group, and that's why I advise you not to load yourselves with things that aren't strictly necessary. We might easily be delayed five weeks before reaching the first villages. Don't forget that we're in the middle of the rainy season and that we'll be satisfied if we can cover nine miles a day."

Next day at the council the men asked for very little in the way of stores. Absolute necessities had been divided during the first days of the rebellion. It struck Andrés that the men had not asked for as much as possible. Perhaps they did not want too much to carry. That was almost certainly the explanation: their moderation was not the result of any moral scruples.

There was one thing that seemed curious to Andrés. Many of the workers went about dressed in rags, and even the simplest cotton shirt in the store should have tempted them. Nevertheless none of them had asked for one. Curious, Andrés asked some of them why. One man replied: "Bah! By the time we get out of the jungle all our clothes will be rags, new ones just the same as old."

Another said: "Do you want me to put on a new shirt to blow up in? Look—when I meet the rural police I'll go for them like a madman. If they get me I won't need a shirt. If they don't get me that'll be beause I've cracked open at least six of those dogs, and then I can pick up all I want in the way of shirts, pants, and boots. And best of all I'll have a good gun and plenty of bullets. So why do you want me to carry around what's in the store? For the time being I've got lots of much more important things to think about than bothering about bargains in the store. As long as my rags still keep my ass well covered I don't have to worry. When I want to renew my wardrobe, the rural police and federal soldiers will be there to wait on me. Get it, Andresillo?"

For three days the artisans' women worked at grinding the limed cornmeal, preparing the dough, and making the tortillas, making bean paste, and getting everything ready for the march. Every man carried at least a *sontle* of tortillas—that is, four hundred of them. That was little enough, for the tortillas were very light and not very filling.

The artisans' women did not like acting as cooks for the workmen. They felt their dignity wounded. Santiago had overheard one of them say angrily but quietly: "How can we have fallen so low that we have to make tortillas for those lousy Chamula pigs? It's a shame that we have to be servants to those Chamulas, who don't even know how to talk like Christians!"

Santiago had waited until the woman's rancor had run out. When she stopped talking, he went up to the group from which her voice had come. "Say, you animals, what are you good for? I ask myself constantly: 'Why have we let them live?' "

On seeing Santiago appear, the women were shaken with terror, having realized immediately that he had overheard their words.

"God damn it!" Santiago went on, "we've done enough for you, too, coming back worn out by the day's labor and still having to cut wood for you, carry water for you, fix the roofs of your lairs—all that when we were dying of weariness. And then, you swarm of bitches, did one of you open your trap to say you were sorry for us? Answer me! Dare to tell me any lies and I'll shove them down your throats with a punch in the face. Now get to work, and right away! Let's see—give me one of those tortillas so that I can see that they're properly made, and if they're not you can fix them up. I'll be back within three hours, you old sows, and each one of you had better have at least ten *sontles* of tortillas ready if you don't want me to beat your hides and pull out your hair. Now get to work and keep your mouths shut!"

"But, sir," one of the women replied timidly, "you know that it takes many hours to prepare the corn. Then we have to grind it, and even if we throw in lots of lime I don't think—"

"I don't give a damn! Let's see how you manage it. I'll give you one hour extra. If the tortillas aren't all ready when I come back, I'll turn you all over and beat you thoroughly. Didn't we often have to do three days' work in one? And when we couldn't, they whipped us and hanged us. And when that happened did any of you say to the bosses: 'Señor, the poor men can't get that work done'? No! And not only that! You enjoyed it and said: 'Give it to them good, those Chamula swine!' "

"I never said anything like that," the blacksmith's wife said.

"Perhaps you didn't, but when others said it you never came out with a word of protest. Well, that's enough chatter. Get busy!"

The women set about the tasks, calling even their children to help them. Santiago walked away. He had no intention of returning in four hours, for he knew that whatever the women did they could not carry out his order.

It went harder with the artisans, the husbands of these women. Matías and Fidel gave them no chance to breathe and told them very clearly what they thought of them. They had to repair saddles, fill water jars, make rope, cut leather straps, and take care of the animals, treating their sores and feeding them. To prepare the departure of so numerous a caravan demanded work without rest, and the men were well acquainted with means of getting action from their employees. They had only to remember how the artisans had treated them. All the same, the workmen were more humane. Obedience was the watchword, but there were no whippings or hangings, nothing much more than a few ribs caressed by the impatient fist of some worker.

In making the artisans work, the men learned something of which until then they had been unaware: that they themselves were capable of giving orders, that they were doing it and doing it well. Until that moment they had believed that in order to know how to command, it was essential to be born a man with light skin or a Spaniard. Now they saw that giving orders was something more simple. And if giving orders to the favorites of the powerful was easy, why shouldn't governing be easy too? Certainly, to govern was not merely to give orders, and perhaps that was why most dictators were such poor devils. Give orders? Anybody can do that, even the most backward Indian. How often an idiot has become a dictator! For the time being, the workers still had a long way to go before they could try their gifts for governing. The Professor told them: "Learn to behave well while we're here. Later, when we've left the jungle, when we can't be sure which is the right side and which is the left, it will be more difficult. Here in the jungle if we meet an army of federal soldiers and rural police, they couldn't hurt us. We'd finish them off in a breath. But you know perfectly well that those sons of bitches will never come looking for us. They'll wait for us in the fincas and the villages. Then we'll have to fight for the revolution, and we won't do it just with words. Revolutions aren't won by words alone. We who are oppressed must fight bitterly to make our resolutions triumph. Whoever tells you anything else merely wants to put you to sleep. He's surely an ally of the enemy, a stool pigeon of the tyrants. Don't forget that, men! Don't ever forget it!"

17

The mass of rebels was divided into eight groups, to which Juan Méndez gave the name "companies." He had been selected as "General" of the entire operation because of his military background. As a sergeant he had more than once had occasion to direct the drill of a group of soldiers whose officer had either drunk himself to insensibility or was too lazy to get out of bed in the morning and had delegated his authority.

Méndez took command of the first company. His battalion companion, Corporal Ortiz, took command of the eighth and last, the one that was to act as rear guard during the march. The Professor was given the title of Supreme Chief of the forces. Andrés was made quartermaster. Matías, Fidel, and Cirilo were to supervise transportation and weapons.

Juan Méndez took Celso as his chief of staff, but Celso gave that fact no importance. He said: "Chevrons? Oof, they make me laugh! I'll be in the front rank next to the chief when the music starts. Then I'll put on my first uniform. They gave me a pistol, but I really have more confidence in my machete."

"As you like, comrade," Méndez replied. "We'll talk about it again later, after the first combat—if we come out alive."

Very few of the men were armed. Pistols were scarce, rifles even more so, and some of the latter were so old that they were breech-loaders. Six of these had been taken from the artisans. The revolvers had been collected by force from the storekeepers and were of the same poor quality. They had never been fired, and their chief value was to frighten. On the other hand, the machetes and axes were all well sharpened. No profound understanding was required to reach the conclusion that the armament of the troop was virtually nonexistent.

When one took into account that the armament of the rural police and the state police devoted to the dictator was considerable, and that furthermore they could count on a good supply of ammunition, one could well consider the march of the rebels against such forces as suicide. The regular soldiers did not carry more than a rifle or a carbine each, but when they separated into small groups they set out armed with one machine gun to each fifty men. With these little toys, bought from the best factories in the United States, they had already given numerous proofs of their skill, suppressing strikes and a considerable number of peasant uprisings. When fifty rural police met five hundred rebels, the result was always more or less as follows: among the soldiers about three men were killed and five wounded, whereas among the rebels four hundred and fifty were killed and none wounded. The remaining fifty owed their lives to very rapid flight into the mountains or the jungle.

The only men in the troop who knew the exact conditions of the struggle that had now been undertaken were the "Professor," the "General," and the "Colonel." The Colonel was Lucio Ortiz, promoted to this rank by decision of Juan Méndez. None of these three made any mystery of what he knew about the possible results of the unequal combat that would take place if the troop of mahogany-workers should meet a column, or even just a patrol, of rural police. Again and again, at night around the campfires, they had explained to the men in detail what the situation was. But neither those who explained nor those who listened to the explanations wavered the slightest in their determination. They had suffered so much, they had borne so much, they had stored up so much rancor and hatred in their hearts, that the struggle, whatever the result might be, seemed to them the only moral comfort possible. To them the idea of coming out the losers was inconceivable. They would win, or they would lose their lives: they saw no other alternative. Their existence had been so miserable, so empty, that to die with the satisfaction of having rebelled seemed to them a thousand times preferable to taking refuge in the jungle in flight from the enemy. Expressing himself like this, Celso was giving voice not merely to his own opinion, but also to that of all the men. They were all convinced that the portals of paradise would open to them if before they died they accounted for five or six federal soldiers.

This fierce hatred of the dictator and his toadies was not a feeling limited to the oppressed. It could be taken for granted that three-quarters of the Mexican people harbored it. This hatred was what was carrying the revolutionary hurricane across the entire country. To it could be attributed the acts of harshness, the determination of the men neither to ask for mercy nor to grant it. No prisoners were taken: the defeated who could not or would not flee were killed. No wounded men remained on the battlefields. The women of the revolutionaries, accompanying their men into combat, scoured the battlefield like furies and finished off the enemy wounded with their kitchen knives. The cause of this savagery was the dictatorship and nothing but the dictatorship. What happened here was what always happens: when the dikes break, the blind forces of nature carry away without pity whatever lies in their path.

Nevertheless, Juan Méndez felt obliged to explain again and again, as clearly as possible, what the situation was. He would say: "If our first company meets two hundred federals, not one of us will come out alive. Not one of us will have time even to aim a pistol—which, in any case, very few of you know how to manage—before a rain of bullets will be falling on us. And then what will we do?"

"What'll we do?" Matías replied once. "Well, I'll tell you, Juanito! If two hundred men fall on us, two hundred victims will be offering themselves to us. And it would be a pity if only two hundred appeared, because the more who face us, the more we'll kill. Right now, if you like, all of you can drop out before things get serious. We'll go ahead and we'll never turn back."

"Neither will I turn back. I'm to lead the fight. All I want is for you to realize what's going to happen to us. I know by experience, and you don't."

"That's possible," Fidel answered. "But then, you used to be a military man. We're mahogany-workers, and now you're one too. And that's not the same as being a soldier. Any idiot can be a soldier! But to be a revolutionary you have to have qualities that are developed only in the wombs of certain women. My mother was one of them."

"Well, to change the subject, Santiago is right: we ought to do away with those artisans. That breed isn't worth a shit!"

A general really acquainted with military matters would have viewed the projected march with dread. He would have foreseen so many difficulties that he would have said: "The devil! With the means at my disposition I'll have lost half of my army in six miles." He would have called together his general staff and tried to overhaul his plans. But Juan Méndez was a revolutionary general who had never even conceived the idea of strategy, of whose very name he was ignorant. "Forward, march!" And his army marched as best it could.

During the dry season an expedition like this, with this number of men and beasts of burden, would have been so complicated that no contractor would have dared to undertake it. In the height of the rainy season it was positive madness.

If they had been reasoning men they would never have rebelled. Uprisings, mutinies, revolutions, are always irrational in themselves, because they come to disturb the agreeable somnolence that goes by the names of peace and order. The men were proving that they were not just simple strikers but authentic revolutionaries, because real revolution does not recognize obstacles. The true rebel, he who feels rebellion down to the last fiber of his being, who leaps over an obstacle even with his last breath, always marches forward—and he who never interrupts his onward march has won three-quarters of the game. Had the men been told that they would have to march for a week through the infernal regions, they would have answered:

"What does it matter? We'll end by getting out of there. And when we get out, we'll be better revolutionaries than before we went in."

The infernal regions certainly awaited them, not for one week, but for three weeks that would seem endless.

Even the slightly raised trails, which usually escape flooding, had become transformed into vast swamps. Rain poured down every three or four hours. The clouds became rivers, and the water fell with such violence as to dig out pools in the forest clearings. Great branches were broken from the trees, and footpaths were converted into streams. Big rocks were swept along by the raging floods and flung against the forest giants, smashing against their trunks and overturning them. When the rain momentarily let up, the sun beat down again on the soaking undergrowth, from which it drew so much steamy vapor that the whole forest became a steam bath in which it was difficult to breathe. When the tops of the trees and the foliage covering the few open spaces began to be dry again, a fine rain would start falling, lasting about ten minutes as the prelude to another storm, another deluge, accompanied by thunder and lightning.

For inexperienced people to have undertaken a long march through the forest in the rainy season would have been a reckless adventure; but for these men, who knew perfectly all the dangers that such a march implied, the mere setting out was proof that they had made up their minds to face the worst in order to carry through implacably to its end the revolution they had begun.

During one of the discussions, one of the rebels had proposed that they should wait until the rains ended.

The Professor had replied: "Certainly we could wait, but there are many others who can't, and they are the peons of the fincas, who want to be free as much as we do, and who want, like us and with us, to march to fight for the liberty of their brothers."

After a time what tormented them was no longer the burning desire to return to their land and their homes. That desire did not leave them, but now a new desire stirred their hearts.

The uprising was a fact, and all the men working in the jungle had joined the first rebels. Every day new groups were arriving to swell their ranks, and this multitude had almost forgotten about the longed-for return home. Now they thought of nothing but the rebellion against the bosses and complete liberation.

More and more they were becoming convinced that if the rebellion did not embrace all their brothers in misery, whatever liberty they won would endure for a short time only. To this conviction, too, they had been led thanks to the able arguments of the Professor.

He had told them a thousand times: "If we rebel and just return afterwards to cultivate our cornfields and take care of our children, we'll bring in one harvest—if we're lucky. But just one and no more. Before we know it, we'll have the rural police and federals on our necks dragging us back here again to be more slaves than before—and forever. That's why our revolution must be powerful and complete. That's why we must either bring the federals and the rural police over to our side or eliminate them. We must not do things by halves or believe in promises. As soon as we fall on the first fincas and the first villages, they will begin to promise us the sky. We must not let ourselves be taken in, because all those promises will be dictated by fear. Everything they'll promise will have absolutely no value if we do not make a complete revolution and carry it to the farthest corner of our land."

"Bravo, Professor! You're right, and we'll follow your advice."

And so it was gradually and on their own initiative that the men had given a new meaning to their rebellion. The desire to return home had given place to the more ardent desire to achieve a complete victory.

Even Andrés and Celso, who, to begin with, had thought only of returning to see their family and friends, now thought of that only occasionally.

"When it comes down to that, they can wait. Don't you think so, Celso?"

"You're right about that, Andresillo. In my house nobody expects to see me back before four years at the earliest. So they will wait. It's better that they should wait a year longer rather than that we should have to start over again. The devil! I'm certain that we'll return home to stay and that we won't have to live in perpetual fear that one day they'll compel us to leave again."

"That's it, Celso. That's what we'll do. Land and liberty—or death!"

18

⚙

⚙   Every day groups of new rebels were arriving from the most remote camps, some of them consisting of five men, others of only three. These men had a really savage appearance. They had run away from their camps a long time before, but had been prevented from returning to their homes by fear of being caught along the trails by some caravan or some contractor who would have reported them. Furthermore, on the paths it would have been easy for pursuing foremen to catch them and force them to return to their camps. Even if, by any chance, they had succeeded in reaching their ranch or village, they would have been seized by the authorities.

Recognizing their fate, the fugitives had abandoned the idea of returning home. They had fled from the camps to escape inhuman treatment and had kept away from trails and roads, living beyond the borders of the law in the unconquerable depths of the jungle. They had lived in caves or in holes dug in the ground, or on the meshed branches of trees covered with dense foliage. Very few of them had gone to the trouble of building even a lean-to. With stones and arrows, taking advantage of primitive slings and bows, they had hunted the few animals whose meat had sustained them. If they lacked something absolutely indispensable—a pinch of salt or a steel arrow-tip—they had stealthily crept by night to one of the camp stores and had stolen what they had to have. Several times the workers in the camps had been blamed for these robberies committed by fugitives and had received the consequent punishment. When the fugitives had not been able to reach one of the camps, they had managed to get what they lacked, by consent or by force, from men they encountered working in the forest. Most often the workers, if they were carrying with them what was wanted, helped out the fugitives, whom they called "the Wild Men."

When the number of Wild Men grew large, the proprietors of the camps in whose vicinity they lived would send five or six foremen to hunt them as if dealing with ferocious beasts. The intention was not to capture them, notwithstanding the constant shortage of labor in the camps. The Wild Men were shot on sight. The hunt was organized with great care, and the hunters took a fine pack of hounds with them to track down the prizes. It was not a mere love of sport or a desire to prevent depredations which motivated these hunts. No, they were trying to prevent others from following the example of the fugitives and thus increasing the number of deserters who left open accounts unpaid.

The Wild Men had no definite plans—only a vague hope that they might be forgotten at the end of a year or two and thus be able to return to their homes. They could have tried to find work elsewhere, but in any lumber camp, hacienda, or coffee finca they would have met the same fate, that of being reduced to servitude and oppressed to the point of being denied the least right to discuss their own living and working conditions.

One other possibility remained to them, provided they could get out of the jungle without being seized: that of joining some group of independent Indians. But only one out of one hundred of them was able to do this. And afterwards, if they succeeded in becoming part of a group belonging to their own tribe, they were immediately recognized. The news sped from mouth to mouth until it reached the rural police, who caught them and later returned them to the contractors. If they took refuge with a strange tribe, they were regarded with suspicion. Almost always they did not know the tribal language, and if they did not have the good luck to marry and thus become part of a family, there was nothing for them to do: they would not be given either land or seeds, and there are no wage-earners among the tribes.

But this situation arose rarely. In most cases the Wild Men would die before being able to get out of the jungle, because the life they lived there concealed dangers a hundred times greater than those menacing the workers in the lumber camps. They were threatened by fever, jaguars, mountain lions, and snakes, any one of which might take pity on them and release them from their painful existence. All the jungle workers knew perfectly well what sort of fate was in store for Wild Men, and it was precisely the terror of such a life that kept them in the camps. Had the Wild Men's existence been a pleasant one, not a single man would have remained in the camps. Only the most resolute, those changed into wild beings by the ferocity of some threatened punishment, had the courage to run away.

Among the groups of rebels who had joined the men of La Armonía after the killing of the Montellanos and their foremen were a dozen Wild Men. Some of them had heard of the rising from old fellow-workers. Others, surprised to see the workers suddenly abandon a whole district, leaving logs where they had fallen and their work unfinished, used all their astuteness and, taking endless precautions, slipped up to one of the offices. There they sometimes met men preparing to leave or came upon the corpses of foremen, eloquent explanations of what had happened.

La Armonía was one of the most important groups of camps of the region, and furthermore was situated right on the roads that led to the big river. It was natural, therefore, for the Wild Men to go to La Armonía.

When they arrived, none of the rebels asked them questions. They were received as brothers. They met men they knew, former working companions in the camps from which they had fled, friends who welcomed them happily as forerunners of the rebellion. The fact that they had had the courage to run away and live beyond the power of the oppressive laws testified sufficiently to their revolutionary spirit.

Three of these Wild Men—Onofre, Nabor, and Isaías—had arrived on the evening of the departure. After recognizing and greeting some friends and brothers of their own tribes, they wandered around in the hope of finding others they knew. During their wanderings they came to the huts where the artisans were held as carefully guarded prisoners. They stopped to chat with the guards, who offered them cigarettes, and they asked: "Why in hell are you looking after those spies?"

"So that they don't get away and go to denounce us."

"Who gave you orders to watch them?" Onofre asked.

"The Professor."

"What idiots you are!" replied Nabor. "If I were on guard here, my watch wouldn't last long. There's a better and surer way of taking care of these bastards, and that's to send them once and for all where they couldn't do any more damage."

During this conversation Isaías had ambled around the huts, which, having no doors, revealed many artisans squatting on the ground playing cards, while others, stretched full length on the earth outside, snored peacefully. Others, their heads in their women's laps, were having themselves deloused. Some of the other women were cooking.

Isaías, casting his eyes over this spectacle, suddenly uttered a loud cry of surprise: "Hey! Come here, quick! Look who's over there, of all people!"

His two companions ran to where he stood.

"Well, I'm damned! Who'd have believed it? Our little friends El Poncho and La Ficha!"

The men in charge of the prisoners came forward full of curiosity. "Do you know them, little brothers?"

Onofre laughed ironically. "Oh yes, we know them. These sons of bitches are the cruelest, most ferocious ass-kissers, the most contemptible abortions, that hell ever rejected. They're the ones to whom we owe having become Wild Men. They're the ones who, helped by a pack of others like them, tried to hunt us down in the forest. These swine are more bloodthirsty than animals, more repulsive than snakes. Even a jaguar might feel the pity they lack. Hey! Poncho, Ficha—come here!"

The two whose names had been called raised their heads

from the game of cards they were playing with other artisans. When they recognized the Wild Men, they turned pale, and the cards fell from their hands.

"Well now," Onofre went on, "you don't seem to be badly off here. You can still pass the time sitting around with your old women and your kids, getting fat as pigs."

El Poncho tried to smile and replied in a scared voice: "Not so fat."

"We've thought for a long time that you were cultivating your cornfields and had got married," added La Ficha, also trying to smile and not succeeding.

The three men turned their backs on the two foremen and returned to the camp, followed by some of the sentries.

"How long have those two foremen been at La Armonía?" inquired Isaías.

"I don't know. I don't belong at La Armonía—I'm from Palo Quemado. Are they foremen?"

"The most cruel and brutal you could find anywhere."

"We killed all our foremen, and the men of La Armonía did the same. If those men are foremen they shouldn't be here."

Nabor let himself go, cursing with the usual energy of cart-drivers, and when he felt satisfied he added: "God damn it! What has happened to you? You act like old women—yes, like old gossips! With you we won't get far. We need to join up with real rebels, not with old women. But even the most stupid old women wouldn't think of fattening torturers and protecting their asses so that the jaguars won't eat them." Then, changing the tone of his voice, he asked the guards: "What time do you have to go to supper?"

"We ought to be eating now. We're very hungry. But we have to wait to be relieved."

"Relief be damned! Who knows what time the relief will come?" said Isaías, laughing. "Go off now and take the time to fill your bellies till they burst. You don't have to die of hunger —we'll take your places here."

The men did not wait for Isaías's offer to be repeated.

"All right, then, we'll leave them with you. The truth is that we're fed up looking after those spies, seeing them drinking their paunches full and making love to their old women and passing the time playing cards for beans and tobacco."

"You're not joking? Tobacco and liquor for these pigs? They never gave us a leaf of tobacco! How about you?"

"Give us anything? Bah! And if you want me to tell you something, comrades, I'll say that it'd be better to finish off all these vermin completely. We ought to treat them exactly as we treated the foremen. What's bad is that it's not us who give orders here. And if the Professor, Andrés, and Celso give orders, we have to obey them."

"Good!" said Isaías. "Go and eat in peace, brother. Hurry! Don't let the others eat it all up! They've roasted a brown deer and two boars. Enjoy them. Don't hurry. We'll take charge of the guarding here. We won't let a single one escape. Tell the General to send our relief at ten o'clock."

"All right, then," said the men. "We'll tell the General that you're on guard. After all, what does it matter to him who looks after them? I think to him it's all the same."

"Leave us your machetes, comrades."

"Sure. Take them. We'll ask for new ones at the store. Why don't you have any? Have you just arrived?"

"Yes. We've been Wild Men for six months. When we ran away, we took our machetes with us, but one got broken, another fell into a swamp and we couldn't get it out, and the last one got left behind the day when the foremen set the pack of dogs on us and left us no time to pick it up. We might have been able to steal a machete from some of the workers, but you know that the poor devils would have had to pay for it. And when we decided to raid a store, we found that the rebellion had broken out."

"You'll find everything you want here, fellows. You only have to ask for it. If you want tobacco, we'll leave you ours. When we get back to the store, we'll get more."

The relief appeared at ten o'clock as had been agreed. The men who arrived to act as guards found the three Wild Men squatting around the fire.

"Everything looks very peaceful here," one of the new arrivals remarked. "As a rule you can hear them bawling and grunting, heated up with alcohol. They still have lots of bottles buried and hidden, enough for them all to get drunk—men, women, and children. The Professor has advised us to let them stupefy themselves with alcohol."

"Don't worry, friends," said Isaías. "Tonight they've drunk more than a barrel, and they're so full, so bloated, that they won't say a word. Your watch will be easy. You can even go to sleep if you feel like it. Not a single one of them will escape. You can be sure of that. Good night, comrades!"

"Good night."

The watch was changed three times more before daybreak. The men did not know each other, nor did they try to find out who came to take their places. What was important was that the watch be kept.

When the first rays of the sun began to shine, one of the new guards observed: "God damn it! They must have been fixed right last night. Not one of them is moving a finger."

Then he approached one of the huts and looked into it from behind a tree trunk. He shouted: "Hey, guys! Come here! The aguardiente they drank last night was as red as a tomato."

"They killed them all, even the kids!"

"Let's look in the other huts."

In the other huts the spectacle was the same: men, women, and children lying stretched out among bottles, splashed with red. It was impossible to mistake what had happened.

One of the men rushed off to the main camp to report what had taken place.

The General, the Professor, the Colonel, Celso, Andrés, Matías, Fidel, Santiago, Cirilo, Pedro, Valentín, Sixto, and some other rebel chiefs were seated in a group discussing the final details of the departure of the first company, which was due to set out before eight o'clock.

The guard gave an account of what had happened in the artisans' huts.

"Are you quite sure of what you say?" asked the Professor.

"Absolutely sure. Not one of them is alive."

"God be thanked that the filth is finished," Celso commented.

"It wasn't necessary to destroy them," said Andrés. "They weren't doing us any harm, and they could have been allowed to live."

"No need to think about the matter," Matías answered. "It's all over. What use would that scum be?"

"You're right, little brother. Now we don't have to watch them and let them grow fat. The truth is that this business of carrying a crowd of spies on our shoulders was not pleasant."

The Professor raised his hand and said: "Why go on talking about it? They were smashed like lice, and they deserved what they got." Then, looking around at his helpers, he added, speaking to Fidel: "Take a dozen of the men and set fire to all the huts. Everything must burn. Nothing must remain if we don't want the stench to be unbearable by noon. And when everything is reduced to ashes, throw a few shovels of earth over them."

19

Of course, the first company was not ready to set out at the hour agreed on. In those remote regions no caravan has ever been ready to march at the hour fixed in advance. This is not the fault of the guides or the organizers of the group but of a thousand incidents and uncontrollable mishaps that always upset even the most carefully prepared plans. In the jungle, as in deserts far from civilization, even the most elaborately constructed plans are useless. It has been decided, for example, that ten mules will be required for the group. The mules are all ready the evening before, but on the following morning three that have broken loose during the night are missing. As there are no walls or fences, it is not easy to find them. If they are tethered securely, the animals cannot look for food or escape from the attacks of wild animals. On the eve of leaving, all the harnesses, the saddles, and the other trappings are in perfect condition, but during the night voracious rats gnaw leather straps through. In the evening the drivers and guides are in perfect health, but during the night a scorpion or a snake bites one of them in the foot, and two or three others suffer an attack of malaria.

On the eve of departure the sun is still shining splendidly, and there is not a cloud in the sky. But suddenly, in the middle of the night, a cloudburst lets loose, inundating paths and tracks, soaking packs, boxes, and harnesses. The night before, everything is well packed, but at the moment when loading is about to begin, it becomes clear that some repacking is required, because the cases weigh more than they should.

At a council of war the preceding afternoon it had been decided that the departures of the groups would be spaced at intervals of one day. Even in the dry season it would have been difficult to lead a numerous caravan through the forest, but in the height of the rainy season it had become a gigantic undertaking.

The troop, which had been increasing without interruption, now consisted of five hundred men and more than one hundred and fifty pack animals—mules, horses, and burros.

To the animals belonging to La Armonía had been added those of the camps formerly administered by Don Acacio and those the men of neighboring camps had brought in with them.

It had been decided to abandon the oxen, which could find sufficient pasturage to keep them alive until the day when they themselves would be able to move along the paths back to the fincas whence they had come. They would know how to follow the right road without any difficulty.

Furthermore, their number was reduced every day because the men sacrificed two or three of them daily to prepare reserve rations. It was Andrés who had thought of taking this precaution. The meat was cut into strips and then dried and salted, producing big enough quantities of dried beef to last for the entire journey.

The whole group was divided into small sections of about fifty or sixty men, each of which was assigned a drove of fifteen animals. Only the first company would consist of eighty men and would take twenty animals, all mules and horses. This company would be the advance guard in charge of preparing encampments for the night. The encampments would be in the full jungle, in an open place between a river and the slopes of a hill, or sometimes even in the bottom of a gorge.

The leaders always had to bear in mind that the animals required pasturage for food and that it might not always be possible to find enough in any one place for one hundred or one hundred and fifty animals at a time. But during the rainy season the grass grows up again with extraordinary speed, even between the departure of one company and the arrival of another, often in less than twenty-four hours. And should there not be enough, all they had to do was press a short way ahead into the undergrowth to find the fodder needed. This, after all, was a minor difficulty. It was the state of the softened soil, converted into mud by the rains, that made it necessary to divide the troop into small groups separated from one another by an interval of one day's march.

The first hundred men would be able, with great difficulty, to make slow progress. But the second would begin to sink in the tracks left by the first, to slide on the sloping places, dragging after them mounds of mud, branches broken from the trees, and loose roots and rocks. For the third group the tracks and paths would be impassable. On the other hand, if the troop was divided into small groups, their tracks would not be so deep and the earth would have time to become firm again in the space of twenty-four hours. The rains certainly would continue without a break, but on sloping paths the water would run off quickly, which could not happen if hundreds of feet sank into the muck, starting erosion that would convert the paths into arroyos.

By the plan finally chosen, the first company would have already made twelve days' progress by the time the last would be ready to leave the main camp.

As soon as the first village outside the jungle was reached, the companies would halt to await the arrival of all the others, until the whole troop was reunited in one place. The first care of those marching in front would be to see that nobody from the village should run to give the alarm to the finqueros established on the road to Hucutsin or Achlumal or to the rural police or federal soldiers of the nearby garrisons. Sooner or later they would not be able to avoid meeting armed forces. But the rebels wanted to reach Hucutsin or Achlumal before confronting soldiers or the police for the first time.

According to the season and the nature of the terrain, mounted caravans usually covered between four and nine leagues daily—that is, from ten to twenty miles. A day in which nine leagues were covered was a heavy one, possible only with a light load. The average day's journey was seven leagues in normal times, and that required tremendous effort.

On the first day out, the leading company could advance only three leagues, and when the men reached the first possible camping place they realized the hardships and penalties in store for them in this undertaking. On this first day they had plowed ahead without a halt, sinking into the mire up to their knees.

Naturally, the other companies were unable to cover even the three leagues achieved by the first.

The General had ordered that each of the companies should spend the night in the encampment prepared by the first. But when they realized that the other companies could not maintain the pace of the first, they deliberated, and the General, in agreement with them, ordered the march of the first company reduced to three hours only. Clearly they could not stop exactly at the end of three hours, because it was essential that they stop in a place suitable for the preparation of an encampment, that it supply drinkable water and pasturage for the animals.

Later they were able to see that the idea of dividing the march, not into leagues, but into hours was really magnificent. In this way the first company had enough time and could throw up good shelters for the night. Moreover, men and animals arrived at the encampment without weariness.

Clearly, only the first company could enjoy this advantage, but on it depended the success of the entire expedition. Three hours' march for the first company without regard to the amount of ground covered was a small matter. For the companies following it, three hours represented the distance to be covered between one encampment and the next. No doubt the three hours would become four for the companies following the first, and the General therefore took care that the three hours should be shortened rather than prolonged. Despite this precaution, the last company had to struggle for eight or nine hours with obstacles along the way in order to get from one encampment to another.

Every five days the whole army rested. Men and animals

could recoup their strength, at the same time giving the paths and tracks time to harden a little, thus making passage across them less painful.

Full advantage was taken of this day of rest. Each company sent two men forward and two back to establish contact with the company ahead and the one in its rear, so that the whole troop could be aware of what was happening.

Not even the most experienced general could have worked as assuredly as this simple, almost unlettered sergeant, who had such officers as the Professor, and such men as Celso, Andrés, Santiago, and Matías, uneducated and lowly Indian boys, born rebels with no personal ambition but that of carrying to triumph the idea of liberty and justice as they conceived it—without compromise or surrender. They wanted that idea carried through whole and complete, and to see it succeed they marched at the head of their men without stopping to consider obstacles. "We want land and liberty." That, and nothing else, was their program.

"We want land and liberty, and if we want that, we have to go and look for it where it is to be found and then fight for it every day to preserve it. We don't need anything else. If we have land and liberty we shall have all that man needs in this world, because it is in them that love is to be found."

The program was so simple, so just, and so pure that the Professor had no need to deliver long speeches to convince the men of its wisdom. He had no need to draw up long statutes or give explanations or recommend to the men the reading of treatises on political economy to make them understand that any man, however stupid he is, will be able to take over the governing of a people, provided he is equipped with machine guns and takes care to see that others have none.

The route that the column followed was crisscrossed by rivers and streams whose overflowing waters had spread out over their submerged banks. Also, it was necessary to go around the many lakes of the region. Some of these lakes were shut in between two mountains where the upper paths were generally found in good condition, because the waters did not stagnate there, and the moisture in the ground was evaporated quickly by the first rays of the sun.

At times the upper paths descended to join one that bordered a lake, so that during the rainy season it was necessary to wade long distances, sinking into muck up to the waist, to find water fit for drinking. This was the one hazard that could most easily upset the well-laid plans of the rebel general staff.

When, at the end of the sixth day, the first company reached the edge of Lake Santa Lucina, the General went up to join the vanguard, of which Celso and Santiago formed part.

"This looks God-damned bad," he said.

"Look whom you're telling that to, General," Celso answered, laughing, though submerged up to his thighs.

"This is the first time our revolutionary march has been halted."

"It's also the first battle we have to fight," added Santiago, who, a few yards from Celso, was struggling against the current of mud.

"I'm afraid," the General said, "that we'll have to wait here for a whole week." Then, having looked around carefully, he reflected some seconds and added: "We might have to stay here three months, until not a drop of water falls."

Celso withdrew slowly until he succeeded in planting his feet on more solid ground.

The General ordered the company to halt and await new orders. Then he sent a few men to find a path that would take them farther from the lake and be more practicable but still would not lead them in the wrong direction. At the end of two hours he received the first report from the scouts: within a radius of three miles there was nothing but swamps and seas of mud.

"It was to be expected," Celso observed. "Otherwise the caravans that follow this route every year would have found other routes."

"That's true," said the General, "but just the same we have to get out of here, find another road. Maybe there's one behind that chain of mountains. That will mean a detour of two or three days, and perhaps that's why the drivers, who always want to save time, haven't looked for it. But we can allow ourselves this detour. We'll arrive on time anyhow, because the fincas we want to conquer, with their land and liberty, won't get away from us because of the delay."

The Professor came slowly up to the group, saying: "Clearly the land won't escape—but liberty? If we want land and liberty, not only must we arrive at the right moment, but we must also arrive together. If we don't, we'll be exterminated. We can win only in a mass, by means of the mass, and with the mass; because nothing will be worth anything if we are not in mass. Let's take a man in the group, any man—Celso or Santiago, for example. Working in isolation, you'd lack the necessary education, the brain trained in the right way to prevent any scribbler in a municipal registry, any shopkeeper, however stupid, from doing whatever he likes with even a hundred of you because of your ignorance, because you don't even know how to read and write. That's why they have always been able to deceive and rob you. But when we work together in a mass, things are different. Then a thousand heads and two thousand vigorous arms make up a superior force. That is why I've been telling you that freedom can evade us easily if we don't form a large mass and if we don't all arrive at the same time. The strongest lion is helpless in the face of ten thousand ants, who can force him to abandon his prey. We are the ants, and the owners are the lions."

"All you say is well said, Professor. But what matters most now is to find a route by which we can get ahead. We can't go back to the camp and wait two months or more until the rains stop and the paths dry up. We've got to continue on our way in order to get there soon and stir up the peons. When they realize our strength and see our weapons, they'll wake up. Well, then—forward!"

It was truly a titanic task to discover a new road through the submerged jungle. They had to make a detour of three miles to the north, driving through virgin undergrowth.

So many hours of the hardest work had been required by the

first company that this afternoon, for the first time since they had set out, the second company arrived in time to camp with the first. But as the original plan of marching separately had to be followed, the second company had to remain in camp three hours the next morning after the first again set out.

The companies that followed the first had no reason to consider themselves favored. Even though the first had the heavy task of finding a place where potable water could be obtained and which at the same time was free of mud so that they could set up the huts of the camp, the other companies had to fight against the state in which those preceding them had left the paths and tracks. Again and again they had to march, without losing their way, many yards above or below the path in order not to sink up to their necks in the muck.

This first fight with the elements was not the only one. The flooding river and arroyos they had to cross caused considerable losses in the little rebel army.

When at last they got out of the dense jungle and found themselves in the first little village, the General announced the losses suffered: twenty-eight men, four women, and three children. Some of the victims had met frightful deaths lost in the swamps; others had been drowned, carried away by the floods. Among the living, over a dozen had a broken leg or arm. Others had big head wounds, and at least fifty were dragging along with the blazing eyes and yellow skin of fever. Of those who were missing, probably more than one had been eaten during the night by some wild animal. It was impossible to say who had died that way: the troop had become used to the cries of the delirious, and it was hard to tell, in the middle of a black night, whether a man was struggling with a real or an imaginary animal. When daylight came, the absence of some man would be noticed. Sometimes, when the rain had not erased them, the tracks of the animal that had visited the encampment would still show.

Twenty horses and mules had disappeared for the same reasons, with this difference: that the horses and mules were not attacked by malaria, but by dysentery, and that nearly all of them were wounded, despite the drivers' precautions, which had been useless in preventing packsores, snakebites, and the attacks of wildcats.

Despite losses, sickness, and weariness, the morale of the troop was excellent. In every company the best of humor prevailed, displayed to the degree and in the way that Indian austerity allowed.

So great was the confidence they felt in themselves, so big were their hopes, and so genuine was the joy they felt at having undertaken that march toward liberty, that they could not recall ever having lived happier hours.

Months, perhaps years earlier they had abandoned hope that their situation would ever improve. For in spite of contracts, promises, and laws, they knew that once they had been meshed into the machinery of the lumber camps they would never be able to return to their homes, or even to see a village. But now, one after another, the companies had reached a village, the first they had seen in many years.

Behind them lay the jungle, with its perils and its horrors. Before them, their homes, parents, and families. Before them, land and liberty! Free land for all! Land without foremen and owners!

All together now, they wept with pleasure when the Professor spoke these words to them: "Listen well, men. Even if we lose this battle, even if we go down to the last man under the bullets of the federal soldiers and the rural police, even if not one of us should ever obtain land and liberty, we will have triumphed. Because to live as free men, even if only for a few months, is worth more than living a hundred years in slavery. And if we fall now we won't fall as peons, as hanged men in flight, but as free men on the earth, as open rebels, as true soldiers of the revolution."

"Long live the Professor! That's the way to talk!" hundreds of voices shouted. "We're free and we're fighting for the liberty of all the peasants and workers, of all honest women and men!"

From the vantage of a branch to which he had climbed so that his voice might reach them all, the Professor looked at the multitude acclaiming him. Then he went on: "You have said it,

men. We are free, but we don't want liberty for ourselves
alone. We must join all the others to fight together for liberty."

"Hurrah for the Professor! Long live liberty! Forward with
the fight for land and liberty!"

Long after the Professor had climbed down from the tree
the shouts of enthusiasm could still be heard.

The last company had arrived. The whole body of men was
reunited. Friends and comrades belonging to different companies met again seated around the same hearth and told about the
sufferings they had endured during the march through the
jungle. In all the groups happiness dominated. Some were playing mouth organs, producing soft, sweet sounds; others
strummed small guitars to accompany the singing of plaintive
songs whose simple, profound words expressed everyone's
simple, profound feelings, words with which they alleviated
the wounds of so many old pains and so much suffering. They
danced, they sang, and they made noise, because the idea of
having been able to come out well despite the horrors of the
forest, with its swamps, the flood of its rivers, and the attacks
of its wild animals had caused an explosion of joy among them.
This was their way of reacting to the end of that exhausting
march.

The little village claimed to be the final point of the forest—
which nevertheless extended into it. The roads were no better
here, and there were places where the undergrowth was impenetrable. Furthermore, the rains might continue for some
weeks. But this would not be torrential rain—only the fine rain
so common in the mountains. During a respite of two or three
days the rain let up completely. Nevertheless, the nocturnal
downpours of the tropics had to be expected. But what could
that matter now that they had dodged the horrors of the
jungle?

A few miles from its edge they found clusters of huts, small
ranches, then fincas; and still farther on, still a considerable distance away, they would see the hamlets of Hucutsin and
Achlumal. From there onward they would pass little caravans,

convoys of mules and Indians on the way to market to sell the products of their labor.

Between these little villages they would still have to cross desert or forest regions covered with thick brush through which they would have to plow for whole days at a time. But the jungle and its dangers were far away now. At last they had been left behind.

They began to see cornfields and patches of frijoles. As they advanced, the cultivated lands became more extensive, until their boundaries were lost to sight at the appearance of the first fincas.

Corn and frijoles! And with them assurance that they would not die from hunger. Until that moment they had sustained themselves with what they had carried away from the lumber camps. Provisions for four or five days more still remained. But the fear of hunger disappeared at the sight of the fincas, with their immense wealth of corn, pigs, sheep, cows, wheat, sugar, and all the things that this crowd of young men desired with all their hearts. For months, and in many cases years, they had been deprived of all those things which make men's lives supportable.

For corn alone was not enough, even though they prepared the ground meal and made the dough, which—by recipes transmitted from generation to generation for centuries—made possible a whole series of foods, including tortillas of several kinds and sizes, some with cheese rolled inside them, and corn-meal-water made aromatic with orange leaves or the little flowers of the anise plant.

At the fincas more than just tortillas and frijoles awaited them. There they would find an endless amount of good things for which it was well worth their stopping awhile. The men were not highway robbers. But a rebellion cannot exist without rebels, and rebels must live if they are to go forward. Rebels are not to blame for the disagreeable consequences that rebellions bring in their train for those who have everything. Those responsible for the acts of the rebels are men who believe it possible to mistreat human beings forever with impunity and not drive them to rebellion.

20

 The first little village they reached on coming out of the jungle was called El Requemado. Thirty years earlier it had been nothing but a lumber camp. Later, when not a stick of mahogany remained standing, despite the promises of reforestation made by the contractors, the friend of a politician had bought the property for a handful of pesos. He had then brought in a few Indian families who worked to his profit under the orders of an overseer. Thus he had tried to transform the camp into a ranch. But it proved so poor a ranch that it did not produce an income for its owner, who, furthermore, never set foot there, preferring to keep on running his business in Jovel. If he got one hundred pesos a year from the ranch, he felt that his expectations had been fulfilled. The majordomo did not receive any salary and lived by selling provisions and other stuff to the workmen who passed through on their way to the lumber camps.

Don Chucho, the majordomo, was seized by terror when the first company appeared. When the rebels began to camp in the vicinity of the ranch, he tried to get them to tell him whether they had been discharged and why they had horses and mules with them and especially why they were traveling unaccompanied by a single foreman. He could elicit only evasive answers. But he was prudent and astute enough to understand that he would do better not to insist. He tried to keep up his courage

by telling himself that nothing of all this was of any importance as far as he was concerned and that if the men had left
the lumber camps it was their own business.

But on the following day, when he saw a new company arrive and realized that the first had no intention of leaving, he
conceived the idea of sending one of his peons to the neighboring finca to inform the finquero of what was happening. Then
his wife dissuaded him, saying: "Look, Chucho, so far nobody
has robbed you. Those men pay you for whatever they need.
If they're not buying much, that's nothing new. That's the
way they always do. And if they have anything on their conscience, that's not our affair. But if they get to know that
you've sent to warn the finqueros, who knows what will
happen to us? I think you'd better keep quiet."

Don Chucho had the sense to know that his wife was right,
and that upset him even more than the presence of the armed
boys camping on his ranch. He knew perfectly well how pistols and rifles had come this far in the men's hands, but he
wanted not to consider (he might have died of fright) what
had taken place in the lumber camps. His wife thought as he
did, and without having consulted each other they carefully
avoided any reference to it. They preferred not to find out the
certainty, for it would have made them die of fear.

Also, his cautiousness was not based on fear alone. Don
Chucho did not attempt anything, because he knew very well
that, even if the rural police were informed, they would never
come to El Requemado to fight the rebels. They would wait in
the outskirts of the important villages, if possible lying in ambush on one of the rich fincas, where surely they could defeat
the rebels. Then the rebels would find themselves obliged to
flee—and Don Chucho knew that they could take refuge only
in the jungle. To reach it they would necessarily have to pass
by the ranch again, and when they returned in defeat, in small,
isolated groups full of rancor, what would be left of his ranch?
Nothing. Not even a wisp of straw. And of himself? They
would not leave even a tiny patch of skin, because by then they
would know who had betrayed them.

The men had not set up their encampment within the ranch because it was not big enough. In reality it was hardly more than a clearing where the jungle ended. A little farther on, along the road leading to the fincas, the General had installed the camp on a wide meadow bordered by the grasses and reeds of the riverbank.

The site was strategic: it cut the road, and nobody could go to or from the fincas without passing through the camp. For the moment, then, they had nothing to fear from either finqueros or rural police. The men could rest for a few days, because they too knew that neither soldiers nor rural police would venture into this region. The jungle was still near, and its undergrowth formed natural ramparts against which the best rifles in the world—or even machine guns—would be useless. There the rebels, barefoot and scarcely covered by their tatters, were the kings; for them the forest held no secrets, and to combat them it would have been necessary to engage in hand-to-hand fighting, the terrible dueling with machetes, stabbings, stones, or even bare fists. And there the iron fists of the cutters—as the soldiers were well aware—were worth more than the best armament. For these reasons the men were completely calm. They were sure that even if the rural police were told of their being at El Requemado they would not come there to fight them.

There was lively discussion in the first council of war called together after the establishment of the camp. But the discussion was nothing like the lamentable deliberations of those men who, in nearly all revolutions, speak and orate endlessly— speak, when they should be taking action, about the way to carry out their resolutions. They talk and talk, and it is these windbags of revolution who end by ruining it. It is during these deliberations that the enemies work, and while the revolutionaries discuss edicts concerning the color of their flag, the counterrevolution falls on the outposts, makes the first columns waver, seizes the sentries, and silences the incorrigible charlatans. Among the rebels there were fortunately no old theorists. They knew nothing of impassioned assemblies or inflamed writings. They argued animatedly, but not about faded and worn-out devices. They talked simply to find out which group should march in the vanguard when the situation, during the march they were getting ready to set forth on, became serious. The company in the vanguard would have the glorious prospect of being annihilated down to the last man when the rural police turned the first machine gun on them. Even without having untied the machine guns from the backs of their mules, the soldiers would account for some men in that vanguard. Had not every soldier been provided with a repeater carbine and a Colt revolver for just this purpose? And had not both federal soldiers and rural police been well trained with this object in view?

The discussion was far from being about the halo of glory that the vanguard would earn. The men still had no notion of the great feats of arms idealized by historians with poetic inclinations. They had not been contaminated by the deformed and deforming spirit of newspapermen and orators. For them it was a question, not of winning glory but of something more concrete and precise: of obtaining their enemies' arms. Not one of them had ever read a revolutionary article or studied histories of revolutions. They had never attended political meetings or known the significance of a program. But experience said to all of them: "If you have arms and your enemies have none, you will win the revolution or the rebellion or the strike, no matter what name you give to the action that liberates those who work. True revolutions are not those which have as their only object the raising of salaries, the division of goods, or the winning of such and such privileges. The true revolutions do not stop until they have achieved justice without deceit."

For the men the revolution signified the end of slavery, of the servitude to which they had been driven by bestial means —nothing more.

From infancy all of them had heard said what later had become clear to them: that he who carried a pistol in his belt or a carbine in his bandoleer had the right to reduce the Indians to servitude, to exploit them, to mistreat them, and to impose his will on them. And as the Indian, the servant, had no pistol in his belt or carbine in his bandoleer, he had to submit and let them lead him away. If he dared to open his mouth in protest, the butt of the pistol smashed his skull, or that of the carbine crushed his ribs. It was therefore completely natural that to them the conquest of arms should represent the triumph of the revolution. To deprive their enemies of arms: that was their watchword and their device.

The company that was to march in the vanguard would be obliged to take the first shock of those who possessed arms. It was evident that at least three-quarters of its men would fall. But the fourth part would remain on its feet to take advantage of the arms won at such a cost. And the rebels were like those lottery-players who are convinced that they will win the first prize: they were all certain that they would be members of the group that would remain on its feet and armed.

The discussion about which group should be in the vanguard was going on with some animation when the General and Celso stopped it.

"God damn it, you bunch of idiots!" shouted the General. "You sound like gossiping old women. The vanguard will consist of the first company. We make up the first company. What then? Now go away and leave us in peace!"

To Celso the General's words did not seem sufficiently energetic, and he let his own voice be heard: "Do you understand clearly? Did you hear what the General said? This is a rebellion, you fools! Rebels act; they don't talk. Within six days we'll all be at the fiesta and never fear, half of us will stay there stretched out on the ground."

"Hurrah!" shouted the men. Some of them added: "You're right, Celso. But the other half of us will have arms and cartridges. Land and liberty!"

Night fell. Attracted by the voices, many of the peons from the ranch had cautiously approached the spot where the rebels were. They would not have dared to do so during the day for fear of the majordomo. They came up timidly, because they did not know how they would be received. The men did not consider them to be their own sort. Earlier the peons had not made a single effort to win confidence or friendship, and the men might well consider them spies who came not to join their movement but to ferret out their intentions and relay them to the majordomo—or even to denounce them to the finqueros or the nearest rural police for a bribe of one peso.

But some of the peons had heard some of the rebels speaking their own language and had recognized them as from their own village. Thus they had learned that they were in rebellion, that they had done away with the bosses in the lumber camps, and that they were getting ready to do the same thing on the fincas. Knowing that much, they were able to confirm it as soon as they entered the encampment. They asked to speak to the leader and were sent to the Professor and the General. They approached the hearth around which the general staff was grouped. Courteously removing their hats, they said: "Chief, do you want to tell us what we have to do?"

"Man," the Professor answered, "I'm not your 'chief.' Now there aren't any chiefs and owners. I'm your comrade. You, the peons of this muddy ranch, are welcome. Land and liberty without overseers and without owners, that's what we want. Land and liberty for all!"

"Comrades, that's what we want too. A piece of land and the liberty to cultivate it in peace. The right to talk freely among ourselves about whatever we like without having the foreman come and smash our faces. That's what we want, nothing more."

"Good. If that's what you want, come with us. We need a lot of fighters, for in a short time many of us will have fallen. Now get ready. Tomorrow we leave."

"But look, little chief—"

"I just told you not to call me 'chief'!"

"Pardon, comrade, let me tell you. I have a little cornfield. If I go with you I can't harvest the corn. I also have three little pigs. What should I do?"

"Didn't you just tell me that you want land and liberty?"

"Certainly I want it. But look, comrade, I also have my woman, and she is pregnant and will give birth within three weeks. I can't leave her here alone."

"Good; then stay here. Stay here, all of you, on the ranch so that they can beat you as soon as you try to raise your voices."

"We could change all that and stay here on the land we work. Because look, every one of us here has a little piece of land to sow with corn and frijoles. But in return for it we have to work three weeks out of four without their giving us a single centavo."

"Do you all have machetes?" asked the General.

"Yes, comrade."

"Good. Then tell me: what do you do if you are cutting down underbrush to clean off the land and you stir up a wild boar?"

"When I have my machete in my hand, there isn't an animal that can get away from me."

"Very good, my friend. You want land and liberty on this ranch, on which you now work without getting a centavo, but —yes—getting many blows."

"That's right."

"Who, then, stands in your way at this moment?"

"You know, comrade, it's Don Chucho, the majordomo."

"And you all have machetes?"

"Yes. And Florencio and Marcos, these fellows who are with me, have more than one. They have two."

"And you all know how to sharpen the machetes. Right?"

"Of course we know how. It's the first thing we do when we get up."

"In that case, get your machetes, sharpen them well, and use them to cut down everything that stands in your way—if you really want the ranch for yourselves."

When the peons had left, the General called in the captains of all the companies to give them the instructions needed for setting out on the march the next day. They had decided that from this point on, the companies would march closer together because they would be expecting their first collision with the enemy at any moment.

When daybreak came, and at the orders of the General, of Celso—chief of the general staff—and of the Professor, the first company would march out at the head. The second and third companies would leave, respectively, half an hour and an hour later. Then would come the fourth and fifth. The last three would form the rear guard, bringing up the animals loaded with provisions. Each man would carry his usual load on his back. The women and the children would follow the company in which their husbands or fathers marched. Modesta formed part of the advance company and on her shoulders carried the same load as the men.

The men did not ask themselves what they would do or what their attitude would be when they reached the fincas. Nor did they stop to elaborate plans for victory over the rural police or the federal soldiers. Why discuss things and waste eternities in useless words? The revolution would triumph, the enemy would bite the dust. To win, to destroy the enemy—that was what mattered. Once that had been achieved, they would have time to reflect and deliberate.

"You can't sell a jaguar's skin before you've caught him," the Professor said to Andrés, who had been advancing a plan for the division of the finca on which he had been born and on which his father still worked as a peon.

"It wouldn't be bad," Andrés answered, "to look in advance for a good buyer for the jaguar's skin so as not to be obliged to sell it too cheaply later."

"Look, Andresillo—for the moment forget the wandering buyers. When we have the skin, that'll be the time to discuss good offers."

In the middle of the night the General called the men of the first company together for the departure. The other groups could take advantage of at least a half hour's more sleep.

It had not rained for four days, but toward midnight, when they were ready to leave, it began to rain again. The rain was fine but dense, and in less than two hours the soil had begun to become mushy again. By the time the General gave the order to start out, all the men were wet to their bones. They had had to work hard before they had succeeded in making fires to warm themselves and heat a little coffee.

The rain let up toward four in the morning. The first company was ready to leave when they saw approaching them the peons who had spoken to them the evening before.

"What is it?" asked the General. "Have you decided to come with us?"

"No, comrade, now that isn't necessary. Now we have what we want. Now we have land and liberty. The ranch is ours."

"Did the majordomo give it to you?"

"No—well, that is to say—when we explained that for many years we had been cultivating the little ranch without pay, he became furious and started to shout that he knew perfectly well what was happening, that the damned lousy fellows from the lumber camps had stirred us up, urged us on, advised us badly, and that if we didn't shut our mouths at once he would take charge of settling with us as soon as the bandits from the camps went on their way."

"And you? What did you answer?"

"Hardly anything. We had sharpened the machetes in advance. When we started toward Don Chucho he pulled his pistol and shot. He killed Calixto and Simón and wounded three others."

"Then it's out of fear that you ran over here?"

"No, my friend. We had thought a lot about what you said, and right now Don Chucho, his wife, and his kids are dead. Furthermore, we took his pistol and his rifle because we may need them. As for his house, we don't want it—it's full of rats. Under these conditions, comrade, little chief, you'll understand that we don't need to go with you. What we have now is all we want, nothing more. If you want to stay here you can do it, because now there aren't any foremen or bosses."

"No, my friend, thanks. We will go on and you will stay here to divide up your land and work it in peace. But tell me: if the rural police come right now and ask for the majordomo, what will you tell them?"

"We'll say that Don Chucho and Doña Amalia became so frightened that they ran to take refuge in the forest. And if our answer doesn't satisfy them, we'll sharpen our machetes again immediately, and we might even make use of the pistol and the rifle that we have now. But you know, little chief, that the rural police won't come here because you'll get rid of them and the federal soldiers on your way. Now we'll go back to the ranch. The men have killed a very big pig, and the cracklings ought to be ready by now. It's too bad that we can't invite you—there are so many of you that there'd never be enough. Good-by, my friend captain. Good-by, all of you, and many thanks. May good luck accompany you!"

The Professor called Andrés and said: "Did you understand that, Andresillo? That is what they call the practical revolution."

"What do you mean by that?"

"Well, simply that the instinct of possession, the idea of property, is now more deeply rooted on that ranch than before. Only the name of the proprietor has changed, and I assure you, brother, that tomorrow or the next day the new owners will be dealing out machete strokes because of the property and will be killing one another off until only one remains, if he can, to enjoy the property. He who remains will be the one who has the pistol. He will be the new owner, and if one of the others succeeds in keeping the shotgun, he'll be the major-domo. As for those who by chance preserve nothing but their lives, they'll be the new peons."

"Then the revolution will have been useless?"

"For these people, yes. The thing has been too easy for them and they have got it too quickly. Ease and speed are not good for revolutionaries. The fields and the pigs will have changed hands, but the ideas will be the very ones that hold up the whole system, which unfortunately will have remained intact. Florencio, and then Eusebio or Fulano; but the owners will continue in their places, because here everything will go on the same way. They didn't show even a glimmer of gratitude for us, who gave them the idea. They would let you die of hunger, and me too, before they would deprive themselves of one bit of cracklings."

Andrés tried to defend the peons, saying: "But how do you expect them to know what they should do if nobody explains it to them?"

"Revolutionaries who have to have explained to them the motives for which they should rebel are poor revolutionaries. The real revolution, the one capable of changing the system, lies in the hearts of true revolutionaries. The sincere revolutionary never thinks of the personal benefit rebellion may bring him. He wants only to overthrow the social system under which he suffers and sees others suffer. And to destroy it and see the realization of the ideas he considers just, he will sacrifice himself and die."

Andrés tilted his head to one side and answered: "Professor, all this is very complicated for me. Just let me become a professor some day. Perhaps then I can understand."

"Don't worry about it, Andresillo. You, the General, the Colonel, Celso, young Modesta, Santiago, Matías, Fidel, Cirilo, and many others among you are the people the revolution needs. You carry it in your hearts, and those who have it there don't need explanations."

A shout was heard in the dawn: "God damn it, Professor, why do you talk so much? Let's get going!" It was the voice of the General looking for his aide.

"Here I am."

"March, comrade! It's the hour for getting out of here. We're going in the vanguard and have a good stretch to cover."

"I was amusing myself explaining to Andrés how those peons, the ones who just left, will be killing one another tomorrow for the possession of two or three more yards of land."

"To hell with them! We have other things to worry about, and we can't stop for such meanness. Perhaps later—"

"You're right, General. We have little time to lose."

"You have said it. Perhaps in a few hours— But now let's get on the road. Quick—we must get to the head of the column! Up there we'll have to be always in the vanguard, Professor. That's the only way we can keep from hearing about selfishness and go on nourishing our hope that the revolution will change not only the system but also the narrow spirit of man."

"Where did you find these ideas, General? I'd like to know that."

"Last night, when the peons returned to their houses, I thought about it. I wandered around our encampment. I saw the fires burning through the underbrush. Bits of the men's talk reached my ears. And the ideas just popped into my head!"

"And excellent ideas they are! By my mother, we ought to put them down on paper."

While talking like this, they were walking as fast as possible, tripping over the roots of bushes, against stones in the road and branches broken off by the rains, sinking at times into mud up to their waists.

The day had begun cold, gray, and wet. It lighted the tops of the ancient trees stingily, while underneath, on the ground covered with the thick foliage of the forest, the darkness was complete.

The men made a strange, monotonous noise as they clumped along, putting their feet into the mud. They groaned, swore, and lamented when they sank in up to their chests in swampy spots or when the least breath of wind in the trees let down on them veritable bursts of water from the branches.

The General and the Professor divined, rather than saw, the silhouettes of the heavily laden men they were passing. At the end of a short time they knew that they were not far from the head of the column. Soon they could hear the potent voice of Celso, who was shouting loud enough to be heard in the inferno: "Gang of burros! What a convoy I've got with me! Are you rebels? Don't make me laugh! You complain and whine more than a bunch of old women. Sons of bitches! You didn't whine like this when you had to march for the bosses and sink in the mud up to your ears for them. Then you worked like oxen. Each one of you did what four oxen together couldn't have done. But then you were working for those bastards. Now that you have to do something for yourselves, here you are whimpering. Swear if you have to, but don't break my eardrums with your whining! Rebels? You're not rebels! Listen to me carefully, you pack of mules. Whoever complains from now on, may lightning strike me if I don't shut him up! Now —get on there and keep your mouths shut!"

The Professor and the General stood stock-still.

"Say, General, it seems to me that you have chosen well in the chief of your general staff."

"So I see. From now on he is a lieutenant."

"Only a lieutenant? I propose that we name him a captain."

"You're our adviser, and if you propose it, I name him a captain."

"Thanks, comrade."

"But now that I think of it, I have one colonel, ten captains, fifty lieutenants, and no major. And so, with your permission, comrade, this afternoon when we reach camp I'll name Celso a major."

Martín Trinidad had started forward again, but just as Juan Méndez made him this proposal he stumbled against a root and fell full length, with his face in the mud. For that reason he was unable to give his immediate approval to the promotion of Celso.